Aiko

愛子

Child of Love

Inspired by Real Events

Dominika Riemer

Aiko: Child of Love

First Edition.

ISBN: 978-83-970414-1-7

Front Cover: 123rf.com/zakhariya

Photography by Katarzyna Kurp

EMERGING
INK SOLUTIONS
Kara Wilson, Editor
www.emergingink.com

This is a work of fiction. Names, characters, and businesses are the products of the author's imagination. The slaughter of thousands of dolphins and other such cruel acts carried out by Japanese fishermen and others in Taiji, however, is real. To the best of my abilities, the details regarding the activities carried out along Taiji's shores as presented by this book have been reviewed by The Dolphin Project.

For all the people in this world who have forgotten who they are.
Open your heart and remember—
We are all children of love.

Chapter 1

異体同心。
Itai doushin.
Two bodies, one heart.

TOKYO, November 2002

WITHIN THE SAFETY OF THE mother's womb and the nurturing waters of existence, life begins to take shape. In the purity of this fluid, an innocent creation gradually forms. Bound to the mother for nine months and connected by more than just an umbilical cord, a life embarks on a miraculous journey.

It is within that amniotic fluid that our personality begins to develop. It is there that our nervous system, skin, bones, muscles, and blood vessels form. It is there that fetal cells migrate into the mother's bloodstream and integrate with her organs. Within that sacred space that is the womb, we experience our first dreams and listen to the comforting sounds of our mother's voice.

Since I can remember, my relationship with water has been unusual.

As a little girl, I adored bath time, eagerly immersing myself in the warmth of the water and playing with rainbow-colored bubbles. It was a euphoric experience watching them dance and vanish into steamy air. The crystal-clear nature of the water instilled in me an innate sense of purity and radiance.

In comparison, the great waters of the wild, like the sea, humbled me. Waterfalls, lakes, and rivers drove me to render respect and fear. But the sea was the worst.

Each step into its chilling embrace carried me farther into the realm of the unknown.

There was something unnerving about not knowing what lay beneath the surface.

Upon that vast expanse, a mirror of infinitude, where the moon's glow danced upon dark waves, I sensed the voices of the deep, a kingdom inhabited by sea creatures untouched by human presence.

It was in that environment that I found a metaphor for my relationship with my mother, Hiroko.

It had been sixteen years since the cord was cut, and I couldn't help but reminisce about our time together. One memory that stood out clearly was the genuine, electric smile my mother would give her customers at the kimono shop where she used to work. Her eyes beamed with pride as she picked up fabrics in fluid movements, allowing the silk to flow over her hands. She offered perfectly matching or complimentary colors and superb quality that her customers, who were more than just customers, loved.

Mother's jewel of a store was hidden in the heart of Senzoku Park in Asakusa. During the busy summer months when my mother needed help in the shop, I and other girls were tasked with serving exquisite *nerikiri*,* often as an accompaniment to the *matcha* served next door in the *chashitsu*.†

Tiny café tables adorned with umbrellas outside offered a shaded space between the kimono shop and the tea room where patrons could mingle, surrounded by the soothing aromas of the tea and the chirping of the birds in park trees.

My mother's customers—the sumo wrestlers, *ikebana* florists,‡ *geishas*, *maikos*,§ and foreigners—were like a reflection of her happiness as she selected the perfect kimonos for them, bringing

*(練り切り) *Nerikiri*: A traditional Japanese sweet made of glutinous rice flour, white bean jam, and Chinese yams.

†(茶室) *Chashitsu*: An architectural space or individual room used or intended for a traditional tea ceremony.

‡ (生け花): *Ikebana*: The art of flower arranging.

§ (舞妓) *Maiko*: An apprentice geisha (usually a young woman) whose jobs usually consist of dancing, singing, and playing the shamisen.

tranquility and purpose into her life. Patiently, they stood in line, devoid of any complaints regarding the sporadically long queues or the duration of their wait, and accepted delectable sweets. Mother possessed a gift, and within the walls of this jewel, she had discovered her true calling.

However, it was not for her to choose her path, for when Minoru—the man society called my "father"—was promoted to deputy manager at the Japanese Tire Company, he decided Mother didn't need to work anymore.

In the slit between the room and the door, I would occasionally glimpse her rummage the closet with kimonos that, with closed eyes, she would touch and revisit bygone memories. When she would open her eyes, she would return to her reality, the house duties of a wife and mother. She never complained about such responsibilities, yet I knew that Minoru's decision affected her more than she realized. With her life's purpose gone, Mother's soul began slowly dying.

They say that everyone has a threshold, a limit for how much they are willing to bear, but my mother seemed to defy that notion. One evening, as I watched her hang up the phone and discouragingly return Minoru's portion of food to a stainless-steel pot, it was difficult not to feel that her entire existence revolved around him. It was a pitiful conclusion, but I could plainly see that she had little control over her own life.

As usual, she put on a facade, acting as if nothing had transpired. She averted her gaze, making a conscious effort to prevent tears from streaming down her face as she made her way toward the bedroom. However, this time, I decided to trail behind her.

"Let's eat," she eventually said, hearing my footsteps.

"So, he's not coming home… again?" I asked, though I already knew the answer. In the long pause that followed, I could almost hear her struggle to keep calm, which I hoped would be a breaking point for her. "Mom, can't you see that you're caring for someone who doesn't care for you?" I lost forbearance for the both of us.

"Someone needs to bring money home!" she exclaimed, trying to find an excuse for Minoru's behavior.

"Money! You can't buy memories with money!" I retorted. "And what is life if not memories?"

But it wasn't only my mother who he didn't care for. The same was true for me. Although rarely home, Minoru had told me all my life what to do. When he did eventually decide to come home, he made sure we knew of his inherency. On these seldom occasions, his armchair would become a throne and the TV remote a scepter while Mother and I became his subordinates. The "king" then would make sure not to keep us bored with his imperious whims and remind us of our places. Mother would bring him a tray of his favorite, never-changing request of simple *gohan*** and *yakitori*,†† and I would clear the plate after his every meal.

He reminded us on every occasion possible that his work first and foremost was the life-blood of the household and that we should appreciate that we had everything we needed. In fact, he knew little of what our true needs were.

The authoritative hold he kept on us was also his way of excusing himself from any house duties. And to a certain point, it appeared expected in our society. But Mother's subservience seemed extreme to me when she stooped to adding sugar to his coffee. While stirring white crystals to dissolve them into the blackness of the caffeine, she would whisper to herself, "This sugar sweetens my life," which I never understood. But one thing I *did* understand was that her life wasn't sweet anymore.

Her electric smile and the lucidity in her eyes had been replaced by the bitterness of her fate, and I just couldn't bear their indifference anymore.

Today was the day.

I would tell her everything. I would tell her how much he didn't respect her, how much he didn't appreciate her, how much…

My thoughts were interrupted by a sudden, unexpected, heavy slap across my cheek.

"Money is crucial. That's why you have food on the table. Don't *ever* say anything bad about your father!" Mother screamed.

Despite our diverging paths, I thought I knew her better.

** (ごはん) *Gohan*: Rice.

†† (焼き鳥) *Yakitori*: Skewered chicken grilled over a charcoal fire.

I had hoped she would understand. But looking into her ice-cold gaze, I realized how wrong I was. Still in shock, holding my red cheek, I wished she could perceive what mistake she had just made.

Instead, she growled vehemently, still looking straight into my eyes, "Never!"

The emptiness in her gaze scared me enough to make me run. So, I did. Deep inside my heart, I hoped to hear her call, "Aiko!" behind me, but there was only dead silence, which soon transformed into the loud pounding of my feet as I ran toward the unknown. That unknown soon became a train station, the same train station that often served as my escape from home.

In times past, I had navigated through the crowds of ghosts, people who thought they were alive, but in my eyes, were more like programmed workaholic robots. And that's what their lives looked like every day from Monday until Friday. The most ambitious ones, or those with less choice, looked forward to overtime on Saturdays and even Sundays. Occasionally some, who missed their last train or were too awash to face reality at home, hid the night in capsule hotels. These tiny pods offered a few hours of dreamless sleep before the "robots" once again rose and returned with coffee breath and dark-rimmed eyes to their monotonous work or to the hypotonic sound and steady movement of the trains. I too sought refuge on a passing metro.

In late evenings, the sound of Minoru's loud snore from the bedroom was a token of my brief liberation. For a few, sweet hours, I would intercept his throne and scepter to become queen of the house. In a hushed tone, I would maneuver the antenna in every direction, desperately seeking a signal that would allow me to obsessively indulge in foreign movies. These films not only taught me English but also served as my gateway to exploring diverse cultures and experiencing life through different perspectives. Even so, my outlook in the morning usually consisted of not more than four hours of sleep where a train's nap was rarely sufficient. That led to dozing off in classes, where my eyelids would keep falling for a few amazing seconds, just to wake up to the sonorous rebuke of petulant teachers. The absence of creativity and the relentless emphasis on rote memorization only intensified my disdain for school and created a greater divide between Minoru and me. He had chosen that institution for me, convinced it was the finest in the city.

However, in my eyes, it felt more like a prison, a place to punish me for transgressions I had never committed.

Luckily, when it came to selecting my circle of friends, fortune favored me. Right within my neighborhood, I stumbled upon a group of kindred spirits, "my guys:" Yamato, Madoka, Spiky, Fumiko, and Ren. Our connection was cemented by our shared disinterest in technology. In the rapidly expanding and tech-driven world of Tokyo, our peers were shackled to video games, new gadgets, and the latest flip phones. However, we opted to revel in our freedom outdoors. We couldn't help but pity others for their decision to vegetate at home and succumb to the perils of loneliness and social withdrawal like a *hikikomori*.[#]

No weather could stop us; we embraced the sunshine and rain alike. We found our refuge in an old, dilapidated building rumored to be set for demolition, not far from our homes in Asakusa. Fumiko stitched colorful umbrellas together to form a makeshift roof, keeping us dry or in the shade on sunny days. Yamato crafted tables and stools from abandoned cedar tree trunks found nearby, which were the most essential pieces of furniture on our estate. In the evenings, we would light the place up with the magic of his smuggled-from-home Christmas lights. In the sparks of their deemed brightness, we would read adult *manga*[§] that had been brought by Spiky's older brother, Hinata. Curious, disgusted, and intrigued, we reviewed the images countless times and joked at the content. Fearing Spiky would snitch on him or elsewise reveal where the forbidden materials were located, Hinata bought us cigarettes.

Madoka and I would often find ourselves engulfed in others' smoke as we joined the rest of the group for a good game of poker. Initially, we would play for a meager sum of yen, but as expected, Ren would swiftly accumulate all the money, for no one could match his skills. When our funds ran dry, we would switch gears and play for kisses instead. This became the most thrilling aspect of the game as we had the opportunity to earn smooches through losses without any lingering guilt.

(引きこもり) *Hikikomori*: A person who has completely withdrawn from society to the extent that they rarely leave their residence.

§ (マンガ) *Manga*: Japanese comics.

Yamato, who was two years older than me and Fumiko, was not only the cutest and boasted a dimpled chin, but he was also a much better kisser than Spiky and Ren. All the girls, including myself, always hoped he would lose.

Spiky, whose nickname had overtaken his real name, was known for his fashionable blond hair styled like the spikes of a hedgehog. He was good at introducing us to new games, many of which he made up himself. One of our favorites required us to split into teams. One team would hide an object for the other squad to find by using clues. Fumiko had rabbit teeth, but that wasn't the only trait she shared with the animal; she was also fast and clever, and everyone wanted her on their team. But to be fair, we would play *janken*[***] to decide which team she would join. We also played other games like Four Square, Hopscotch, and *Ohajiki*[†††] during the warm spring and summer days.

But those carefree days were long gone now. With the sting of Mother's slap compelling onward, I had no intention of meeting with anyone from our group. I wasn't in a hurry and had no specific destination in mind, so I took the first train whose doors opened to admit me and sat in the closest empty seat. It was only then that I realized how sore my cheek was, and I couldn't help feeling bitter and disappointed at the thought of my mother's injustice and ignorance. After all, I had tried to open her eyes to the sad reality of her existence.

As the train passed through Shibuya Station, I couldn't help but grin, recollecting well-to-remember evenings I used to spend there with my friends, exploring the hidden gems of the small side streets.

I got off the train and looked out at the busiest intersection in the world which welcomed thousands of feet every day, spreading like ants, in different directions.

The monstrous, glassy buildings were adorned like a mosaic, with screens of varying sizes and content that changed dynamically, resembling a colorful kaleidoscope.

I knew the smells of grilled *teriyaki* meat, spicy and sweet perfumes, suffocating cigarette smoke, and occasionally a hint of

---

*** (ジャンケン) *Janken*: Japanese rock-paper-scissors.

††† (お弾き) *Ohajiki*: A traditional children's game similar to marbles played with colored glass or plastic.

sweat; it all mixed in the alleyways to create a thick scent that filled every nook and cranny. It wafted into the nostrils of people from all over the world who were in the same place at that moment—Shibuya. A place that had seen it all.

Japan with its many rules was more merciful at night. In the darkness, people could finally bury their *hatarakiari*[‡‡‡] lifestyle and set loose their true desires. Seeing the worst of the worst, some would call it "hell," while others knew it as "paradise."

Young, drunk locals, as well as tourists, unleashed their inner beasts there. The street bars were filled with shouting, singing, dancing, and the occasional vomiting before its entrance. Skateboarders weaved between throngs of people.

Shops with unique, *kawaii*[§§§] clothing filled shop owners' pockets with fat yen as they gained fans from around the world. Meanwhile, bars, pachinko parlors, and electronic shops attracted the attention of teenagers with their vibrant and blinking neon lights.

Adolescent, scantily clad girls promising to provide the most amazing night tempted even the most faithful.

Drunk Scottish men, bold and daring, lifted their innocent kilts to reveal naked buttocks and flirted shamelessly with Japanese Lolita women on the streets. At the same time, courageous gays covertly displayed affection that could be misinterpreted as warm friendship by outsiders.

Teenagers with the appearance of human dolls, desperate to stand out and express themselves, left behind their obligatory school uniforms for yellow and purple wigs, elf ears, gothic clothes, and vampire-like contact lenses. Some even went to drastic measures, such as getting silicone forehead implants, rib removals, titanium horns in the skull, pointed teeth, and tongue bifurcation. Others, with enlarged eyes, rhinoplasty, and painful diets promoted by ubiquitous magazine covers sought acceptance and validation from society.

Despite the pain, hard work, and money spent, these individuals were willing to do whatever it took to not be neglected or unseen. Often, that desire for recognition covered up feelings of

---

‡‡‡ (働きアリ) *Hatarakiari*: Worker ant.

§§§ (かわいい) *Kawaii*: Cute.

loneliness and confusion, as people prioritized their looks and fame over the contributions of scientists, writers, and philosophers. Often the more different and unique they became, the more lost and unhappy they were, hiding behind their masks as lost and miserable souls.

In search of answers, behind doors of mystery, some would turn to palm readers while clowns, half-naked teens, and ex-pats from every part of the globe tried to make their way through the crowds, at times bumping into one another.

Old, wrinkled businessmen, hunted for their gazelles like lions, frequently leaving strip clubs with young, cute girls or visiting Department H fetish parties.**** In the mornings, their wives at home often pretended as if nothing had happened.

On such intoxicated nights, there was little time to ponder on poverty, the unfairness of the world, global warming, starving children, earthquakes, or the latest headlines of never-ending bad news. Instead, there was time to talk about an auntie's death, a sister's fight, a broken tooth, an unplanned pregnancy, the break-up of a best friend, and issues regarding a boss. These conversations often ended with smeared mascara, vomiting, and sometimes thoughts of a trip to *Aokigahara suicide forest*†††† or perhaps one-night stands in *love hotels.*‡‡‡

And these nights, which ended on a high note with tales of newfound love, the arrival of a long-awaited baby, a work promotion, or a new, attractive partner were filled with boisterous laughter, concealed excitement, and occasionally, silent, accidental flatulence.

On warmer days, some cafés offered outdoor tables that remained available late into the evening, accommodating a plethora

---

**** (デパートメント H / デパ H / デパチ) *Department H*: The longest-running fetish night in Tokyo that runs monthly held at Tokyo Kinema Club in Uguisudani in Tokyo. It is usually very gay-friendly.

†††† (青木ヶ原) *Aokigahara*: Also known as Blue Tree Meadow or the Sea of Trees is located on the northwestern side of Mt. Fuji. Due to its density and remoteness and folklore regarding senicide (the practice of abandoning or killing the elderly), the place is well-known as Suicide Forest and has been the site of countless of suicides over decades.

‡‡‡ (ラブホテル) *Rabu Hoteru*: Love Hotel, a short-stay hotel operated for the purpose of intimate and clandestine meetings and stays. They are usually used for sexual activities.

of visitors and tangled languages punctuated only by a Japanese waiter's politeness and patience.

Lost in my thoughts and bitter toward the world, I found myself wandering aimlessly in an unknown street. Confused and disoriented, I realized that I must have unconsciously followed the crowd.

The cold November breeze cut through my light cotton shirt and thin jeans, chilling me to the bone. With no money on hand but feeling frozen, I was compelled to warm myself and made my way down the stairs to an *izakaya*§§§§ that I had just passed.

The smell of moldy bricks wasn't particularly inviting, but I couldn't imagine going back out into the frigid night, so I made my way to a small table in the corner of the entrance. This was my first time visiting a strange bar in an unknown place without money and completely alone. I imagined it was how Madoka had felt doing her walk of shame, an event she described to me as a journey full of guilt.

But it seemed like my night took a turn for the better when a good-looking stranger approached me and insisted on buying me a drink.

I wasn't particularly talkative, but my admirer was as he masticated a toothpick between his teeth. I paid more attention to an abstract painting on the wall above his head, trying to make sense of it, but he seemed satisfied with my company as he was likely seeking an outlet for his broken heart after his school sweetheart, Himari, left him the previous Monday. His tale was complex and reminiscent of a Brazilian soap opera, like the ones my mother often used to watch.

Tired of hearing the same painful events of his love life on repeat, I decided it was time for a trip to the washroom. As I stood, I felt dizzy. I was sure it was from that fourth Asahi. Despite my unsteadiness, I gathered what little composure I had left and made it to my destination.

"Are you okay?" called an angelic voice. The question had a slight accent and came from a girl washing her hands in the sink next to me.

---

§§§§ (居酒屋) *Izakaya*: A Japanese bar that also serves various dishes and snacks.

"Eh, I'm fine," I replied, trying to understand the purpose of her query. I worked to make my answer sound confident.

"Just to let you know, we are sitting opposite you if you need anything. My name is Sayaka, by the way," the girl said with a sweet smile before flitting from the washroom, the scent of flowers trailing behind her.

There was something unique about this girl. It was not only her unusual accent that made me assume she hadn't grown up in Japan but also her appearance that suggested she wasn't fully Japanese. Her slightly oblique eyes were a deep but dim blue and contrasted with her dark, wavy hair and white, Hollywood-like smile. Seated at the table across the bar, she was ravishing and stood out from the three around her.

Observing my every little step and trying my hardest not to trip in front of the slightly blurred crowd, I made my way to the table.

My wooer's cheesy remarks and compliments regarding my "beautiful eyes" and "sexy body" were retribution to my ears. And when he leaned in to laugh, his alcoholic breath reeking, or to whisper something, I felt his wet tongue, like a repulsive snail, attempting to slither into my ear. I decided it was enough.

Feeling uncomfortable and slightly scared, I stood with the intention to tell him to back up. It seemed he conveniently forgot that we were speaking in Japanese, and instead, he pulled me toward him and aimed to sneak his fingers under my shirt. Abruptly, his hand was halted by a stronger one belonging to a familiar face. It was one of the guys sitting at the same table as Sayaka.

I took the moment to sprint toward the staircase that had, hours prior, helped me escape the cold of the November evening. Echoes of insults and the sound of approaching footsteps trailed behind me, inducing a sense of panic that propelled me to accelerate. Puddle water splashed beneath my sneakers as I sprinted. The weather had taken a turn. Raindrops fell from dark clouds and city lights shimmered in their reflections. They cascaded onto my face, mingling with the silent tears I struggled to contain. Amid this chaotic scene, a familiar angelic voice reached my ears:

"Wait! Wait!"

Feeling nauseous, I stopped to find the girl from the pub's bathroom, Sayaka.

"Oh, my Lord, you are fast, girl!" she said breathlessly through a smile. She leveled a grave expression at me. "I told you to come to our table if you weren't okay. Where are you heading?"

"As far as possible from that crazy guy." In the irony of the situation, we both started laughing.

"I know a good place, let's go."

It was a long walk, but it passed swiftly under her umbrella, and I lost count of time as we carried on talking. Along with briefly confiding in Sayaka about what had happened earlier at home, I learned that she was eighteen and had been in Tokyo for only four months. She had come along with her Swedish ambassador father and Japanese mother, which confirmed my assumptions that she was mixed.

An air of positivity and hospitality enveloped us as we stepped inside her family's grand villa that was nestled within a diplomatic district of the city. The tranquil symphony of the wind sweeping through the front porch windchimes provided a comforting backdrop, evoking a heavenly and familiar ambiance.

The lavender fragrance of freshly-laundered washing permeated the space, harmonizing with the gentle caress of a refreshing, crisp breeze that filtered through the partially ajar windows. Yet what I cherished most was the comforting warmth that emanated from the heated, dark wooden floor to soothe my freezing feet.

Sayaka's parents were at a business party, and like me, she was an only child, so the entire villa belonged to us. After a brief tour of her house, we headed to her room on the first floor.

"I hope your friends will be all right." I took a sip of a hot chamomile tea and snuggled into the plum-purple wool sweater I had borrowed.

"Oh yes, don't worry," she said confidently and added a smirk. "Remember? It was three against one, so I think they should be fine."

"So, how long have you known each other?"

"Those guys from the bar?" I nodded. "Well, I just actually met them tonight," she laughed and, seeing my astonishment, added, "But to be fair, they seemed nice and helpful, right?"

"You are crazier than me, Sayaka!"

"Don't worry! They won't beat him up. They aren't violent. At least, they didn't seem to be. They will teach him how to respect a lady, peacefully… I think."

I hoped her doubts were a mockery of the whole grotesque situation. Her words made me feel slightly better, but I couldn't shake the guilt and responsibility for what had happened at the pub.

In a state of shock, fear, and slight intoxication, I succumbed to impulsiveness rather than employing logic. Little did I envision that after enduring a slap from my mother, the evening would unfold with even more unforeseen events.

Yet there I was, inside the abode of a complete stranger, divulging intimate facets of my life to her. Remarkably, it felt fitting.

"It's really hard seeing my mom act so passive," I admitted. "She prefers to bury her head in the sand, thinking it's easier that way. She lives in fear and it controls her every move. She just doesn't want to hear the truth. But the worst part is seeing her hurt, and knowing I can't do anything about it. I've tried to approach, to talk to her so many times, especially when she's crying, but I think of her never-changing excuse. 'Aiko, it's just something in my eye. Maybe you can help me remove it?' But I never used to find anything in there.

"At first, it used to make me really sad, but then I built a wall to protect myself. I pretended everything was fine and went on with my life. And then I realized it wasn't her pain that hurt me, but the fact that it didn't bother me anymore. Until today, when I exploded. That anger must have been growing under that wall all these years. But the most painful…" My voice started to shake and I knew I wouldn't be able to hold back my tears any longer.

Sayaka cautiously handed me a tissue and stood up to further open the window. She then retrieved a lighter and a pack of cigarettes from underneath her bed's mattress. "Want some?"

I declined, shaking my head. I never liked the smell of cigarettes, especially when Minoru would smoke them around the house.

To my surprise, the smell of these was different, subtle yet spicy and intriguing. She noticed my confounded expression and explained, "They don't smell too bad, right? They're from Indonesia. They're called Kretek, cloves cigarettes. They're cheap, less than a dollar per package, so I bought a few before I left for Japan." She

hesitated and then added, "I am sorry. When I'm stressed, I smoke. I have this sickness called empathy."

"Sickness?"

"Well, I know it's not a sickness, but sometimes I feel like it is. I sense people's emotions deeply and it can be overwhelming, especially when I can't do much about it. Every word you say I feel as if it's my own. Sorry, let's continue. The most painful is…" She gazed into my eyes, and I could see the depth of her sickness. It was bizarre but for the first time, I felt truly understood—by someone I had just met.

"The most painful thing is that I have nobody to look up to. Sometimes you just need a role model, you know? Especially when you're feeling lost and need guidance."

She filled the silence with only a few words, but they were the ones I needed most. "I am sorry."

"I've always dreamed of looking at my mother and saying with pride, 'This is my mom,' but I just can't." This was the first time I had ever shared my feelings about my mother with anyone.

Time, rain, and fresh air had washed away my insobriety, so it wasn't the alcohol that let me open myself up so much and speak the truth. Although I used to believe that expressing emotions freely with friends was a sign of weakness, I felt liberated and content.

It was an indescribable feeling of trust, openness, and relief that I experienced as I let my words flow like a river.

"I love her. She's my mother. And I always will. I just wish she could understand me, that she could see the world in truer colors. She was not always like that. She just forgot…"

"Forgot what?"

"To live."

Sayaka took a long breath and sighed. "Aiko, I'm sure your mom cares about you a lot. She shows it in her own way, and you show your love back in your own way too. There's this big gap between your generations. She's got these habits from when she was young and from her own life experiences, plus she's still got a lot of Japanese culture and traditions in her. It's like a cycle that keeps going. Being an adult with all those responsibilities must be tough, and being a woman and a mom, that's a lot too! But sometimes I worry we take life too seriously. Life's too short to stress about

everything and try to make it all perfect. 'Cause let's be real, it's never gonna be perfect.

"Sometimes it's like, you gotta accept what you can't change and work on what you can. You know your mother best so you know the situation better. Either she is ready to grow or she's not there yet. But until then, don't hold out hope for anything big from her. Just take her as she is. The less we expect, the happier we are. But hey, our own view of things matters too. You might see yourself one way, but your mother might see you differently. So, which one's the real you, Aiko?" Sayaka gazed out the window and then back at me. "And last but not least, you don't need a role model; you already have all the answers. Listen to your heart and you will know."

As I stood under the shower's hot water, Sayaka's words replayed in my mind. The water washed away my sadness, leaving me feeling purged and cleansed. Although everything in Sayaka's house was unfamiliar, I felt a sense of bliss. Despite my frustration with my mother's behavior, I knew I was in the right place at the right time.

Gazing out the bathroom window, I noticed the crescent moon partially obscured by passing clouds. I remembered the words of the poet Shreya Maurya. "Talk to the moon or even the sun, both will tell you it's okay to disappear when things don't go right. But it's important to come back and spread your light."

And at that moment, I felt ready to spread my light.

Chapter 2

井の中の蛙大海を知らず。
I no naka no kawazu taikai wo shirazu.
A frog in a well does not know the great ocean.

January 2003

AFTER THAT EVENING WITH SAYAKA, I began to perceive my mother in a slightly altered manner. Though I still struggled to comprehend or fully embrace her actions, I made the conscious choice to grant her the space she needed, hoping that eventually, she would rediscover her true essence. I started treating her with greater respect and kindness, and in response, she gradually extended to me a modicum of trust and freedom.

During my early teenage years, I had possessed an insatiable hunger for life and held the belief that I had a profound understanding of existence, oftentimes surpassing that of my peers. Yet I soon discovered that foreign films served as a mere introduction to the profound script of life. With each passing encounter with Sayaka, my awareness expanded, and I came to the realization that I had been confined to a narrow sphere of existence. She unveiled the world to me from a fresh and invigorating perspective, dismantling the notion that age dictates maturity. It made me reflect on Minoru, who, despite being nearly triple her age, paled in comparison to her sagacity. Sayaka possessed wisdom far beyond her years, prompting me to occasionally question if she hailed from this very planet.

I had never met anyone like Sayaka. Her world was new, exciting, and challenging, and nobody truly understood it. But she knew I was on the path to being a part of it. Despite her knowledge, she was humble. Our favorite topic of conversation was travel. After school, we spent hours in small cafés, restaurants, and pubs, hiding

from the cold winter days, and discussing the places I'd never seen before. Listening to her, I felt like I was reading a fantasy book and she was the main fairy.

Her father's job, which required her family to migrate often, allowed her to live these incredible experiences that seemed like fantasies. But it wasn't just her colorful world that drew people to her; it was her positive attitude toward life that many lacked. She often said, "Perspective is everything, and you can always change problems into challenges, failures into lessons, rejection into redirection, and pain into power." Life is often merciless and throws challenges and adversity our way, but Sayaka knew how to keep moving. I felt proud and lucky to be her friend and couldn't wait to introduce her to my own group of friends. In many ways, we were different from other teens; but in others, we were just like them. We enjoyed partying until dawn, smoking, and gossiping to escape from home and school issues and responsibilities.

Among all the memorable moments we shared, I held a special fondness for our karaoke nights, when we would reserve a private room. We would indulge in copious amounts of beer, taking advantage of the tempting yet perilous all-you-can-drink specials, and feast on generous servings of *edamame*[*] and *yakisoba*.[†] Every night brought a unique blend of experiences and, despite our diverse backgrounds, we formed a tight-knit family, belting out tunes together. Our repertoire spanned across continents, harmonizing with the melodies of European hits, like U2, and Queen and seamlessly intertwining with Show Ya, Atsuko Maeda, and countless other songs we unearthed throughout those enchanting evenings.

The pinnacle of those nights undoubtedly belonged to Madoka and her awe-inspiring performances. Her voice, simultaneously angelic, smoky, and mellow, possessed a unique quality that emanated from the depths of her throat, carrying with it vibrations of seemingly uncharted melancholy. We couldn't help but question why she hadn't graced the world stage with her remarkable talent. Despite our constant encouragement for her to participate in talent

---

[*] (枝豆) *Edamame:* Green soybeans, usually steamed.

[†] (焼きそば) *Yakisoba:* Fried noodles, usually with vegetables and meat.

shows, however, Madoka preferred to stay with "her guys," her only audience. Among us, no one could even come close to her, particularly Ren, whose lack of singing talent never failed to elicit laughter.

While my own voice may not have been exceptional, I still derived immense joy from singing.

When it was my turn, I sang ballads while relying on a thick, well-worn book for guidance. As I closed my eyes, I transported myself to a different realm where everything and everyone ceased to exist. Even the posters of music stars on the red-painted walls would blur, resembling Picasso's art. It was my date with music and nothing else mattered.

As fun and nostalgic as they were, these nights were a way for us to silence our problems with the help of music and Kirin Lagers beer and to be artistically vulnerable in front of each other. But among all the excitement was our biggest fear: the karaoke bar's manager, Hyun-Soo, whom we secretly called "Macho." His signature appearance was the loud tapping of his cowboy boots as he walked toward our room, impatiently knocked on the door, and stood with his arms crossed in the door frame. He would twitch his lips, causing his thin mustache, which he was quite proud of, to dance. At closing time, he never hesitated to give us a cold and unwelcoming look and made no effort to hide his desire to be rid of us as soon as possible.

Despite Macho's hostility, we didn't want to go anywhere else. There was something about the place that made us feel at home. And it wasn't the half-torn, kiwi green couch or the sticky floor from sweet cocktail spills. It wasn't even the fact that he would turn a blind eye to our being underage to keep the business going. It was our comfort zone, our second home, our sanctuary that we had cherished over the last couple of years. And that was the place I wanted to show Sayaka most.

On rare occasions when Macho was in a good mood, he would join us for a few "on the house" beers, which would slightly reveal his Korean accent. On these few and seldom nights, we would leave at dawn, squinting against the daylight that had been obscured in the smoke-filled, dark rooms and only appeared at the main door, where the busy streets of Tokyo were filling again with people hurrying to work.

One freezing January night, however, Macho was not in a good mood, and as he stood at his favorite spot in the door frame, peaking at his watch, we knew it was time to leave. It was a huge shame, not only because we were at the peak of our fun, but because it was Sayaka's first time at our karaoke place. Even so, there was not much we could do.

At this stage, as always, Madoka would reach for the empty beer bottles that mostly ended up on the floor and put them on the table. Pedantic Fumiko would align them in a perfect row while I gathered all the other trash to place in the bin.

But tonight our "usual duties" were suddenly interrupted by Sayaka's firm yet soft voice, "You must be Macho."

Hyun-Soo looked abashed, as did we, especially since he was unaware of the nickname we had given him. I wanted to crawl underground and vanish into nothingness, and I believed the others felt the same.

With impatience and fear, we waited for what would be said next.

"I heard a lot about you," She continued. At that moment, we moved our eyes from Sayaka to Hyun-Soo, whose mustache moved slightly upward. But Sayaka spoke again, taking our attention back to her. "Only good things… Could I see your watch?"

We were all surprised when Macho sat next to Sayaka and proudly showed off his golden accessory.

"I stopped wearing one some time ago," she stated, examining it. "I used to live in Congo." Sayaka glanced at our confused faces. "Central Africa. Wow! What a beautiful place! The nature! I've never seen soil redder than there! And the women! Not only attractive but so strong! In the villages, for many miles, they would carry baskets full of cassavas, bananas, sugar cane, or even heavy charcoal and firewood."

Something about the way she spoke was addictive; it was easy to get lost in her stories. Was it her intonation, the content, the passion with which she spoke, or the vividness and detail of her tales? Maybe it was all these things combined. Whatever it was, when she spoke, it always brought silence to the space around her.

"My father's friend, Mark, was working as a UN pilot. He would often fly to the bush where Pigmy people lived." Always aware and present, she noticed our yet again bewildered faces and

explained, "Pigmy are an ethnic group. They are known for being really short, adult men are on average less than one hundred fifty centimeters."

Even though the Japanese aren't the tallest people, the Pigmy did seem very short, I thought to myself as the others, assuming the story would be longer, slowly started taking their seats again.

"So, Mark and the other pilots would give them blankets, clothes, and aid. One day, when Mark landed in one of the Congo forests, a local man asked him, using body language, looking at his watch, what it was. Mark looked at it and contemplated how to explain to this man what a watch was. He used a local translator and finally, he said in the easiest way he could describe it, 'It tells you when to eat, when to go to work and return, and also when to sleep.' Proud of finding the perfect words to describe a watch, he waited for the man's amusement. The man shook his head, pointed at it, and answered him with irony in his voice, 'This small thing tells you what to do?'"

At first, we started laughing at the story's conclusion, but then we slowly stopped and each of us sank into our thoughts. Eventually, there were more stories and more Kirin Lagers "on the house" that night. And from that day on, Macho never had a bad mood around us, and I never saw him wearing his watch again.

Chapter 3

人間には３つの顔がある。１つは自分の知る自分。２つ目は他人が知る自分。もう一つは本当の自分。

Ningen ni wa mittsu no kao ga aru. Hitotsu wa jibun no shiru jibun. Futatsume wa tanin ga shiru jibun. Mou hitotsu wa hontou no jibun.

People have three faces. The first face you show to the world. The second you show to your friends and family. The third face you never show to anyone. It is the truest reflection of who you are.

Koukou Kyoushi [*校教師*]

March 2004

AMID JAPAN'S BREATHTAKING NATURAL BEAUTY and the tranquil serenity of its temples, where perfection and aesthetics existed in every form and where attention to detail was evident in so many aspects of local life, I was both frightened and amazed by how few people took the time to appreciate these wonders and traditions. So few stopped and smelled the rainbow of flowers or gazed at the stars in the navy blue sky. Sadly, most of their moments were spent in the office or at a train station, racing against time.

Overwork was a significant issue in my country, and it even had a name—*karoushi.** The frustration and exhaustion of working long hours, often up to nineteen hours a day without a moment to eat breakfast or dinner, was leading many to a dismal fate. Secluded and drained, they sought fleeting solace wherever it lurked, resorting to heavy drinking or yielding to other vices to numb their stress, often collapsing in unexpected locales like streets or bars. In the worst cases, they would attempt suicide and repeatedly, tragically, succeed.

---

* (過労死) *Karoushi*: Death from overwork; an occupational death.

The toll of overwork was both physical and mental for many. They were pushed to their limits, exploiting their desire or need to simply survive, not even motioning to thrive.

"It's frightening how easy it can be to take one's own life," Sayaka mused one March day. "Sometimes it doesn't take much. The line between tolerable and unbearable pain is very thin. Humans can be strong, but they can also be incredibly fragile. Living under constant pressure and stress. They are on the edge, and then the worst is they can't see a way out. But if only they realized that there's always another tomorrow. We never know what the future holds."

"That unknown, which gives hope," I finished Sayaka's thought.

"Exactly! If only they knew," she agreed, emphasizing the bleakness of this existence. "There are so many absurdities in the world. In Japan, for example, people appreciate togetherness, but there's also a strict hierarchy. And they often care about others more than themselves. My mom, who used to be a flight attendant back in the eighties, always said that if there's a decompression in the plane, you must put on your own mask first, then take care of the others. But if you try to help someone else before you put yours on, there's a chance you both could pass out from a lack of oxygen. Yeah, so it's something to think about..." She sniffled as she always did when she spoke from the heart. "What kind of life is this, to keep pleasing others before you make yourself happy? We only have one life. Why waste it like this?"

Sayaka opened my eyes to the sorrow of this irrationality, something I had never fully considered before. When you're rooted in your homeland, it's easy to miss the bigger picture. But having an outside perspective, like hers, helped to shed light on these issues.

We discussed these heavy topics, but also lighter subjects. My favorite tale was about how her parents met.

"Well," she began, "when Mom was still new to Japan Airlines, the manager put her to work in business class on a flight to Hong Kong without any training. One of the cabin crew had called in sick, so she had to fill in. She had no idea what she was doing, so you can imagine how nervous she was. The crew used to give nicknames to passengers to make it easier to recognize them when serving. My dad was one of them, and the girls called him 'Dimples' because of the deep indentations on his cheeks. That's where I got mine from." She paused and smiled as if she wanted to present them again. "He

was seated in Mom's area of responsibility, so she had to serve him. He asked for tomato juice, and, believe it or not, her hand was so shaky from nerves that when she passed it to him, she spilled it all over his white trousers."

"Oh my God! He must have been so pissed," I concluded.

"He wasn't that pissed since they're married now," she remarked, chuckling, to which I nodded in agreement, joining in the laughter.

Our connection was always a source of immense joy fostered by our shared sense of humor. We reveled in the art of cracking jokes and exchanging amusing anecdotes during our everyday interactions. However, there were also moments of comfortable silence, where we would simply coexist, engrossed in our individual activities. I would peruse the books Sayaka had brought from her travels, while she meticulously filed her nails, immersed herself in comics, or even indulged in a brief nap. Just like the Spaniards, she cherished those blissful siestas.

In search of a more daring escapade, unbeknownst to my mom, we would clandestinely "borrow" kimonos from her closet. Once adorned with vibrant garments and complemented by carefully applied makeup, we would transform ourselves into Geishas. Sayaka exuded an air of authenticity, resembling a true diva as she skillfully balanced a cigarette between her lips, while I resorted to using a breadstick, cleverly simulating puffs of faux smoke by blowing cold air.

We would giggle at strangers, blowing kisses and winking at them. Our antics would often make them respond, and we'd run away laughing. Despite the discomfort of wearing tight kimonos, the joy they brought us was worth it.

For our favorite vintage shopping, we would visit second-hand shops in Shimokitazawa, also known as Shimo or Shimokita among locals. This place had a rich history, a unique underground vibe, cozy bars, restaurants, live music, retro bohemian shops with vintage garments, and old record stores. It attracted a diverse crowd of people from different subcultures and backgrounds.

As we passed by Shibuya, we never failed to pet the statue of Hachiko, the famously loyal dog who had been immortalized in bronze. We held his unbelievable story dear and cherished this opportunity to express our love.

Just down the road, we would often stop at Zaya Café for ice cream.

"Do you see that waitress running back and forth?"

Assuming I knew who she meant, I looked around just to make sure we were thinking about the same person. "You mean the one who just spilled a coffee a minute ago?"

"Yes, that's the one. Do you know that it often happens to her? Why do you think that is?"

I answered with a guess, "Maybe she's just clumsy?"

Sayaka scratched her head and continued, "That might be part of it, but I don't think that's the real reason. It's okay to spill coffee—we all mess up. But if you watch her, you can see that she is the only one always rushing. It seems like she thinks being fast is more important than being friendly and natural. I find her service robotic. Trying to please unnaturally. No eye contact. No listening skills. It brings the opposite effect. Fast doesn't always mean right."

"How did you see it all? I haven't really noticed."

"I like observing people. She reminds me of how not everyone in Japan values *shokunin*[†] and *omotenashi*,[‡] which is a shame. It's the business card of Japan and would be great to be implemented everywhere. Anyway, if you have a calling for a job, it won't feel like a struggle."

"And how do you find that calling?"

"It comes in its own time and everything just feels right. It's like you've found where you belong… Just like with love…"

"Did you find yours?" I asked, curious.

"What? A job or love?" She smiled and I saw a glimmer in her eye.

"Let's start with love," I said.

"Well," she sighed, and I didn't know if I had asked the right thing.

"If you don't want to talk about it, it's okay," I added promptly.

"No, no, it's not that. It's just not a happy ending. I promise I'll tell you another day. In its time."

---

† (職人) *Shokunin*: A craftsman or artisan.

‡ (お持て成し) *Omotenashi*: Hospitality, reception; A Japanese expression that roughly describes concepts of hospitality and mindfulness.

Trying to lighten the mood, I moved on to the second topic, "What about the job? Did you find your calling?"

"I kind of did."

"And? What is it?"

"Being a never-ending tourist," she replied with a grin.

"Oh, that's a great job!"

We both laughed.

A week later as I sat waiting for her at our favorite and unchanging Zaya Café, I stared at the spilled coffee on the table next to me in thought. Sayaka was late. If it had been anyone else, I would have left. Despite not always providing the best service, we hadn't found a better matcha ice cream in the entire capital. However, my desire to consume the dessert was fading with each passing minute. A huge clock on the funky, delicious-looking pink wall, wasn't lying. She was late. Again. Since I met her, she had never been on time. This was starting to irritate me more and more.

The entrance door kept opening, but she didn't appear. After a tall, male tourist, a group of uniformed school girls and two businessmen had walked through in the last twenty minutes. I was becoming increasingly frustrated at not catching a glimpse of her. To make matters worse, a cheerful couple entered, and their laughter only added to my annoyance.

Just as I was about to stand up in frustration, Sayaka finally walked in, her face grim with worry. She quickly sat in front of me, removing her scarf and hanging it on the back of the chair. In one breath, she said, "Aiko, remember I was telling you about that girl from the Indian slums that I used to visit?"

I didn't need long to recall who she was talking about. It was Mahika, a bright girl with aspirations of becoming a nurse. Sayaka had smuggled books for her to secretly study English and basic medicine against her parents' wishes. With the little knowledge she had gained, Mahika had helped her neighbors with hypertension and anemia, and in time, anyone who needed help in the slums. These were usually minor problems, like high fever or diarrhea, but she had even assisted in childbirth. But I wasn't interested in how Mahika was doing, and I couldn't understand why Sayaka was bringing her up now.

"We used to go there with my friends I met in the ashram. Mahika was the smart girl who…" she began.

I interrupted her, "I know who you're talking about."

Sayaka's face was pitiful as she continued, "Carla wrote me a letter to say that Mahika's parents have decided to marry her off to a man twice her age because they can't afford to have her around anymore. She's only fifteen years old! She's become depressed and desperate, but there's nothing she can do. I'm just so frustrated. Sometimes, I can't understand this world anymore…"

"To be honest, I don't care about what happened to Mahika. You were late again. There's always some explanation. It's irritating, annoying, and tiring," I said, watching as Sayaka looked shocked. It took her a few seconds to respond.

"Aiko! You're not being serious," she exclaimed.

"Yes, I am very serious," I replied with no mercy.

"You're acting like you're the center of the world," she retorted outraged.

"Really? I thought the same thing about you," I snapped, becoming increasingly agitated. "I'm tired of you disrespecting me. I even ignored my friends for you. At least they value my time!" I finished, standing up and moving my chair back with a loud screech on the floor. "What kind of life is this to keep pleasing others before you make yourself happy?" With satisfaction, I quoted her own words against her and walked out of the café.

It didn't take long for me to regret my decision, but there was no way I was going back. I marched toward the train station, thinking that if I returned, it would be a sign of weakness. As if I would give up or admit that I was wrong. But I knew I wasn't mistaken.

I could only hope that Sayaka would look for me soon, apologize, and we would sit in front of each other at Zaya, enjoying our favorite matcha ice creams, as if nothing had happened.

Sayaka was aware of where I lived, but we rarely hung out at my place. Not only was my apartment small, but even though my mother had met her and really liked her, I didn't feel comfortable inviting my friends over. And Sayaka understood this.

As sunset turned to sunrise and another sunset, a deafening silence echoed between the four walls of my room. The unbearable loneliness and the fear of losing Sayaka weighed on me.

As much as I wanted to be upset with her for the sheer lack of respect she had shown me and for the last awful words she had spoken to me before I left, I found myself losing focus on those reasons. My anger and hurt started to fade away until I finally stood from my bed and decided to face her.

Swinging my denim jacket over my shoulder, I rushed to the door. To my surprise, Sayaka was already there, as if a telepathic force had brought her to my doorstep.

I let her in, and she walked straight to my balcony with a lit clove cigarette. After a moment of silence and smoke from her mouth which disappeared into the crisp air, Sayaka finally spoke. "I thought about what you told me, and you are right. I should have been more considerate of your time. I'm always late. I know that." She sighed and took a deep breath to continue. "And as much as I don't like being a slave to time, I will do my best to change that habit. Time is the greatest gift a friend can give one another. We can never recapture our time, and that is something I wanted to apologize for."

I was surprised and didn't know what to say at first, but a huge relief washed over me after her confession. My thoughts, deeply stored in my heart for days, finally transferred to words as I said, "I am so happy you came. I left you behind, alone in front of everyone. I felt so ashamed to embarrass you like that. In fact, I was afraid I had lost you forever... especially when you said I'm not the center of the world." I paused for a loud guilty sigh.

With a hurt ego, I hoped she would put a balm on it.

"Aiko, have you ever heard of this saying? 'People have three faces. The first face, you show to the world. The second face, you show to your friends and your family. The third face, you never show to anyone. It is the truest reflection of who you are.'"

"Yes?" I said doubtfully, trying to comprehend what she was trying to tell me.

"I showed you a third face, Aiko," she began. She gave me a moment to ponder over it, but upon seeing no response from me, she continued. "Can't you see that I am just being honest with you? Sometimes, even if it hurts? That I have no limits on what I can or

can't tell you? What is the meaning of friendship if I only tell you beautiful things? Is this how we can elevate each other and become better versions of ourselves? Through lies and pretending? There would be no room for becoming better. Anyone can flatter you and sweet-talk you. Anyone can hang out and party with you until dawn. I know, I've been there—waking up in the morning with the worst hangover, surrounded by smoke and poison from the night before, with vomit and an unbearable stench filling every corner of an unrecognizable place.

"But the sluggishness of your brain and the pain are not as bad as the pang of consciousness of the lost memory, as if you're watching yourself on the most pitiful theater stage. And everyone around is actors playing their roles. Nobody really knows you. Even, yourself. Not everyone is willing to be truthful with you. The question is, are we ready to hear the truth? For months now, I have shown you the purest reflection of who I am, without any filters."

"What you said was hurtful," I interrupted, still in a victimizing state, as she gashed out her cigarette on the balcony railing and gazed blankly at the horizon.

"No matter which country we come from, we share common traits. One of them is seeing our problems as the biggest ones. We often lack humanity, understanding, compassion, empathy, and modesty. The truth is that we all sometimes behave as if we are the center of the universe. Aiko, I don't mean that each of us isn't special. It's exactly the opposite—we are all special because we are so different. Funnily enough, despite our differences, we are so alike at the same time. We have the same needs. We all want to be loved, respected, needed, healthy, and happy. We are all connected, in fact. And as I said before, we shouldn't please others all the time and put them in front of our own needs, but also we shouldn't only care about ourselves, but find a healthy balance. We were created to help and love one another."

I tried to grasp her words. They were new and unknown to me.

"Tell me—when you used to help in your mom's kimono shop, that girl, Fumi, used to do everything to spoil your hard work, sneaking behind and saying lies to your mom about you. Right?" It was a rhetorical question, as she continued, "But when she was finally dismissed and Hikaru came to take her place, everything went smoothly and you made amazing sales together because of your

teamwork with her. Remember how your mom was proud of you?" I nodded, slowly understanding what she meant. "That's a perfect example of how human relations can work. When we help each other, we can achieve great things and life becomes much more enjoyable. But if we are careless about others, life can become a struggle and even hellish. It's that simple. Sometimes the simplest things are the hardest to understand. Life isn't difficult, it's people who make it difficult."

I immediately thought of Minoru and Mother.

"So, when we open our eyes a bit wider, we can see that we have much more in common with our neighbors than we thought. Our problems may not be as bad as they seemed at first, and many people have it worse than us. We're not the only ones in this universe. That's what I meant by saying you are not the center of the world." Sayaka cleared her throat before she added, "It's hard to admit one's mistakes, but you were right. I am not the center of this world, either. And I understand why you are pissed. That's why I came to your house to apologize for being disrespectful and not considering your time. I shouldn't make excuses," she added.

"And I am sorry for not seeing the bigger picture. For not caring about the greater problems, like the ones Mahika has to go through. We can't even compare our problems with hers! You are right, you always are…"

"No, Aiko, I don't have all the answers. Sometimes, I feel like I've seen too much. Too many places, too many people, too many situations. Like I've seen it all. Yet paradoxically, I often feel like the more I see, the less I know," she admitted.

With that brief and unexpected confession, I found myself struggling to accept that I might have had unrealistic expectations of Sayaka. In my mind, she was perfect, the ultimate truth, a goddess. However, she showed me something even more valuable. By embracing her weaknesses and struggles and by daring to question the world and challenge the status quo, she was authentic and astute enough to not accept life at face value or blindly follow societal norms.

"Being of mixed heritage can be amazing and challenging. Sometimes you feel like you belong everywhere and nowhere at the

same time. Even when you think of the word *hafu.*§ Does it mean I am only half of a human? And what about the other half? I know many people don't pay attention to these details, yet for some, these details are everything they've got. They would only understand if they were in our shoes," she said.

"So, it's not a country, tradition, or culture, that defines who you are then?" I asked, eager to understand her better.

"Many people think that, but through my experiences, I've come to realize that we are all just children of this Earth," she replied. "People love to put themselves and others in boxes, to use labels, especially when it suits them. But can't we all simply belong to Mother Earth, as one?"

That conversation took our friendship to a higher and deeper level. It proved to me once more that true friendship was not only about partying, drinking, or telling each other meaningless stories but about growing together, even if it meant temporary pain. It was about accepting one another without unrealistic expectations and idealizations. Nobody is perfect, and that's okay.

Even though Sayaka never put a watch on her wrist, she made an effort not to be as late as she used to be. And that effort meant everything to me. I, in turn, took the time to be more aware of the world around me, to look at various perspectives, to question what wasn't clear, to think before I spoke, and to look for answers.

That evening, we stayed up until dawn, talking about nothing and everything.

And we cried. Shedding tears for Mahika, and for all the girls and women across the globe who are oppressed by men. They are unable to make their own choices simply because of their gender. We cried for the stoning, beating, bullying, and mental abuse that left no bruises, only scars etched onto their hearts forever. And we

---

§ (ハーフ) *Hafu*: A biracial person, especially one who is half-Japanese; literally means "half."

shed tears for the abused men who go unnoticed and unrecognized by society.

We wept together for the suppression and societal pressure on the Japanese population, especially the ones who needed to obey, conform, and prioritize public approval, even if it goes against their true feelings. Our tears flowed for the victims of the suicide forest, for the loneliness experienced by *hikikomori*, and for those who, despite having the gift of sight, are blind to the limitations they impose upon themselves by following the system without questioning it. They are blind to the fact that there are greater rewards than pleasing a boss or sacrificing their own happiness for the sake of others.

And we mourned for the victims of racism, individuals who endure suffering simply because of variations in their skin color, something not chosen by them.

We also cried for those with disabilities who are so often subjected to bullying, misunderstanding, and disrespect and are seen as inferior beings. All they desire, like anyone else, is love and acceptance.

And we mourned for the victims of war, individuals whose basic necessities have been taken away. Instead of hearing the joyous explosions of fireworks, they endure the deafening blasts of bombs. Children who often have not only lost their mothers, but also their fathers, siblings, and friends, and have been left to live in poverty amid the destruction caused by war. They exist day by day, with no promise of a tomorrow.

And we shed tears for those struggling with addiction, trapped in a vicious cycle and relying on substances to solve their problems, only to wake up the next day, in an even worse state.

We wept for the most vulnerable among us: children and animals who often lack the ability to protect themselves and who, after growing up in abuse, not rarely continue this cycle with limited chances to escape.

And we mourned for those living in fear, lacking the courage to embrace the truth and love instead.

And yet we found tears for the oppressors as well, for the system and the families that trap them in this course. We cried for their weaknesses, blindness, and ignorance, and for those who simply do not know any better.

We grappled with the circumstances and injustices of the world but found no answers.

It was a cathartic experience, but we knew that our tears would not save the Earth. We knew we wouldn't rescue the whole world. We understood that change must begin within ourselves.

So, we made a promise to always strive to be a better version of ourselves and to support each other in this journey.

There is always a calm before the storm. And as Japanese, we could always feel it in the air.

Typhoons were nothing new to our country, but every time one was about to hit, I still couldn't help but feel anxious and terrified. No matter how much we prepared for its arrival, we could never guarantee Mother Nature's intentions.

With its relentless winds and heavy rains pulling moisture from the oceans, the typhoons made landfall, causing mass flooding and ripping apart tediously planted harvests. With hysteria and lament in their throats and shock and dread in the depths of their eyes, people looked upon the outrage of water that took everything they had worked their whole lives for in no time.

Cars with weak alarms wailing, hard-to-identify flying debris falling off roofs, broken trees surrendering to almighty Nature's whims or, one would say, punishments for some, floating to the unknown destination—nothing was spared. Lives were lost in seconds.

Victimized, lonely, and petrified people in the emptiness of deprivation, waking up to a nightmare of their reality, counting with unbearable pain and disbelief their impossible and unimaginable losses. The peace and harmony of one moment are taken by the chaos of another.

In the midst of the disorder, even those who didn't suffer personal losses, driven by their inherent empathetic nature as Japanese, rallied together in shared grief for their neighbors' calamity. Amidst the wreckage of what were once cars, meticulously tended houses, serene Zen gardens, flower pots, kitchen utensils,

treasured dolls, and faded family portraits, people united to rebuild and embark on a fresh beginning.

In Japan, with around twenty typhoons per year, the year 2004 brought particularly severe damage with typhoons Songda and Tokage leading the way. While it did not impact Tokyo, countless other towns were affected. Despite the widespread destruction caused by these monsters, Sayaka and I experienced our own personal tragedy that overshadowed the misfortunes brought by the forces of nature.

And though there was no falling debris or collapsing roofs, I felt just as much chaos and turmoil when Sayaka received news from her father that they would soon be moving to Lima, Peru.

"That's an ambassador's fate," she could only explain. Still reeling from the shock, Sayaka tried to compose herself as she began packing her luggage. Her wrecked suitcase was adorned with an array of colorful stickers, some scratched from all her travels. Rubbing off my salty tears and trying to hold her own, she lit a cigarette. "I knew this day would come, but I didn't expect it so soon."

The idea of letting her go was excruciating and heart-wrenching. Yet deep down, I knew that our meeting was fate. Our friendship was not coming to an end. With tear-filled eyes, we pinky swore to keep in touch by writing letters to each other.

The two years I spent with Sayaka irrevocably changed me. I was fortunate to have met her. We were more than just friends; we were more than family. We were not afraid to show each other our third face.

As she passed through the ticket gate and walked through the crowded airport, I spotted her head among the hundreds of unfamiliar ones. She was rushing as she was running late for her flight. And I knew then that she meant more to me than words could express.

At that moment, I realized she was the person I needed to guide me. Before she disappeared into the sea of heads, I bowed after her and whispered, "*Arigatou*."**

** (ありがとう) *Arigatou*: Thank you.

Chapter 4

一期一会。
Ichigo ichie.
One opportunity, one encounter.

February 2005

FOR SOME TIME, I STILL had my close group of friends, but things were not the same. They accused me of neglecting them in my infatuation with Sayaka which gradually led me to realize how much we had grown apart in our choices of conversation and values. Spiky and Fumiko were often preoccupied with talking about fashion, trendy looks, and the lives of celebrities while rolling cigarettes. Ren would frequently skip our hangouts to be with a girl he had just met from his school, and the rest of the group spent their time playing poker and gossiping about people I didn't know.

While we still enjoyed our time together, something was missing.

It felt like I was moving forward while they were staying behind. It seemed they were content with the status quo while I had broken free of it in many aspects. After several attempts, I sadly concluded that they were not ready for change. I knew that there was not much I could do and that I could not influence the paths and destinies of others.

Regretfully, we grew apart. But the real climax arose with the destruction of the base within which we had built memories over the years. Years of tears, laughter, first kisses, and shared experiences, from playing poker to falling in love and experiencing heartbreak—all gone in seconds, reduced to ramshackle bricks and balls of dust left behind.

Although we didn't frequent the base as much as we used to and we knew the day would come eventually, nothing could have

prepared us for the emotional impact of watching it fall into a million pieces.

Standing there, with tears in my eyes, feeling hopeless and most of all helpless, I watched as our estate was demolished, like a house of cards in a windstorm, a sad reminder of the recent Japanese typhoon catastrophes.

With audible sighs, we realized the fragility of things beyond our control, although no one admitted it aloud. We knew it was the end. As we said our goodbyes amid the sound of falling debris from the building, I understood that it was the last time we would be together. The group dynamic was gone and there was no longer a sense of "the guys."

This marked the beginning of the end. People were coming and going, and there was nothing I could do about it.

Like Sayaka's family—who was moving to Peru—my own decided to change residence and move elsewhere within Japan. During one of the few evenings when Minoru was at home, he sat in his armchair in the living room watching NHK news on our brand-new Sony TV while Prime Minister Junichiro Koizumi's speech was playing. Still blindly gazing at the TV, he informed me of his plans in a casual manner, as if nothing were amiss. He had received a better job offer in Shizuoka; he was moving our family there. Additionally, I was going to start university in Hamamatsu, over eighty kilometers away from our new home, to study medicine and become a doctor.

This instantly reminded me of one winter evening when, after having too many savory Ishikawa sakes, he had admitted to still carrying anger and blame toward his father for the poverty that had shattered his youth dream of becoming a well-respected doctor. He was determined to live vicariously through me.

Once again, he assumed what was best for us and his needs dominated our lives, leaving me with no escape from his unfulfilled desires.

The house we moved into, unlike our Tokyo abode, was in a secluded area. It was far more spacious than our apartment with an open kitchen, a commodious living room divided by *fusuma*,* and small bedrooms. The house boasted thick, oak floors, except for the bedrooms which had tatami, and a fresh, minimalistic but very Japanese personality.

Well-kept narrow *engawa*,† separating *shouji*‡ and outer storm shutters, were hidden under a dark silvery roof that provided shade on scorching days. Bonsai trees with their perfect trim in the tiny greenish patch at the front of the house were showered by generous sunlight and bid a warm welcome to guests. A small marble fountain that attracted musical birds brought a feeling of tranquility. However, the atmosphere inside the home, within our family, was quite the opposite.

Everything returned to its routine when Minoru found a new throne for his sake evenings; Mother found a corner in the kitchen for her solitary cooking times. While birds sang their pleasant melodies outside, Minoru shouted painful epithets directed toward me and Mother. But his words were nothing compared to the yawning chasm Sayaka's departure had left in me.

They say that smell is the strongest of all senses. I didn't know if that was a fact, but I knew my heartbeat quickened when I smelled the familiar scent of Indonesian cigarettes on the first day

---

* (襖) *Fusuma*: Rectangular panels in Japanese architecture that can slide from side to side and redefine rooms.

† (縁側) *Engawa*: The wooden strip of flooring before windows and storm shutters inside traditional rooms.

‡ (障子) *Shouji*: A door, window, or room divider made of rice paper or washi over a frame of wood, usually held together by a lattice of word or bamboo.

of June as I returned from my lectures at the Hamamatsu train station. The feeling of déjà vu and nostalgia washed over me as I tried to find its source. I scanned the faces of the people around me, hoping to find Sayaka puffing out clouds of clove aroma from her round, full lips. It had been close to half a year since I had received her first and last letter, and it was unbearable to accept that she could have forgotten me so easily.

I sent her a letter with our new Shizuoka address. Lima was an ocean away, and she always tended to lose track of time. But to that extent? It was hard to comprehend. Had she come back to Japan and not told me?

Hope quickly turned to disappointment and regret as I realized that the source of the smoke was coming from a young *gaijin*§ who stood a head taller than the rest of the crowd. I approached, drawn by the familiar scent, and closed my eyes to bask in the memories it evoked. But my moment of peace was interrupted by a voice speaking in English, asking, "Do you want some?"

I opened my eyes to find a familiar pack of cigarettes held out in front of me, accompanied by a huge smile from its owner.

So, there I stood, facing a tall, blond-haired foreigner offering me a cigarette in English. It had been a while since I last used it. Gathering my courage, I fumbled a response. "I don't smoke."

"Oh, sorry, you looked like you wanted some."

I could have sworn I saw a hint of a smirk on his face, which irked me slightly. I didn't feel like explaining to him the reason behind my love for the scent of Indonesian cigarettes, so I gave him a stiff smile, hoping he would stop talking to me. It then dawned on me that he was breaking the law, but despite my disinterest in continuing the conversation, I felt a twinge of pity for him, getting into trouble or facing a potential fine.

"It's not allowed to smoke here," I whispered. In spite of the astonished looks from commuters, he casually crushed his cigarette with his Vans shoe on the train platform.

He gave me a half-smile and smoothly changed the topic. "I'm heading to see Mount Fuji. Where are you going?" I was familiar with the directness of foreigners thanks to Sayaka's stories. Instead of answering, I glanced at his enormous camera, which he noticed

§ (外人) *Gaijin*: Foreigner.

and exclaimed with excitement, "It's a Nikon D70, just released a year ago." He took a proud look at it and continued, "I'm planning to go to Miho Beach to take some shots of the great mountain."

I knew Miho Beach and often went there for a break from my intense school lectures. It was a way for me to take a virtual trip back to my life in Tokyo and the memories I cherished with my friends. However, there was no one I missed more than Sayaka. While I yearned for the others, it was Sayaka who had had a significant impact on my life. After meeting her, nothing had felt the same, and I could never go back to who I was. I had matured over the past years into a person I hardly recognized.

On days when I visited Miho Beach alone, I would see her bright, deep blue eyes reflected in the waters of Suruga Bay. And I would cry, unlike most Japanese, in public, simply because I felt like it. Crying helped me feel free and purified me. On windy days, my tears were stunned by the angry waves, while on calmer days, I received a compassionate gaze or, more rarely, an ironic smile, and sometimes even a tissue from passing by strangers.

Now, this foreigner was going to *my* beach. It felt like he was walking with shoes on into my house. And possessively, I felt annoyed. Aggravated enough to protect my sanctuary, I decided to follow in the same direction as the foreigner when he again asked me where I was going. Additionally, there was no rush to go to my intellectually empty house where nothing awaited me but my mother's negativity and my father's preaching. Most importantly, I didn't feel like studying for tomorrow's exam.

It seemed to surprise the foreigner as he asked, "That's great. Can you show me the way from the bus station to the beach? I understand there's a bit of a walk."

I nodded and he smiled. Amid our awkward silence, he caught me off guard with an unexpected religious confession, "I am Christiaan. And you?"

I replied curtly, "Well, I think religion is my own business."

His sudden laughter puzzled me until he explained, "It's my name. Well, Chris in short. What's yours?"

I instantly felt heat spread throughout my body and imagined my face turning tomato-red. I could see him trying to stifle his laughter.

"I am Aiko," I answered quickly, eager to put an end to my embarrassment.

"Like the name of the emperor's daughter?" he asked, looking at me without any shame and adding with a bold and rakish wink, "Princess."

This left me confused, but I was impressed with his knowledge of Japan. I wondered where he was from but kept that question to myself.

As we stood there waiting for the train, he finally said, "I heard that trains in Japan are never late!" He was correct, trains in Japan were rarely late. People were focused on each other's satisfaction and respect as a collective unit.

But not all countries were like this, as I remembered Sayaka's stories about the railway system in rural India. They were not only consistently late but there were times when people had to wait hours for them and sometimes even had to sit on the rooftops because of a lack of space inside. It was hard to grasp, and I was still amazed by the diversity of our world.

When the train arrived exactly on time, I noticed Chris fidgeting; it was obvious he wanted to cut the neatly formed line of people. But since I was standing in a queue, he joined me, waiting for his turn. Despite this, he continued to search for an excuse.

"Too many rules here. I'm an artist, not a robot," he finally said, admitting his true thoughts. "And I'm also impatient."

Although I did agree with him to some extent, I felt like I needed to challenge him. "Good luck," I responded.

"Excuse me?" Chris asked, appearing puzzled.

"Good luck with no patience in your life," I repeated.

"Are you patient?" he inquired.

"Very."

The train was packed with people, but it was a little girl with pigtails sitting a few rows from the door that caught my attention. Looking out the window with excitement while her feet swung back and forth, she suddenly gave me a smile that conveyed the innocence of childhood.

"Is she alone?" Chris asked, gazing at the child.

"Yes."

"At her age? She doesn't look more than six years old," he said in disbelief.

"It's normal in Japan. Even younger children travel by themselves to and from school. They are very independent," I explained.

But that wasn't why I was observing her. I realized she was the only truly awake person in the train car.

Everyone else was either sleeping or appeared to be on the brink of dozing off. A man with thick, black-rimmed glasses had his head on the shoulder of the person next to him, only realizing it was a stranger when the train's loudspeaker announced the next stop at Kakegawa Station. Embarrassed, he awoke with a start and apologized to the man with a sheepish smile and a bow.

The foreigner also noticed the situation, glancing at me to confirm if I had seen it as well before throwing me a cheeky smile. But this was not an unusual sight. It was just as common as seeing foreigners eat on the train, which was happening at that moment as Christiaan removed a sandwich from his backpack to snack on.

"It's not really polite to eat on the train in Japan," I whispered to him, trying to avoid further embarrassment.

"But I'm hungry," he replied.

I passed him a sardonic smile. "You can do whatever you want, I'm just telling you how things are here."

He considered the dilemma, but like a little kid, eventually decided to take a quick bite of his sandwich. Although he rapidly put it away after the nibble, he didn't seem bothered and it appeared that the people around him were more uncomfortable than he was. Fortunately, the awkward moment was coming to an end as we approached our stop.

"We're getting off at the next station," I informed him.

Now standing at the bus stop, I was just fifteen minutes away from home, and I suddenly had second thoughts about going to the beach with this stranger. However, I remembered the reason why I had decided to come in the first place; I was determined not to back out now.

I took a seat on the bus but stood up a minute later to offer it to a young lady.

"Why did you let her sit? She doesn't look much older than you," Christiaan asked.

"Can you see the heart-shaped keychain with a mother and a baby hanging from her backpack?" I replied. He glanced discreetly

and nodded. "That means she's pregnant, but since it might be in the early stages, you wouldn't know. The chain is to let people know."

He looked at her and then at me, amused. "Japan is one special place."

Throughout the arduous journey that consisted of a train ride and a shorter bus trip, we stood side by side. We hadn't engaged in much conversation during our two-hour expedition, save for a few casual exchanges and his insatiable curiosity about Japan. His random questioning didn't bother me in the least. Surprisingly, time whisked by faster than I had anticipated, and before I knew it, we found ourselves en route to the beach, traversing a magnificent pathway adorned with ancient pine trees.

"Fuck!" he exclaimed in excitement, followed by an innocent, almost remorseful look as he added quieter this time, "Pardon my French. It's just hard to describe the beauty of this place other than to use the f-word."

But he was right, and nobody could deny that there was something mesmerizing about Mount Fuji. The breathtaking view was a blend of vigorous waves of jet black and navy blue and lava rocks that glistened beneath cascading water droplets. In the background was Mount Fuji, its snow-top peak glorious in the sunlight.

"So, you're French?" I naively asked as he shared with me another generous smile.

"Nah, it's just an English expression. I'm actually Dutch. I'm from Holland, Europe. Have you heard of it?"

My world map understanding had improved after I met Sayaka, and I had come across that country, but that was it. My knowledge about the place ended there and I truly hoped not to be asked more. To my relief, as if reading my mind, he added, "I don't expect you to know much. It's a small country with big people." He paused for a smile and continued. "But if you want to know more, feel free to ask me."

"Thanks." I quickly changed the subject. "You're lucky, by the way. You can't always see Mount Fuji. It's often covered by clouds or fog."

"Yes, I am lucky," he smiled again and looked deeply into my eyes, which made me feel uncomfortable, "Can I?"

"What?" I was uneasy and confused about his intention.

"Take a photo of you?"

Then, without my consent, in a matter of seconds, he spun the camera into his hands and took a photo of us together.

"Hey! What are you doing?"

"Sorry, if you want, I can delete it." He seemed genuinely apologetic with his contrite face.

"It's fine," I said dismissively while he took off energetically to finally do what he had come there for.

After wandering the shore for a while, we sat on the cold sand and Chris began showing me some of the shots he had just taken of the mountain.

"So, you're a photographer?"

"Well, if you're asking about my profession, then no. I'm a banker. Or rather, I was... I resigned a month ago. I couldn't stand being in the office from eight to four o'clock. Not my cup of tea. Five years of my life looking at a computer screen was more than enough. So, I bought a camera and decided to finally make my dream come true—travel. Japan is my first stop. I've always wanted to come here for some reason." He paused for a second as if he was waiting for some reaction, which he didn't get so he continued. "Now you know everything about me. Well, almost everything… How about you?"

I chuckled. "I can't beat your story."

"What do you mean?" he asked.

"Well, your story seems much more interesting than mine. I have never even been overseas," I replied, embittered.

"Come on. Each of us has our own story and path, so don't say that. Comparison is the thief of joy. Besides, you are still so young... I assume." He ran an appraising eye over me before continuing. "You will see. You will travel. You are just at the beginning of your life. There are so many chapters to come."

He was right, I knew it. After Sayaka's farewell, I had forgotten about my dreams and how to smile. But now, he had brought it back to my face for the first time in a long time.

As I walked into my house, I couldn't help but notice the familiar smell of burning incense left by the previous owners. Though it wasn't unpleasant, it was always present and hard to miss. This time, however, my attention was drawn more to the tiny pebbles that were lodged between my toes, a reminder of my trip to the beach. I quickly removed them as I made my way upstairs to my room.

Once there, I reached for my favorite birthday present, a world atlas given to me by Sayaka on my seventeenth birthday. As I flipped through the pages, I searched for information about Holland, but couldn't find it. For a moment, I thought that maybe the stranger I met at the beach had said Poland instead. But as I turned the pages one last time, I discovered that Holland was also known as The Netherlands.

Before I could delve deeper into the book, I fell asleep. The alarm clock startled me awake sometime the following morning.

Despite trying hard to catch up on my exam topics on the train to school, I kept having to return to the beginning of the chapter. My thoughts were not focused on the lower and upper limbs, but rather on the stranger's smile. Christiaan had asked for my number, but I didn't have one, as I was faithful in my belief against technology and didn't own a phone. Even if I did, I convinced myself, I wouldn't have given it to him as we had only just met. But he was persistent and shouted goodbye, saying, "Tomorrow… Same time! Same place!"

Without thinking, I blurted out, "No! Sorry!" and now I was trying to convince myself that I had made the right decision.

But if it was right, why couldn't I shake off the thoughts of Christiaan? He continued to pop up in my mind like a recurring memory, and I couldn't seem to find a reason why. Now I truly needed Sayaka who, most of the time, seemed to have an answer for everything.

During the exam, my head pounded and the questions seemed to make no sense. I knew I was likely to fail, but that wasn't what worried me. The fear of never seeing Chris again gnawed at me.

So, in a spontaneous decision, at the last minute, I jumped off the bus in Shizuoka before it could reach my home, much to the confounded face of the driver. I knew I had to go to Miho Beach, there was no other way.

After a long ride, I finally arrived at the same bus stop I had been at just the day before. As I approached the beach, I felt a mixture of excitement and anxiety. The longer I walked along the shore, the more conflicted my emotions became. The beach seemed longer than usual. After pacing back and forth three times, I took a break and sat on the hard, uncomfortable rocks in front of the angry waves that mercilessly crashed onto the uneven shoreline.

The sun was setting, casting a beautiful array of red, pink, and purple hues that reflected off the horizon and making the water appear even more cold and lonely. The only thing I could discern were the silhouettes of a few people in the background.

Sighing heavily, I gazed out at the sea, feeling disappointed and angry with myself for bothering to come to meet a stranger. I was searching for answers, trying to reconcile with my destiny when I got up to walk back to the bus station. But only a few seconds later, I heard a panting voice behind me.

"Hey, are you in a hurry?" Before I even turned around, I recognized Christiaan's deep voice. I wondered how and when he had arrived, but the answer didn't matter after all. The warmth in my heart overpowered my body's chill and racing thoughts when Christiaan stepped toward me. This was a new and overwhelming feeling, scary yet electrifying at the same time, and I felt as if I had lost my voice. Despite that, I couldn't take my eyes off him.

I was bewildered by what was happening to me and I wondered if Christiaan could sense my emotions. The cool breeze from the sea didn't alleviate the heat spreading throughout my body. In an attempt to calm the storm within me, I quickly said, "I think I failed my exam."

He responded swiftly, "That wasn't what I was asking, but I'm sorry to hear that." He never broke eye contact, making me both nervous and exhilarated.

"And I think I failed because of you," I blurted out in one breath.

As he took another step closer, my heart raced even faster, threatening to jump out of my chest. Christiaan placed his cool hand on my heated cheek and gently pushed my hair away from my face, tucking it behind my ear. I struggled to swallow as our gazes met. "I'm sorry for causing you trouble. I will make it up to you," he said. His eyes seemed to penetrate my soul, leaving me vulnerable

and open to his next move. Before I had a chance to respond, his lips met mine.

He was tender and slow, holding my head and running his fingers through my hair. Then, he grabbed me closer, passionately interlocking his mouth with mine and biting my lips from time to time. It was almost painful but extremely pleasant as he seemed to know when to intermingle softness with the swelling sensations. The spearmint flavor of his tongue and the softness of his outer lips explored mine in the infinity of excitement. My feet felt unsteady and my head began to spin in this unfamiliar, alien world.

In a trance-like state, we couldn't let go of each other. The warmth of his breath, the familiar scent of his body, and the touch of his skin brought a feeling of being home. Where we belonged a long time ago.

In the cold evening air, we felt an adventitious fire that kept us warm until night, which we spent in each other's arms…

Chapter 5

いつも飢えてたの、私。一度でいいから愛情をたっぷりと受けてみたかったの。もういい、おなかいっぱい、ごちそうさまっていうくらい。一度でいいのよ、たった一度で。

Itsumo uetetano, watashi. Ichidode iikara aijyou wo tappuri to uketemitakattano. Mou ii, onaka ippai, gochisousamatte iukurai. Ichidode iinoyo, tatta ichidode.

I was always hungry for love. Just once, I wanted to know what it was like to get my fill of it—to be fed so much love I couldn't take any more. Just once.

Haruki Murakami
Norwegian Wood

HAMAMATSU, October 2005

WITH ITS NATURAL WONDERS SUCH as parks, *onsens*,* lakes, and magnificent temples, as well as Hamamatsu Castle,† the prefecture offered plenty of attractions for visitors. But for me, the greatest of all was Chris' apartment. It was our little kingdom where we were the monarchs and could rule as we pleased. It was our sanctuary where we could hide from the outside world and be known to no one but ourselves.

We engaged in our own little conspiracy. We knew there would come a time when we would have to reveal our secret, but for now, we couldn't risk Minoru discovering our relationship. But there was another reason as well. In the fear of our limited time on Earth, we didn't want to waste a single moment of it in anyone else's company.

---

* (温泉) *Onsen*: Hot spring.

† (浜松城) *Hamamtasu-jou*: Also known as Shusse-jou, which translates as "Success Castle."

We were fortunate that even the apartment's owner, a middle-aged car garage proprietor, was not aware of my presence as he was a rare visitor. The tenth-floor flat stood among other skyscrapers and was a twenty-minute bus ride from my university. Despite its small size of only twenty-five square meters, it was still big enough for Chris to be disorganized. But it didn't bother me at all. On the contrary, I found satisfaction in searching for missing pairs of colorful, to-brighten-my-life socks, as he called them.

I would pick up cotton pillows from the retro carpet and arrange them in a perfect row on the couch and neatly stack important-looking forms and papers on the side of the desk. This made me feel needed. In the mornings, I regularly found dried toothpaste on the nozzle as Chris never put the lid back on, but I was glad to wash it off the white cramps and twist it back on. And after each shower, the bathroom would flood as he wouldn't properly pull the shower curtain to avoid water leakage. But even that didn't trouble me, and I would wipe the floor after his every use.

With my patience and dedication, his apartment looked like a brand-new place, sparkling clean as if prepared for a sales agency advertisement. And then again, within a few hours, when he would mess it up once more, with Hachiko's puppy-like gaze, he would only say for his justification, "You know, it's an artist's thing, my princess."

And indeed, he was an artist. He had an eye to catch a moment. His photos of landscapes reminded me of the best quality postcards with always the right angle, perfect light, and great choices of objects. But he was still best at photographing people. Capturing their stories and emotions frozen within the creases of their wrinkled faces and unique glances, only to live eternally within the A2 prints, crowned him a true master of his craft.

Despite all his imperfections, I loved him for who he was and wouldn't change a thing about him. Even in those evenings when he disappeared into his cave.

Sitting in the kitchen on a wooden chair, I would admire his masculine silhouette which, in the darkness, was unveiled in the moon's reflection. There he would have a "date" with his favorite Jameson whiskey and kretek cigarette, gazing outside the window while his deepest thoughts remained secret. At times, it would bring

loneliness and fear inside of me. Fear of the unknown. What was he thinking?

My anxiety melted away, however, in the safety of his embrace. There were days when we wouldn't even leave the bed, and I remained lost in the soft and slow touch of his fingertips on my body as if they had invisible wires that gave me goosebumps and shivers in my soul. He always seemed to know how and where to touch me, and we fit together like yin and yang, superglued for hours, losing track of time.

The feeling of safety and happiness within me was something I had never experienced before, and a sense of belonging slowly bloomed within me. At times, it was overwhelming, and I struggled to express my feelings. So, on one of those days, I picked up a pencil and paper and began sketching Chris as he peacefully napped. His closed eyelids were partially covered by a strand of thick hair, his mouth was relaxed as he breathed in and out in a meditative rhythm. Like stars in the clear desert sky, I gazed at his skin decorated by moles, gracefully covered like a nude Greek god by white bed sheets. And I thought of the indescribable innocence and purity of the unconditional love I felt toward him.

In the quiet sound of the pencil's scratches, I struggled to capture the essence and oneness of that instant. The moment would eventually pass, as it always did, unlike the drawing which would stay as a reminder forever.

As I was making final adjustments to my shading, Chris unexpectedly caught me in the act. "Let me see, let me see," he murmured, his heavy eyes squinting as he gazed at my sketch.

"No way!" I exclaimed, feeling too bashful to show him my scribbles.

"Come on," he said, knowing where I was most ticklish. Bringing his huge Apollo-like torso upright and laughing, he playfully tickled my toes.

"No!" I screamed, hoping he wouldn't peek, and added through an uncontrollable scoff, "It looks more like an elephant's ass than your face!"

Chris couldn't stop laughing and, amid his hysteria, I was able to grab my sketch and throw it in the bin. As humorous as the situation may have seemed, it was disappointing to me. It was a

reminder of my childhood memories and the talent I once had. I was shocked at how inadequate my drawing skills had become.

In the background of Chris' laughter, I made a promise to myself to re-learn how to draw. I wouldn't give up. And as the weeks passed, my sketches began to improve. With time, persistence, and patience, I rediscovered my passion for drawing. I never left home without a pencil and paper and found inspiration everywhere—the train station, class, parks, or even on seemingly boring streets. I would stop to illustrate anything that caught my eye, and as reserved as I was with words, I finally found a tool to express myself.

But in the evenings, it was all about the hugs. There was nothing more serene than being embraced in Chris' arms. Whenever I felt overwhelmed or a little shy, I would look into his eyes and breathe in his distinct scent. I had always believed Westerners smelled different from Japanese people. Chris would simply chuckle and, with a mischievous grin and sparkling eyes, tell me it was the scent of love. He didn't care for my musky perfume and insisted it was unnecessary, that it hid my natural body scent. But I would tease him and say, "My perfume or my fart? Which one do you prefer?" And he would laugh, shedding tears of joy, and tell me how absurd I was.

I remembered it vividly, the day Sayaka finally confided in me about her first and only love, whom she had lost touch with during her travels. His name was Liam, an Irish boy from Dublin, whom she met while living there with her family.

"How did you know you loved him?" I asked her eagerly. As she pondered her answer, a multitude of questions swirled in my mind. Was it the way he held her hand or the way he kissed her? Or perhaps it was his stunning sapphire blue eyes that she spoke of with such passion?

But Sayaka's response was simple yet profound, "I just knew." Her words hung in the air, and she was lost in her memories for a moment.

Only now, as I gazed into Christiaan's large, green eyes did I truly understand what she meant. I just knew.

"Most of the names in Japan have a meaning. How about yours? Does Christiaan mean anything?" I asked one lazy Sunday morning as I lay in his arms.

"Well, it means a follower of Christ," he replied.

"Oh, okay. So, you're a Christian then?" I asked.

"Well, I think religion is my own business," he retorted. I was taken aback and slightly offended, but before I could react, he held me tighter and giggled. Confused at first, I quickly realized that he was referencing my response from the day we met at the train station, and we started laughing. He didn't forget anything. When I playfully slapped his arm, he responded with a newfound seriousness. "Well, my parents are religious, so they gave me this name. But I don't follow any religion. What about you?"

"It's actually quite similar to my story," I replied, feeling a strange connection to him despite growing up miles apart. "I was raised with the philosophy of Shintoism, but I don't really follow it or any religion. I believe in God, or some kind of divine energy, but not in any particular religion."

We agreed that religion had often been built on the blood of innocent people and sometimes had caused more division than unity. "I believe in a religion called love," Chris said, staring into my eyes before kissing me passionately. My heart pounded with emotion.

Despite our religious views, we acknowledged that it had brought captivating architecture and gripping traditions to many diverse places. Sayaka's photographs from her travels had been a testament to that, and I couldn't help but admire the beauty of all the temples, mosques, and churches from all around the world.

Christiaan and I were in awe of the Japanese shrines we visited. I was particularly drawn to the traditional *jinja*‡ with *torii*§ gates, often made of cypress wood or stone, while Chris preferred the Buddhist ones. As we walked through the *torii* gate, which marked the boundary between the earthly realm and the spiritual world, we had a little tradition of kissing each other instead of bowing. We pretended it was our wedding gate, and we always did it with love

---

‡ (神社) *Jinja*: Shinto shrine.

§ (鳥居) *Torii*: A traditional archway most found at or within a Shinto shrine.

and affection. Some people looked at us with mysterious smiles, but most were outraged at our seemingly inappropriate behavior in a holy place of the *kami.*[**] Nevertheless, we just smiled innocently, catching them off guard. We knew that God understood our love, and that was all that mattered to us.

As a child, I had particularly enjoyed the part of the Shinto ritual where I needed to clap my hands after throwing a *saisen*[††] coin into the *saisenbako*,[‡‡] ring the bell to ward off evil spirits, and purify myself to finish with two bows. Even though I couldn't remember the last time I prayed to kami myself, watching others pray with such passion and peace gave me a sense of belief and hope that everything was going to be all right.

The individuals around me appeared almost angelic, projecting an image of purity and leading seemingly faultless lives. However, my thoughts turned to Minoru, who meticulously lit incense during prayer, and it dawned on me that he was far from being a saint. This realization had initially pushed me away from faith. As time went on, I came to comprehend that hypocrisy, exemplified by Minoru as its reigning monarch, permeated the lives of others as well.

As I pondered on the geographical limitations imposed by religion, I couldn't help but imagine that if I had been born in Pakistan, I would most likely be a Muslim, but if I had been born in Ireland, I would probably be a Christian, specifically a Catholic. Sayaka told me of various people blindly following the cycles of their families' beliefs, yet often not even implementing their religion's rules in daily life.

And then there was Chris. In his arms, I felt true love. Through him, I realized that the "religion of love" was closest to my belief system too. Religion was based on structure, but love had none. In matters of love, there were no rules to follow. Life was full of absurdities and unanswered questions, but once I let go of the rational commands of my brain and allowed my heart to take the lead, everything seemed to make sense. Love was present in small gestures, jokes, gazes, and hugs.

** (神) *Kami*: God.

†† (賽銭) *Saisen*: Money offered to gods or bodhisattvas.

‡‡ (賽銭箱) *Saisenbako*: Offertory box.

Throughout my life, I hadn't been fortunate enough to receive many of those. It wasn't until I met Chris that I realized how addictive and therapeutic they could be. With him, every hug was new, fresh, relaxing, and freeing.

When we weren't cuddled in bed, we would set out to explore Shizuoka's hidden gems. It would be me with my paper and pencils and Chris with his camera that he never left behind. Surprisingly, some of the places were new to both Chris and me.

Shizuoka was a popular tourist destination, mainly due to its most prized gem—Mount Fuji, or as the locals called it, *Fuji-san*. Every day, masses of people arrived by foot, big coach buses, trains, and even helicopters, eager for adventure and the perfect photo opportunity to admire the symbol of Japan's empire, regardless of season or weather.

We too, but more modestly, often took strolls on our beach of many past and future memories to come to regard its strength and splendor, though it was frequently hidden by capricious fog. In the summer, when the sun was at its peak and unbearably hot, we would take a dip in the sea to cool down, followed by a refreshing aloe vera massage for each other.

One sunny August day, relaxing at the sea's shore, I glanced at my fingers, feeling embarrassed as they had become wrinkled from the salty water. But Chris, as usual, read my mind and gently took my hand in his, looking at it with tenderness and saying, "That's how I want to see them one day. Only your hands, Aiko." At that moment, I knew there was nothing I needed to be self-conscious about in front of him. Not even the secret I had held for so long. My fear of the depth of the sea.

There was a limit, and that limit was my waist. There was no way I was going any deeper, not even with Chris, a man I intimated trusted who stubbornly urged me to go farther. I felt safer with my feet planted firmly on the ground, whether it was pavement, sand, carpet, or grass. Even out of a bicycle's pedals, I could jump off the solid ground as Chris patiently taught me how to ride his bike.

While in the Netherlands, Chris had his bike stolen three times. One of them was mysteriously found in the depths of a Rotterdam canal a day later, which wasn't uncommon. But in Japan, he felt confident enough to leave his bike without a lock. Even though theft was rare and crime was relatively low here, I still admired his

level of trust and belief in humanity after his previous encounters. I, on the other hand, didn't possess that same confidence, particularly when it came to my secrets. Nonetheless, I knew my fear of the sea was safe with Chris.

I trusted him completely and enjoyed spoiling him. Being a huge fan of sushi, I frequently made him homemade sushi rolls which he jokingly referred to as "sushi for lazy people." These rolls consisted of rice and any desired additions stuffed in seaweed and eaten like a sandwich. To add to the fun, we would often go to *kaitenzushi*,[§§] where we could enjoy the most colorful and delicious pieces of art as they circulated on a long, common table, satisfying both our hunger and our eyes.

However, it was during our first meal at an Italian restaurant that we shared a special moment. As we took our first bite of the perfectly crusted pepperoni pizza straight out of the oven, Chris and I simultaneously expressed gratitude for the food in our own ways. He said it in English, while I used the Japanese expression "*Itadakimasu*." Our smiles couldn't be contained, and my goosebumps signaled to me that this would not be our last date.

When I told Chris about the Japanese concept of *hara hachibu*,[***] he shared a similar approach to meals, even though he didn't have a name for it. He too would eat until he was almost full, recognizing that it took time for the stomach to signal satiety. Before each bite, he would take a deep breath and savor the taste and texture in his mouth. It was hard to believe it was a coincidence to think so alike despite coming from two different parts of the world.

Although it may have seemed like we were just having ordinary outings, every moment we spent together felt sacred to me. Even something as simple as walking through dark parks on the coldest nights felt safe and comforting with Chris by my side. Playing checkers, a game I usually found dull, became exciting when I was with him. The birds sang more enchantingly around him, and the sky was never bluer than when we were together.

After I parted ways with my friends and after Sayaka's farewell, I had never communicated as much with anyone as I did with Chris.

[§§] (回転寿司) *Kaitenzushi*: Conveyor-belt sushi.

[***] (腹八分) *Hara hachibu*: Eating with moderation, eating until eighty percent full.

Despite some language barrier issues, the language of hearts remained the most powerful. He helped me understand that my anger and scars from childhood covered my passion for life and freedom that I had deep inside of me. No one else could ever see it, not even if we spoke the same language. Over time, Chris and Sayaka, both of them from foreign lands, noticed, cared for, and nurtured me.

Like a cherry blossom on a sunny spring day, I bloomed while many others were still closed in their flower buds, hurting in loneliness among crowds of other buds. No one cared like Chris, no one else saw me like Chris.

Unfortunately, after dancing with him in autumn's rain amid the crowds of Shibuya and despite not consuming any alcohol but feeling drunk from happiness within, I became sick. It started with an innocent sneeze and ended with pneumonia.

"Sip this," he said, noticing the grimace on my face. "I know it doesn't taste the best, but it will help you."

Doesn't taste the best, I ironically thought to myself as I was too puny to talk. The brew tasted horrendous, and I was hoping that it was worth my effort toward recovery. With every cough, he looked at me with concern and care, which gave me a dose of strength. My eyes were sensitive to light, so even during the day, we stayed in the darkness behind a heavy curtain. My nose was ruby red and dry from tissue use, and my mouth was mostly open, trying to gasp for air that wouldn't flow through blocked sinuses. Although I badly needed rest, I couldn't relax until Chris brought giant, fluffy pillows so I could lie in a semi-upright position. But what truly soothed me was his soft fingers, which landed on my nose and moved tenderly toward my cheeks, then back to my nose and up to my temples. That was the last thing I remembered before I sank into a deep sleep.

I woke up in a fright, tears streaming down my face, a feeling that was completely foreign to me. As I lay there, sweating and parched, I could see nothing but the pitch-black, lonesome, and eerie darkness. Suddenly, I heard Chris's brisk footsteps, and as soon as he took my hand, a wave of relief washed over me.

"Chris!" I cried out, my voice shaking. "I-I..."

"It's okay. I'm here, my princess." He leaned over and planted a kiss on my feverish and damp forehead.

"Thank God," I gasped. "I had a nightmare. I dreamed that you had left Japan… You left me."

Overwhelmed with the sense of emptiness brought on by the nightmare, I gazed at Chris, silently pleading for comfort.

"You silly," he laughed, "I could never leave Japan!" I let out a quiet sigh, tears still in my eyes, and felt my heart ease with his words. But then he added in a somber tone, "Where would I find toilets like these in any other country? Only in Japan can you dream of having a warm seat during long diarrhea." I wasn't in the mood for jokes, and he quickly realized it, offering me an apologetic, warm smile.

Perhaps it was naive and strange, but it had never crossed my mind before that we could be separated. Some things in life seem certain, and our togetherness was one of them. From the moment our lips met, we were inseparable. Even when we were physically apart, I knew we would always think of each other until our next meeting.

But the nightmare had felt so real. And despite not remembering all the details, the overwhelming feeling of emptiness lingered.

"Promise me that it will never happen," I implored.

"I promise."

Chapter 6

惚れた病に薬無し。
Horeta yamai ni kusuri nashi.
There is no medicine for lovesickness.

SHIZUOKA, September 2006

"I BELIEVE THERE MAY BE something concerning about Aiko," I overheard Mother say to Minoru one night after dinner. "She's so moody. Sometimes she smiles for no reason, and other times she looks like she's cried the whole night." My body immediately tensed up, and my heart began to race, hoping they wouldn't hear its loud pounding from behind the *shouji*. "Also, she is rarely at home. I never see her. She claims she sits in the library after school and visits her old friends in Tokyo, but these sleepovers away from home…" Mother trailed off.

As I recalled the many times I'd fibbed to my mother, I felt guilty watching her silhouette from outside the kitchen window when sneaking out from home. But those feelings always faded away hours later as I lay in Chris' arms.

"Does she pass all her exams with good marks?" Minoru interrupted.

"Well," she hesitated for a second, and to my relief, finally stated, "As far as I am concerned, she does. Yes."

"Then, let her be. The most important thing is that she is studying and passing her exams with good marks. Remember, she needs to complete her studies. That is the most important," Minoru summarized.

Luckily for me, I was gifted in absorbing knowledge from lectures, so I didn't need to study much outside of class. I just had to concentrate and listen to professors, and my brain would soak up all the information like a sponge. But Minoru didn't know that

about me or a million other things. He never took the effort to get to know me; his time was reserved for things that were more significant to him, most of which I didn't know or care about.

Among the neatly arranged pile on Minoru's desk were numerous vibrant *meishi*[*] from men he had encountered on his life journey. I remembered that there seemed to be little space left among these cards for the drawings I had so painstakingly created to earn his approval.

There was no time for him to read me a bedtime story or take me on his lap for a simple, genuine hug. There was no singing, dancing, cooking, or baking together. No Sunday picnics, birthday parties, or forest treks. He cared only about himself.

It wasn't much different with Mother, especially after she stopped working at the shop. She always seemed busy running aimlessly around the house. Feeling completely disconnected from my parents and their somber, impenetrable behaviors, I wondered who they were and who I was to them. Sometimes, I felt like I didn't want to know the answer after all. I didn't belong there. Sorrowful and scary as it was, it also made me feel lonely. I questioned the value of family.

When I was home and no longer surrounded by unconditional love, I truly missed Chris. Despite the wrenching weakness I felt while being sick with pneumonia, which I soon forgot, I couldn't overlook how solicitously Chris took care of me. And even though I was still upset at him after yesterday's dramatic quarrel, it took me a good few seconds to remember why we had argued. The recollection of him leaving me a mountain of laundry to fold brought back a repulsive memory.

This was the third time such an event had happened in the last two weeks.

This time, however, I had become fed up with being his maid again. When I furiously started kicking and throwing his clothes around the room, he dared to call me crazy. It was enough for me to slam the door behind me, take firm steps toward the lift, and leave him with his never-ending mess. Yet… I still missed him.

---

[*] (名刺) *Meishi*: Business card.

His unorganized socks and hard toothpaste were no longer fun. Flinging the door, shouting at each other, grudges, and petulancy for trivial affairs had not been rare recently.

Ironically, the more I tried to clarify something, the more misunderstandings arose; the fights often spiraled out of control. As much as he brought out the best in me, he also brought out the worst. Yet… I still missed him.

Hopelessness shrouded my understanding. Sadness muffled my laughter. Despite my efforts to appear strong, it wasn't easy. Every time we fought, I felt like my world was falling apart. Fear gnawed at me that it would be the last time I saw him. Despite his pride, I knew he felt the same. We didn't need words to understand each other. We communicated on a deeper level through our eyes that were linked to our souls. I adored his, which were like a chameleon's skin, changing color with his clothes or the weather. At times they were turquoise, sometimes emerald, or even pastel-saturated, but the one constant was their depth.

Nobody ever looked at me the way he did, which made me feel exceptional. But I hadn't seen any of that lately as he had been avoiding eye contact for a while now.

We could lie in bed for hours and do nothing, but I never felt guilty for wasting my time. On the contrary, it was the most valued time. And I thought nothing could change that.

But time wasn't gracious and dutifully reminded me that I don't have all I want under control. Coupled with torturous disappointment and frustration, I kept failing to fix the pieces of broken glass.

In the first few weeks after we had met, Chris would adore how I slurped my noodles, and at times, would join me in this cultural way of eating soba, which he knew so well. But with time, it started to irk him.

"You guys don't have manners," he said.

"Manners? Do you call a cultural thing a 'lack of manners?' Come on, you know better than that, Chris." I couldn't believe my ears at his unfair and ridiculous judgments.

He became withdrawn, hiding in the corners of his tiny flat, giving me lame excuses to linger at home.

My jokes suddenly stopped being funny, and I couldn't recall the last time we had laughed together. Yet I still missed him…

It became hard to recognize the man I knew, and I could feel that there was something not quite right. Feeling like Chris was expressly looking for arguments, I became more unhinged and frantic which, as a result, made him get what I assumed he wanted. We fought. A lot. It was painful. I didn't understand why and what was happening and the only person who could help me comprehend it was ironically on the other side of the spectrum.

I was in a relationship, but I never felt lonelier.

But it was his camera, which he hadn't touched for two weeks, that worried me most.

Chris had always been critical of his own photographs. His greatest source of frustration was his inability to capture the moon in all its beauty. Instead, he would simply gaze at its luminous glow against the dark night sky with his own eyes. Yes, the night was his time. The time when he could be himself without any barriers.

As the lurid glow of the moon cast a haughty contrast with the ebony sky, another wave of fear washed over me as I lay in bed. These feelings had become more frequent in recent days, but tonight was the strongest yet. I knew there was no more time to waste, no more strength to pretend that everything was fine.

Despite my uncertainty about how to excuse my sudden and late-night departure from the house, I was determined to finally face my fears and reveal the truth tonight.

Listening at the door, I heard Minoru's caviling to Mother yet again and seized the opportunity to slip out. As I closed the door behind me, I couldn't help but feel a twinge of pity for my mother. But I knew there was nothing I could do to help her; she had chosen to live the life she was living.

Taking the last train to Hamamatsu, I promised myself that I wouldn't leave Chris' place until I got an answer.

The darkness of the night, no less the view of Chris' door, brought a sense of dread to my heart. To my surprise, the door was unlocked.

Clean clothes were still scattered around the bedroom, but Chris was nowhere to be seen. Taking a few hesitant steps toward the kitchen, I spotted him sitting in his favorite chair, slowly sipping his whiskey. My heart began to pound harder, but I summoned the courage to ask him the question that had been haunting me for weeks. I knew it was now or never.

"Can you tell me what's going on, Chris?"

Since yesterday's argument, Chris had been treating me like a ghost—as if I weren't present in the world around him. Even with my unexpected appearance, he didn't react. The silence was unbearable, and I couldn't take another minute of living in the unknown.

"Chris! Speak!" I shouted, my voice echoing through the empty flat.

The scream that I had grown accustomed to hearing was actually a cry for help. Help that I thought only he could provide, but instead, with a strange calmness in his voice, I received a quick and unbelievable blow, like an executioner's guillotine.

"We can't be together, Aiko."

The room filled with deep stillness and the silence became deafening. It took me a few seconds to comprehend what he had just said, finally answering a question that I had waited for so long to hear. Instead of feeling relief, however, I was filled with a sense of denial, as if I had misheard him.

Had it not been for the cold shiver that ran through my body and the spongy feeling my legs took on, I would have thought it was a nightmare, one that I would soon wake from in Chris' arms, as it was in the old, good days.

Instead, a tsunami of shock filled my mind, body, and soul.

His words were like a hard slap to the face, like a cold bucket of water on a body that had just been bathed in an *onsen*. And I had brought this upon myself.

After the first wave of turmoil, I couldn't imagine there could be anything more painful to be said, but I was wrong.

The hangman had no mercy, and without looking at me, he added, "I am leaving Japan."

"Chris," I stressed his name, the way I always did—gently and with love this time, to remind him who I was to him. To remind him that I knew him and that we were not strangers.

Now, vexed by the outcome, I tried to touch his palm, but he removed it before I could feel its usual warmth. His icy gaze and stiff body were relentless. Feeling hot and cold flushes alternately, I couldn't catch my breath.

"What are you saying?" But this question and the hundred others that followed hours later remained unanswered. My screams and lament, begging, and even my humbling as if before a king on a throne, kneeling before him, were all met with the same fate—silence. This hush was followed by emptiness and an unendurable physical and mental torment.

I thought I knew him better than anyone else, perhaps even more than he knew himself. But I couldn't recognize my soulmate. In a matter of seconds, we went from being one to being two strangers. That realization, which I couldn't grasp, was agonizing to its core. Why? That question haunted me to my core.

Was I so wrong? I had trusted that we understood each other without words, yet he could also hurt me without them.

"You broke the promise!"

Drowning in an ocean of torture, loneliness, and incomprehension, I left, crying, slamming the door, and hoping he would come to his senses soon.

Chapter 7

空が青を失ってる。
Sora ga ao wo ushinatteru.
The sky is losing its blue.

A WEEK LATER, I FOUND myself staring miserably at the same spot on the floor.

The silk top, which I had worn when I last saw Chris, now hanging carelessly on the chair, was yet another reminder of my misery. His body scent still clung to my clothes; his beaming smile still materialized before me when I closed my eyes.

Chris had left me with fears, hopelessness, and betrayal. Nightmares haunted me at night while anxiety and depression weighed my heart in my waking hours. They were cruel mementos of reality. Reality without him in my life. From spending every single moment with him to being utterly solitary, I had fallen into a pit of loneliness.

Even though it hadn't been ideal between us recently, I would never have envisaged Chris breaking up with me and leaving Japan. And no matter how I tried to comprehend his motives, they didn't make logical sense to me.

Blaming him for all the failures, just to regret my own faults seconds later, I felt I was becoming insane amid the chaos of nonsensical existence.

It seemed that I had no influence on his decisions and how he felt, further proving that we were not one, as I had been so certain of. Suddenly, the last fifteen months felt like they had never happened.

But they had… And the idea of not having Chris in my life was impossible to bear, so I kept contriving ways to have him back. I just couldn't give up without a fight.

Now that some time had passed, perhaps he had thought it through and realized it was a mistake, but with his ego at its forefront, he was too constrained or terrified to admit it. Probably, he was waiting for my move.

In my head now, I had way better scenarios for us and would change so many things if I had a second chance.

Trying to grasp the past and searching through memories stored in the recesses of my heart for reasons of failure, I felt I didn't deserve love.

There were regrets I couldn't forgive myself for. Why when he had annoyed me that autumn day for a thing I don't even remember now, didn't I kiss him after he asked me to? Why, with fury in my eyes, had I called him an idiot and not even apologized for a trivial misunderstanding that I can't recall the details of? Why had I ignored him for the whole day with no apparent reason, other than being angry with the world and taking it out on him?

It seemed he was not the only one with "ego on its forefront."

Had I not engaged in the selfish whims of a child, would this have turned out differently? Or maybe if I hadn't visited him that evening and asked for the truth, would we still be together?

In desperation, I tried to find a glimmer of hope.

If only I could turn back time… All I could do was try to talk to him one final time. Face to face…

Despite feeling drained and weakened, lost, and incredibly hurt, I knew I had to find answers amid all the madness.

I didn't know where I found the strength, but I managed to retrace my steps and make my way to his place—the same place that had turned from an oasis of peace into a living hell in just a few short weeks. The same place I had just left running away a week prior.

As I waited for the lift, I took a deep breath. A feeling of discomfort swelled in my chest. I grew restless when I realized the elevator was taking too long to arrive. Suddenly, I heard slow footsteps coming from a stairwell and saw a shadow following them. An older lady, perhaps in her eighties, with sharp eyes that met mine emerged.

"The lift is broken. It's been out of order since yesterday afternoon and I don't know why they haven't fixed it yet. You'll have to take the stairs." Then she added with a hint of briskness in her

tone, "But it's not a huge hassle for someone with young legs like yours, unlike my old ones."

I mumbled a thank-you.

She paused in step, concern spreading across her face. "You look sad."

I held back tears, knowing that if I let one fall, the floodgates would open. It surprised me that this stranger, this old lady, could see through me in just a few seconds of our meeting.

And then, as if to cheer me up, she added, "But there's something about you, young lady. You look like you're on an epic mission in life."

Yes, I was. I had to give this last chance to me and Chris. But I left that thought to myself, as she wouldn't understand it.

Despite my detachment from her visions and my obvious hasten, I maintained the practice of Japanese custom. I bowed to the old lady while simultaneously uttering, "*Arigatou*," before mustering the courage to ascend the stairs on trembling legs. Climbing ten floors was a grueling feat, but it paled in comparison to the sheer exhaustion brought on by the decision to push open the door.

That was a fear unlike anything I had ever experienced. It surpassed even the anxiety I felt during my final exams in high school when utterly unprepared, I had perspired profusely for the entire one-and-a-half hours, grappling with questions that made little sense to me. It exceeded the dread I felt when Minoru caught me mid-stretch, inadvertently revealing my newly-pierced navel. It even surpassed the fear that consumed me when a classmate lifted my skirt, shamelessly exposing my underwear to the entire class.

I pressed the door's handle but found it locked. A hot flush of blood ran through my body.

As I stood outside Chris' door, I rehearsed the words I had prepared for him; they felt like a tongue twister and made no sense now. With a heavy heart, I knocked.

There were no footsteps nor did a familiar voice call out.

Tears uncontrollably streamed down my face at the thought of him being gone already.

My knuckles, deep pink from the hard knocks, started to ache, and I had a terrible headache from all the crying that had accumulated throughout the week. But what made me weep even

harder was the doormat that read "*Youkoso*,"* which I now slid down to in infirmity. I had bought it for Chris to make him feel welcomed in Japan just a month after we met at Hamamatsu Station. But now, I knew I wasn't welcomed at all.

Questions about why he had left, where he went, whether he would come back, and if he had met someone else swirled in my mind as I wept in despair at the unknown future.

As a ghost, he came into my life and as a ghost, he left it.

Falling to my knees, I looked out the corridor's window at the pale sky, shouting through my tears in despair of silence, "God, whoever you are, give me strength! Give me answers! Help me!" But even as I cried out, the answers didn't come. So, I turned to the poem I had written for him the previous night and quietly read it once again.

There is this silent cry
That only you yourself will understand.
That smell
That touch
That vision
That sound
will trigger the deepest memories.

And these memories will be your own, lonely memories
That only you yourself will understand.
There are these feelings in your heart and loneliness
That only you yourself will understand.

The feeling of missing it badly,
So badly,
That only you yourself will understand.

If you would only know what I know.
See what I see,
Smell what I smell,
Hear what I hear,
Feel what I feel,

---

* (ようこそ) *Youkoso*: Welcome.

That pain. The pain of pains. Pain in the crown. Glorified.
That only you yourself will understand.

There is this fear,
There is this emptiness,
That only you yourself will understand.

I can't smell,
I can't touch,
I can't see,
I can't hear,
I can't feel anymore.

It almost feels like it never happened...
It only comes as a memory now.
That lonely, solo memory
That only you yourself will understand.

The glimpses.
Déjà vus.
The flashbacks of your life.
A life that is so easy yet so complex.
We come alone to this earth.
And we leave alone this earth.

Love.
That only you yourself can understand.
Or maybe... can't?

I held onto a glimmer of hope, wishing that perhaps he wasn't prepared to open the door just yet, maybe out of shame or due to his absence from the house with the possibility of returning soon. With a mix of uncertainty and anticipation, I slid the poem beneath the door and departed.

Weeks passed without any response from Chris, and the unknown continued to cause havoc. Amid the uncertainty, the once colorful Shizuoka turned gray. Even the fun *kaitenzushi* lost its charm, and the food became flavorless. My usually sensitive palate couldn't be tickled by the hottest wasabi. And despite being hungry, I struggled to swallow my saliva. I only ate not to starve. Even on cloudless summer days, the sky seemed to lose its blue hue while the sand felt devoid of texture. The shrines that used to be charming now seemed dull, and the bird's chanting melodies faded away.

I kept asking myself, "Why me?" But no answers were ever revealed.

Chris had broken his promise, and I felt deserted. If this was love, I didn't want to love ever again. Like a mantra, I repeated this sentence in my thoughts.

I questioned my own feelings. Had I imagined this love or had it been real? What was love anyway? Was it something we feel through our heart, body, and mind, or something we tell ourselves we feel? Was it what we've learned from the world of cinema and books? Can we control or suppress these feelings? If so, how?

Exhausted and in contemplation, I found nothing to satisfy the ever-growing number of questions that proliferated within me.

I didn't want to think about him, yet that's all I wanted to do. It felt as if self-torture was the only way to survive.

Despite my hatred for him, I found myself wandering the paths we used to take in Shizuoka, Hamamatsu, and Tokyo, hoping to chance upon him.

Everywhere I turned, memories of him flooded my mind: the scent of freshly mown grass in the park where we used to walk, the sound of the waves crashing against the rocks, the taste of raw salmon, the view of looking deeply into each other's eyes and holding hands tightly, random couples, the sunrise's warmth, and the sunset's chill. Now they were a collection of miseries.

I longed to remember my life before him, but it felt like there wasn't one. Instead, I wanted to breathe the air he breathed and walk the ground he walked.

There was just no switch to press and forget him. It seemed as if we were bound together forever, no matter what. Like untrimmed

trees, perfect in their imperfections, was our connection. He owned my soul and had taken it with him when he left.

Life can take unexpected turns, as I soon discovered.

Just when I thought things couldn't get any worse, I learned that Minoru lost his job and had begun to spend a fortune at geisha houses, which I learned from a friend who is a *Maiko*.

Understanding how crucial it was for Minoru to support my education, I grew increasingly concerned when he started hinting at his inability to afford it any longer. I knew we were faced with a grave situation.

As the months passed, I heard nothing from Chris—no sign, no news, no letter. Just unbearable silence and emptiness. I couldn't help but wonder where he had gone and what had happened to him. And other agonizing questions started to plague me, causing me more pain than I ever thought possible. From hope to disappointment, anger to pain, I cycled through a range of emotions that seemed to control my every thought. And unfortunately, Minoru's words rang true: "You see, a human can adapt to anything."

And he knew he had no other choice than to conform to this plight as our funds dwindled and we could no longer afford the luxuries we had. In the background of his drunkenness and Mother's obvious depression, Minoru had to sell his beloved car, save furiously on electricity and the quality of the groceries, and meticulously count every yen. Ultimately, the inevitable happened—I had to leave the university.

Yet it was not our increasing poverty that tore me apart, but the silence from Chris.

Each day was like a punishment. It was survival. It felt like a lost battle, and I wanted nothing more than to disappear, to vanish where no one could find me.

They say, "Hope dies last." Well, mine finally died that ugly Thursday when I looked in the mirror and saw indifference in my eyes. No longer did my gaze hold the sparkle that Chris had always admired.

"Your eyes are like these two black stones," he had once said at the beach, holding up two pebbles he found on the shores of Suruga Bay, "and they always shine, like the sun that reflects in them."

The apathy that had taken root in my heart for almost two years now was so overwhelming that even when my father decided to arrange a marriage for me with his old friend, a thirty-eight-year-old fisherman from a small village in the south of Wakayama Prefecture, I barely registered it.

Leaving my life in destiny's hands, I knew that nothing good awaited me anymore. I was too weak to be angry. I was too weak to be sad. I was too weak to cry. I was too weak to check the letterbox anymore. I was too weak to believe. Everybody and everything left me. Even hope.

Chapter 8

意味ある苦痛ならわたしは耐えられる。
Imi aru kutsuu nara watashi wa taerareru.
I can bear any pain as long as it has meaning.

Haruki Murakami
1Q84

November 2008

MINORU DECIDED HE COULD NO longer afford to keep me around. Following the old Japanese tradition of *omiai*,* he showed me brief pictures of my old groom-to-be, which I couldn't even look at. But he didn't ask my opinion. He spoke as if the decision had been made. I was too weak to disagree.

Mother, as usual, had nothing to say to him except to acquiesce, yet she did spare a few words of advice for me. "One day, you will understand, Aiko. Life is about surrendering to your fate. There is nothing like real love. Love brings only pain… You will get used to him or maybe even learn to like him in some way."

The day before I left for Taiji, my belongings of twenty-two years on this Earth packed into two suitcases, I sat on my small, metal-framed bed with its freshly pressed linen sheets. Looking out at the slowly dancing keyaki tree leaves, I reminisced about the sweetness of childhood innocence.

As I indulged in my memories, I laughed at the paradoxical notion of how much I had yearned to grow up. The sound grew louder, seemingly attempting to camouflage the tumultuous thoughts that plagued my mind.

---

* (お見合い) *Omiai*: Commonly mistaken as an "arranged marriage," *omiai* are usually interviews wherein a potential bride/groom can meet one another and decide if they wish to move forward.

I recalled the mischievous joy I had felt when I secretly adorned my mother's cherry red lipstick, believing it made me appear mature. I thought back to the momentous occasion when I had transitioned from watching cartoons to films featuring real actors, embracing a newfound sense of adulthood. And then there was the revelation that Santa Claus was nothing more than a myth, which I discovered with a mix of fascination and disappointment.

Oh, the yearning I had to spend time with older kids, driven by a desire to accelerate my journey into adulthood. Particularly with Kawasaki, who possessed an uncanny knowledge of everyone and everything and who held the esteemed position of leader within our neighborhood's gang of children.

Kawasaki had been the epitome of cool, the one all the kids aspired to be like. It wasn't just because he owned the best collection of Pokémon cards; in our innocent eyes, he possessed a multitude of extraordinary skills. In our imaginations, Kawasaki excelled at soccer, rivaling the great Hidetoshi Nakata. He had the prowess of a seasoned mechanic, effortlessly changing car tires. With the agility of a nimble monkey, he scaled trees with ease. And during games of hide and seek, he could vanish as if he possessed the power of invisibility. It left us baffled, wondering where he could be hiding.

Lost in my thoughts, I found myself reminiscing about my mother's former job at the kimono shop. A deep desire had grown within me to earn my own money and attain the independence she had once possessed. While my memories of childhood and my parents were fragmented, I retained enough to recognize that I had once inhabited a world filled with vibrancy and boundless excitement.

However, as I contemplated the freedom I had relinquished by leaving behind that realm, my laughter transformed into tears and eventually escalated into uncontrollable sobs. I felt powerless to halt the flood of emotions. Who would understand my plight anyway? My mournful cries consumed the room, casting a shadow of darkness. Even the moon seemed to conceal itself behind the keyaki tree as if mirroring the gloom that engulfed me.

"Aiko, wake up, wake up," Mother's voice roused me from my slumber. Still feeling groggy and fragile, I slowly opened my heavy eyelids to see her concerned face peering down at me. "It's time. You need to catch your train in three hours."

As I looked at my reflection in the white-framed mirror on my bedside table, I saw the telltale signs of my pain—empty, puffy eyes, and a blank, pale face. But I tried to cover up the scars of my hurt with some foundation and powder and gather my strength.

With my suitcases in my weak hands, I glanced back at the door closing behind me as I left the house.

But before I turned away, my eyes landed on the mailbox. Inside, I held onto the small hope of finding an apology letter from Chris, and I couldn't resist opening it one last time before leaving.

But it was empty, just like my heart. By way of pain and disappointment, I whispered my goodbye to it, concluding that chapter of my life.

Deep down, I knew I would never return to this place. My parents no longer existed in my world, even though they waved at me as I boarded the train toward my inglorious future. As it pulled away, I spotted my mother through the train window. Tears streamed down her face for some reason. For me, it was just an empty gesture.

As the world moved forward around me, the giant orange sun rose, the wind rustled the leaves on the trees, and the clouds lazily drifted across the sky.

People rushed to find seats on the train while others held onto metal handrails, standing and chatting with one another while views outside the windows changed like a colorful kaleidoscope. But my world had stopped.

I couldn't pinpoint when it had happened. Had it been when I last saw Chris? Or when the postman had arrived with a gas bill instead of a letter from him? Somewhere along the way, I had lost hope.

And as time passed, I often wondered why I didn't escape at one of the stops. Was I scared of becoming homeless? Or was I afraid of the unknown? What held me on that train all the way to Taiji? Was it indifference, or was my body paralyzed, refusing to

obey? Or perhaps, deep down, I still had a glimmer of hope for my life?

Sayaka once told me, "Everything happens for a reason," but despite my efforts, I couldn't imagine any.

And whatever the answers were, I ended up there, in Taiji, a small train station which, in contrast to the bustling suburbs of Tokyo, was entirely dead.

Only two people disembarked there—an old man with a jacket too large for his small frame, leaning on a walking stick that echoed loudly with each step, and me. He disappeared behind colorful murals of whales and dolphins, returning the station to its muteness.

Standing in the desolate train station, my sense of reality became even more tenuous. A wave of fear washed over me, chaos and turmoil erupted in my mind, and a thousand thoughts and doubts about the unknown future followed.

But through the cumulus clouds, the rays of the sun tried to break through the dark purple sky, giving me a small hope that perhaps I would finally taste the freedom that had eluded me for so long. A new tomorrow, a new possibility, a new man.

Perhaps my new husband would sweep me off my feet and help me forget about Chris. Maybe his kindness would rekindle my shattered heart.

I never desired a grand life, nor did I need to be rich or famous. The only thing I wanted was to be happy.

The turmoil of my thoughts was disrupted by a man. When in the far distance, marching quickly in my direction, he kept gazing straight at me, I realized in dread that I might be looking at Hisoka, my future husband, a stranger with whom I would be spending the rest of my life.

This overwhelming notion paralyzed me, and all I wished for was to disappear. But I couldn't and had to face this reality. In the inevitable moment to come, he brought a fishy scent with him. Revealing his dirty nails to take one of my bags from me, now in close proximity, he couldn't set his gaze on me.

I, on the other hand, couldn't help but steal a glance at his chiseled, model-like cheekbones and rugged facial features that were softened by a subtle beard on a sun-kissed and healthy-looking face. His pursed lips gave him a stern and hostile aura, although there was something intriguing about him. But not intriguing enough to forget

about Chris at once. And even if I was inclined to fall in love at first sight, it would have been difficult, given that he always avoided my eyes.

As we traversed the hilly town, the air resonated with the cacophony of Hisoka's car engine, intermittently accompanied by the sound of him dabbing his forehead with a handkerchief to combat the sweat. Each of us fixed our respective gazes solely through the front window of the white van, observing the scenery that unfolded before us.

We passed a handful of charming houses, a butchery, a boutique, a couple of yellow tsunami evacuation route warning signs, a grocery shop, and a bookstore. The journey to Hisoka's place, including a brief stop at the petrol station, took us a mere fifteen minutes.

The house was much smaller than our Shizuoka home with a solitary tree and a few withering flowers in a small patch of grass right before the entrance. Above a pair of men's heavy rain boots was an *omamori*, † which was believed to ward off bad luck. Nevertheless, I couldn't shake off the negative vibes.

The noisy creaking of the wooden floor echoed with my steps, making me feel unwelcome and out of place in this unfamiliar environment. The cracked shabby walls, old-fashioned, dusty, and dark-colored furniture, and tiny windows, one of which faced the solitary, leafless tree, didn't make me feel any better.

"You must be tired. This is our bedroom." Apart from ensuring my name at the train station, these were his first words to me. Putting significant stress on the word "our" made my heart skip a beat, but it wasn't a pleasant kind of feeling. Fear was starting to set in as the reality of the situation sunk in.

Despite my discomfort, I was too exhausted to dwell on my thoughts. I placed my bags neatly beside the tatami mat and waited for Hisoka to give me some privacy to prepare for bed. To my surprise and relief, he indeed stayed away, and I found even greater solace in the fact that he never joined me in the room.

The entire trip to Taiji felt surreal, almost like a dream. If I hadn't woken up in the middle of the night to find myself in a strange house, I would have thought it was a nightmare.

---

† (お守り) *Omamori*: Amulet, similar to a talisman.

Instead of weeping, I clenched my teeth, trying not to wake the stranger snoring on the couch in the next room. I swallowed a few salty tears and curled up in the fetal position, trying to fall asleep again and hoping I would never wake up.

Unfortunately, my prayers went unanswered, and I was abruptly awakened at four-thirty in the morning by the sound of the sliding door opening to the bedroom I was sleeping in.

"I'm going to work now. When I come back, please prepare our lunch. I left some fish in the kitchen fridge. Afterward, we will go sign the marriage papers," Hisoka announced. And then he left.

It had been a while since I had experienced any kind of emotion, but the last words that were spoken brought a new wave of shock, disgust, and dread.

Despite my exhaustion, I could sleep no longer. As the sun began to rise, shyly breaking across the curtain, I observed the cracked ceiling with a geometrically-perfect spider web and a little victim, a tiny fly, fighting for its life. I felt a deep empathy for the fly's misery and its trapped existence, and I tried to understand how my own life had turned out this way.

With an abundance of time on my hands, I took a closer look at the room from where the night's snoring had hailed. It was supposed to be a living room, but to me, cluttered with mismatched items and covered in dust, it felt like a chaotic, cheesy museum.

The entire house was filled with a pungent fishy odor which was even more pronounced than the night before. It didn't take long for me to realize why after I stumbled upon the tiny kitchen situated beside the living room. It was littered with dried seafood lying on a small ceramic table, some hanging on hooks like decorative ornaments. The ones that had been eaten were left as bones in the overflowing garbage bin.

As I searched the fridge for the fish I was supposed to cook for lunch, I was dismayed to find it almost empty. But what was worse, I had no idea how to prepare it. It was absurd for me to be left alone in a new place without any guidance and be expected to cook. I firmly decided that I wouldn't do it, even if it meant taking a stand against my future husband's wishes.

As time dragged on, I wandered aimlessly around the small, confined space, unsure of what to do with myself. I eventually decided to turn on the TV.

I couldn't recall the last time I had watched it, and the episodes of various dramas, news segments, and silly commercials only solidified my belief that I had no regrets about not watching TV for all those years.

A soft grunting noise interrupted my restless state, and I realized that I had fallen asleep on the couch. It was my future husband, who still couldn't bring himself to look me in the eye.

He spoke quietly, breaking the silence, "We need to get going soon."

Now, I had the courage to take a longer look at him. His age showed on his wrinkled, tawny face; his forehead was covered by salt-and-pepper bangs. Despite his slightly humped nose, I couldn't deny that he was still a fine-looking man.

"I'm sorry. I didn't cook. I-I overslept," I apologized remorsefully.

A flicker of disappointment crossed his face, although he maintained his composure. "Never mind," he replied. "We'll eat after the ceremony. Let's get ready."

A subtle tickle of a brush left soft, rose pink on my cheeks; a smooth, charcoal-black perfectly-drawn line on my closed eyelids; and a velvet, kissable red lipstick coloring every inch of my lips. Hair styled under a large coiffured wig. Padding and wrapping to create a shape along my body. Then, the first layer, *nagajyuban.* ‡ Next, *kakeshita*§ followed by an *obi,*** which was tied in a most precise way to metaphorize a woman to a wrapped gift.

The final layer of the heavy coat, the *uchikake*†† with its patterns of plants, animals, and treasures to bring good luck for the future

---

‡ (長襦袢) *Nagajyuban*: A garment of light fabric, usually worn under the kimono.

§ (掛下)*Kakeshita*: The inner robe of a wedding kimono.

** (帯) *Obi*: Kimono sash.

†† (打ち掛け) *Uchikake*: Woman's bridal robe with trailing skirts worn over a kimono.

with a beloved one, were steps before wearing a *shiromuku*,[#] the pure white, wedding kimono. And to seal the look of it, a large, white *wataboshi*.[§§]

That's what I had imagined when planning my wedding with Chris. I instead looked in misfortune at my long sleeve, prosaic beige shirt, and mediocre maxi cotton gray skirt.

In place of walking behind shrine masters performing peaceful, ancient, and melancholic music on flutes to walk through the *torii* gate to have a traditional Japanese "wedding before God" and a purification ritual of sharing and exchanging with the groom three differently-sized cups of sake, just before thanking kami and exchanging the rings, I ended up in a municipal's office with two witnesses whom I had never seen in my life.

Yet the most tragic aspect of it all was the person standing beside me. Instead of Chris, with whom I had so clearly visualized the smallest details of our wedding ceremony, was Hisoka… a total stranger.

I wanted to scream and roar, but I had to keep the torment to myself and feign that I was fortunate to receive flowers and gifts from a few joyful newcomers.

Within minutes, I went from being a single woman to a wife. With a tremulous hand, I signed two sheets of paper that I didn't have time to read. This time, Hisoka made sure to remind me of my new role.

That night, I didn't sleep alone anymore. In the middle of the night, a thunderstorm raged outside. Chris used to make me love them; every time I heard one, he would hold me in his huge arms and comfort me despite my screams at each booming rumble. He had adored how innocently I feared them, and as a result, I loved how safe I felt around him. But tonight, Chris wasn't with me. Instead, I was in a house with a stranger, someone Minoru had sold my body to.

"He can imprison my body, but not my mind," I repeated this sentence in my head as I noticed the door open to the room.

(白無垢) *Shiromuku*: White kimono.

§§ (綿帽子) *Wataboushi*: White cotton hood.

Hisoka's silhouette appeared in the doorway, and it took a few seconds for me to swallow and try to calm my rapidly beating heart. I closed my eyes and pretended to be in a deep sleep; unfortunately, it didn't deter my new husband. Clumsily, he stepped on my small finger, and I tried to hide the pain between my clenched teeth as he lay down next to me, far too close for comfort.

Dread took control of my heart, which started to beat even faster. Could he hear it? I could feel his cold, rough hands sliding into my pajamas and touching my naked body, finishing on my nipples. I froze, still pretending to be asleep. He kept touching me all over. Then he jumped on top of me and moaned and chugged; I knew he was determined to do it. He came instantly, which somehow gave me a sense of relief.

In many societies, it is said that for a woman to be accepted and respected by the community, she should wait for the right age, the right person, and, most importantly, a marriage certificate before giving herself to a man. If a woman sleeps with a man before the union, she is often criticized and called derogatory names, losing honor in the eyes of others.

However, it seems, the same rules do not apply to men.

When a man sleeps with a woman before tying the knot, it is considered ordinary. Moreover, often the more women he beds, the more admiration he receives from his friends, not rarely to be hailed a hero, a Casanova, and macho. Whilst he proudly glorifies his achievements, other men ask him for advice to become like him.

But what if gender differences didn't matter? What if people could live their lives the way they wanted without being judged for their choices? What if two people in love could express their feelings without being labeled or criticized? They wouldn't count the number of dates, listen to priests or tradition experts?

What if they didn't need to wait for societal expectations or a piece of paper to allow them to express their love? What if their connection and intuition were stronger than any conviction or label? Where they could be above any of that. What if they could simply

listen to their own hearts and bodies, following their own time and space? Where they were not only driven by desire or needs but by a shared frequency, they would be on the same wavelength, connected by an inner knowing.

Where, with just a gaze into each other's eyes, they would know. The physical and emotional sensations of excitement, goosebumps, raised heartbeats, fast-pumping blood, and shivers of the body through sweat would combine with understanding, total trust, confidence, and devotion until they became one.

Merged in a holy unit, they would experience the infinity of body to body, mind to mind, and soul to soul's pleasures, flying together to a place that no words could describe in the ecstasy of the pineal gland, in a sacred event called love.

Where it was more than just a desire, more than fetishes, more than just aiming for an orgasm. It was about the journey, not the destination. It was all of that and more. They would laugh and cry alternately, moan and pant, yearning to understand and cope with the overwhelming amount of feelings that were overcoming them.

And in the end, they would decide to recapitulate it with a powerful feverish hug that meant more than anything…

But for me, that all was long gone.

And through Hisoka's loud snores, there were my silent sobs that only God could hear.

Chapter 9

二人で同じベッドで寝ていても目を閉じるのは一人だ。

Futari de onaji beddo de neteitemo me wo tojiru no wa hitori da.

Two people can sleep in the same bed and still be alone when they close their eyes.

Haruki Murakami
Hard-Boiled Wonderland and the End of the World

TAIJI, February 2009

IT HAD BEEN THREE MONTHS and three days since I arrived in the town and I knew no one except a few shop sellers with whom we exchanged daily greetings.

At times, I would stand in front of the mirror in the bedroom and try to hold imaginary conversations with my reflection, or at least give it a friendly smile as I practiced bidding it goodbye. But even then, I would feel disappointed with myself for failing. I missed the deep conversations I had shared with Sayaka and Chris, but I also yearned for the lighthearted banter we shared, where we could mock meaningless topics. Both had made me happy because it was the company that mattered. Yet they were gone now, and I was left with myself.

Losing my identity, I wasn't sure what was worse—feeling nothing or being overwhelmed by agony. In my senseless existence, I just didn't know who I was anymore, like a baby who must learn everything from the beginning but without any guidance.

Now, putting on a mask in fright of not recognizing myself and the emptiness I carried, I had never felt more lost in my life. Eventually, I could no longer bring myself to look in the mirror.

But in the locals' eyes, I must have come across as a haughty and conceited townsperson who hailed from the capital and didn't have the time to socialize with them, the peasants.

Perhaps that was why they never approached me or tried to get to know me better. And in a way, it was a reprieve. The fewer questions, the better. That meant less exposure. Exposure to a life I didn't even own.

Even though Hisoka was a Taiji local since birth, he didn't have many friends. The few he had were just other fishermen from around town. Thus, our social life remained barren. My only loyal companions became bitterness and solitude, both of which refused to leave me.

Every town has a unique scent that sets it apart, and Taiji was no exception. The powerful and distinct aroma of humidity and fish permeated the air, traversing through its narrow streets which were flanked by compact houses with roofs faded in shades of red, gray, and blue nestled among lush hills and mountains. The town embraced the azure expanse of the Pacific Ocean, its rocky bays adorned with boats and ships bobbing in the water. Upon my arrival, which now felt like ages ago, I had accurately sensed the tranquility that enveloped the town. Taiji proved to be one of the most serene places I had ever visited.

In contrast, I remembered the chaos, hastiness, and rat race that people lived in the metropolis of skyscrapers like Tokyo or any other major city in Japan. There existed two extremes in the country. Nobody was rushing in Taiji. Everyone appeared to be living in slow motion.

But for me, time became my worst enemy, even though Chris used to say, "Time is an illusion." It wasn't for me in Taiji. I would conceive every single second loudly ticking on the faded, black clock that had hung precisely in the center of the kitchen's wall.

Each morning, Hisoka would faithfully awaken at four-thirty in the morning, unless the weather was inclement or during some holidays. Depending on the season, he dressed in a specific fishing

attire, often donning a grass-green raincoat and worn black gum boots. To ensure he had something to eat on the go, I would prepare a takeaway breakfast for him the day prior. With his meal in hand, he would step into his white *keitora** and make his way to the harbor.

Usually, the boats set sail from the dock around five or six o'clock, heading toward a slowly brightening sea painted in delicate pastel hues—a sight I could only imagine. The details of his job remained a mystery as he rarely spoke about it when we were at home.

As a result, to my satisfaction, I didn't see him most mornings. However, in those rare moments when he left home later, I needed to wake up to prepare breakfast and tea for him, which he adored. The aroma of the tea always took me back to the kimono shop Mother worked at.

Suddenly, I missed her and her wisdom, especially when she experienced moments of contentment. Being a person of few words, she was usually meek, but when the time was right, she knew what to say. By fair means or foul, I could say, she saved me in a way. If it weren't for the advice she gave me after a fight with Fumi, I don't know how I would have dealt with such distressing moments as an early teenage girl: "When you feel like crying, when you feel sad, and even if the reason might seem trivial to others or even yourself, try to find something to do that you like."

That day, I had taken a book that had been collecting dust in my room's dresser, packed it, and promptly left for the shop. At first glance, the novel had seemed shallow and short, but as I read it during breaks, I discovered it contained many hidden pearls of wisdom. It had taken my imagination away from Fumi's nitpicks and made me truly understand the importance of not judging a book by its cover.

Soon after, karma had caught up with her, and she had been dismissed for being rude to a customer. But I had known it was her negativity, jealousy, and hatred that attracted her failure, and my patience, transparency, and ignorance toward her that attracted my victory. As I stood with the book in my hands behind a mannequin

---

* (軽トラ) *Keitora*: A mini truck or type of pickup truck; also known as a "light truck."

wearing a navy blue, cotton *yukata*† decorated with salmon-pink cherry flowers, Fumi had given me a final miserable glance before leaving for good. Although I felt sorry for her, I knew she needed to learn a lesson. I wished my mother had listened to her own counsel later in life, as she had changed so much that I could hardly remember her true nature.

Despite my anger and disappointment toward her, I remembered her advice and occasionally turned to the books that Sayaka had brought from her trips. With their juicy stories, they often helped pull me through the despairing reality I lived.

At night in Hisoka's tiny home, my subconscious was less merciful and often plagued me with nightmares that I wished to forget the next morning. The only consistency in my routine was my body's clock, which usually woke me up around six every morning, leaving me to stare at the same dilapidated ceiling until my stomach reminded me of its needs. I would then prepare myself breakfast, which most often consisted of natto, rice, and occasionally miso or vegetable soup, and tuna salad. At exactly nine o'clock, I took my contraceptive pill daily, which I had gotten a prescription for a few days prior to my departure to Taiji. I kept it hidden in the folds of my book on the shelf, out of Hisoka's poor sight.

Even on the brightest and most glorious of mornings, joy always managed to elude me. My days were mostly spent curled up in bed, my gaze fixed on the world beyond the window. Occasionally, a plane would grab my attention, its thunderous roar reverberating across the land as a white contrail painted a trail in the sky. During those fleeting moments, an intense longing would wash over me, a desire for an unoccupied seat on that aircraft, an escape to a distant island where I could vanish without a trace. The absence of motivation to rise and face the day persisted, weighing heavily upon me.

But the evenings were the hardest. The gloomy murk seemed to intensify my worries and pain.

To survive another day, when Hisoka would finish watching his evening news, I often found myself flipping through the channels, desperate for a distraction from my own thoughts. Unfortunately, all I could find were local programs that offered little entertainment.

---

† (浴衣) *Yukata*: A light cotton kimono usually worn in the summer or used as a bathrobe.

At times, accompanied by a small bucket of matcha ice cream, I would think back on Chris' remark, "Green tea ice cream? You guys are crazy about green tea! I have never seen this in my entire life! Everything is green tea! Perhaps you even have green tea popcorn!" Of course, what he didn't know was that, in fact, we *did* have matcha popcorn. We had that and matcha chocolates, tea biscuits, and more! When I had revealed that to him, he had laughed even harder with his pink gums showing. His chuckle always made his eyes sparkle with genuine joy.

There were days when my memories of Chris filled every inch of my soul while other times they slowly faded away. The worst was being left alone with my mind which I couldn't escape.

And as much as I didn't want to remember him, at night, he would occasionally visit me in repetitive dreams. Standing in the far distance, I would see his silhouette walking toward me through a bank of mist. He would suddenly stop a few meters from me, as he could walk no more. It seemed some hidden force was controlling his movements.

He was trying to tell me something, but every time he opened his mouth, he was unable to utter a word. Frustration was evident in his eyes, and the pain I felt throughout my soul was almost unbearable. I became uncertain as to whose pain I was feeling—mine or his.

With a sorrowful expression on his face, he attempted to reach me with an outstretched hand. When I tried to give him mine, he vanished into the dense fog's eternity.

And that was it. In its unbelievable briefness and woe, it couldn't feel more authentic.

And if not for the loud hammering of my pounding heart, which brought me back to my bed in the Taiji house, I would have thought it was real.

I couldn't understand why he visited me in my dreams or what they meant, but I knew there was some eerie connection between us, despite our regretful ending. I wished I could bring him from my dreams, but he always slipped between my fingers. If only I could have let him stay a little longer…

Yet paradoxically, I knew that thinking of him was leading me nowhere but to a world of sorrows and unanswered questions. Faced with this never-ending torment, I had two choices—to spend

my life mourning, feeling like a victim, and sinking deeper into despair, or to distract my thoughts by immersing myself in books and a whirlwind of work.

Although it wasn't easy to pull myself out of my misery, I knew that if I didn't try, I would drown in the abyss.

So, when my eyes grew tired from reading the tiny letters, I threw myself into household chores as an escape from my preoccupied mind.

Sorting laundry by color, ironing, and even folding Hisoka's collection of handkerchiefs into perfect squares, meticulously sweeping the floors of endless dust, collecting Hisoka's old newspapers to recycle in exchange for toilet paper at the corner store, doing modest grocery shopping, taking care of the plants in the garden, washing dishes, and the least pleasant task—preparing fish by removing scales, pulling out bones, and filleting and drying them. I did it all to forget my reality.

One of Hisoka's favorite meals was lunch, so depending on the season and how successful his fishing was that day, he would come home between eleven and twelve to join me, despite my disaffection. He left shortly after to return to the port for another hour or two to fix the net traps and prepare for the next day of his work. Rarely would he come back home empty-handed, as the better part of the time, he would catch fresh tuna, sea bass, horse mackerels, squid, octopus, and, if he was lucky, bluefin tuna. The majority of our meals consisted of seafood, which I learned to prepare in every possible way. The smell of frying fish often lingered in my hair; I replaced my favorite dresses with comfortable tracksuits.

Although Chris liked me most naturally, I still found pleasure in drawing a quick line of black eyeliner behind my eyelashes and a rose-pink blush on my cheeks. But here in Taiji, I found it pointless to wear make-up or dress up as I used to with my alluring, funky, and quirky clothes. They had mostly been given to me by Sayaka before her farewell to Peru.

My favorite was a liputa dress with a tribal African cut and an eye-catching blue, red, and gold geometric design which she had bought at a local market in Congo. Its cotton material was strong and light, making it comfortable for mild days. But I didn't wear that dress at all even on mild days. It politely hung among my other captivating dresses and tops in the bedroom closet.

Days in Taiji were long and monotonous; the only thing that changed was the weather. Winter, with its seven to fifteen degrees Celsius, was slightly brisk, yet much warmer than Tokyo's climate while summers were much softer and mellow with refreshing breezes from the sea. Hisoka had explained over dinner on my first week in Taiji that despite the temperate weather, "we must be careful. We tend to have strong typhoons."

Hisoka, despite living in such a picturesque town, entertained a dull and uneventful routine. While he was a stickler for order and I had grown accustomed to his lack of spontaneity, the house was filled with silence or the TV's piffle. His narrow views on life left little room for engaging conversation, and we were limited to exchanging necessary information. Apart from a marriage paper, we lived more like students who shared a flat; we had nothing else in common.

Hisoka was a shadow in the background of my story while I was a shadow of his. And I accepted that we would never share anything but a bed.

From the moment I saw him at the train station, despite the beauty he carried outside, I quickly realized that he would never understand my thoughts and perspectives on the various topics that I could discuss endlessly with Sayaka and Chris. I understood that he would never really feel the softness of my skin on a deeper level nor would he ever notice the glimmering dark depths in my eyes, much less the extent of my heart's capabilities. There was no possibility of him opening it as Chris had. I just knew we were from two different worlds.

There was no chemistry between us. Worse, I could sense that he had no experience with women before me. Over time, I realized that Hisoka was not a bad person, as Minoru had repeatedly told me before our marriage. But there was just nothing inspiring about him. On the contrary, he was exceedingly tedious and predictable to the point that I often presumed what he would say or do.

As I vegetated there, alone with my thoughts, I couldn't help but think of Mahika, Sayaka's Indian friend, who had shared a similar fate.

The extreme loneliness and grief slowly consumed me, and I wondered how much longer I could continue like this.

Chapter 10

虎穴に入らずんば虎子を得ず。
Koketsu ni hairazunba maru wo ezu.
If you do not enter the tiger's den, you cannot capture the tiger cub.

May 2009

DURING RARE MOMENTS WHEN HISOKA felt inclined to be sociable, we gathered with his fellow fishermen and their spouses. However, among the colleagues, there was only one, Katashi, who occasionally graced us with a visit alongside his delightful wife, Masami.

"Aiko, I have a little surprise for you," Masami exclaimed with infectious excitement one afternoon. The sunny day had put Hisoka in a splendid mood, sparking his sudden desire for socializing. As we relaxed on a cozy outdoor couch in our backyard, we treated our guests to edamame, *Kaki no tane*,* and local beers. Masami, who not only loved a good chat but also recognized that I was struggling to establish myself in the area, effortlessly filled the conversation void. Her soft and melodious voice carried the pleasant tones of anticipation. We had unknowingly settled into a natural rhythm where I listened attentively while she engaged in delightful prattle. It turned out to be a perfect arrangement for both of us.

Although I couldn't call her a friend, as we had only met a couple of times over the course of my six-month stay in Taiji, I noticed that despite her naïve but concomitantly singularly stubborn personality, she was rather a genuine and fun person to be around. She was petite in size but robust with dreams.

Once, with the help of Hisoka's homemade sake, she had confessed to me that it was her fantasy to become an actress. Tipsy, with sparks in her eyes and an inscrutable smile, Masami had

---

* (柿の種) *Kaki no tane*: Soy-flavored rice crisps mixed with peanuts.

repeated the same sentence a few times. I could remember by heart her tangled tongue's monologue on how she had worked hard and dedicated herself to becoming a part of the high school theatre club, where she was mainly offered leading roles. But with her dream came an even greater one…

It was during the play *Romeo and Juliet* when acting as Juliet that she had met Romeo at a Capulet family masked ball and they had feigned a kiss. In fact, it had been Shingo, a schoolmate one year her senior. And it was then that she hadn't needed to act to fall in love with him. She had known he was the one for her.

In desperation, she had been willing to do anything to repeat that scene to make him see what she saw—their future together. Even if it cost her acting reputation.

Despite sacrificing her dream for him, there had already been someone else in his life. An older, "not very comely"—according to Masami's telling of the story—pet food shopkeeper who used to appear from time to time in front of the school.

It had broken her. In distress and as a rebound to ease her pains, she had begun seeing Katashi, her classmate with a twitching eyelid, who had loved her shyly for years.

By the time Shingo had realized her love for him and, more importantly, his love for her, it was unfortunately too late to turn back time and fate, as she was already married to Katashi.

In the face of all these failures, and with an involuntary hiccup, she revealed that she still hoped to go to Tokyo and become an actress, which was hard for me to imagine with Katashi in her life. And she knew it too. Perhaps she pictured herself beside Shingo, whom I assumed she still loved given the way her eyes shined while talking about him. But despite her bitten nail cuticles, she was good at hiding her disappointments, I observed, as her pretty, round alabaster face always had a bright smile.

As I imagined her enduring each day beside a man she didn't love, I couldn't help but wonder how she coped with the pain. It was a feeling I knew all too well. She seemed to maintain a zest for life that I couldn't quite muster.

"I feel so lethargic and demotivated," I confided to her. "How do you manage to have so much energy and joy, Masami?"

"*Kaizen*,"† she replied with a chuckle, noticing my confusion. After repeating herself, she added with a hint of disbelief, "Are you Japanese? It's the concept of making continuous, incremental changes. Even small changes can make a huge impact over time. It will all fall into place. It's better to take small steps than no steps at all. With consistent effort, you can achieve anything in life."

She paused to regard me with pity and a bit of sorrow.

"I just knew it, Aiko, you seemed like you needed some entertainment badly. Imagine, I have lived here all my life and I never attended these dolphin shows they have here in Taiji at the Whale Museum!" Masami opened the next bottle of beer and leaned into me. "Are you ready for a surprise?" I forced a smile and nodded, feigning excitement. "I have two tickets to the show from Katashi! It's sure to be great fun!" she exclaimed while our husbands droned on about their own mundane topics.

Sometimes, looking back at my past, I felt like none of my experiences were real. All the events I lived through with all my senses and all my heart felt like they belonged to someone else. It was like watching a movie of my life. It felt like a mirage. With the help of time and my own denial of self-preservation, my memories were gradually fading away.

My new life took over and as I let it flow to its rhythm, I was gradually forgetting who I used to be. I didn't bother to understand anything anymore. I didn't plan anything anymore, as it seemed that life had its own plans.

And as boring as they were, I knew that anything would be more exciting than another copy-paste day in Taiji. Despite my penurious knowledge of dolphins, apart from imagining them as "cute creatures," I felt rather indifferent about them.

"So, when is that show?" I took my first sip of the beer and looked with a mischievous smile into Masami's tipsy eyes.

"Cheers. To the dolphins!"

"To the dolphins!"

---

† (改善) *Kaizen*: A philosophy or set of practices that focuses on the continuous improvement of processes, usually in business. It has also been applied to healthcare, life-coaching, government, and other industries.

Next Friday, we found ourselves sitting in an outdoor coliseum-like venue. Instead of a podium, there was a midsized, half-oval pool. And in place of Greek gods and goddesses in long white dresses, four dolphin trainers stood in tight light blue diving suits, preparing last-minute adjustments before the start of the show.

As I regarded the chaos from the stands, I tried to recall the last time I had been a part of such a throng. It dawned on me that I didn't miss Tokyo's crowds all that much.

I noticed a nearby girl in a frilled, watermelon-red dress with a ponytail drop her entire scoop of chocolate ice cream on the cement floor. If not for the stern look on her mom's face, she might have picked it up and continued licking it.

But it was not the girl who captivated my attention. I couldn't help but notice a tall foreigner making his way toward a seat.

If his hair had been a shade lighter, he would have looked like Chris. *It's been a while since I've seen a Westerner*, I thought to myself.

Witnessing the gentle kiss he planted on his Japanese partner's forehead, a pang of emotion surged within me. It served as a poignant reminder that couples of mixed nationalities could indeed thrive.

Glancing indifferently in my direction, I noticed the lack of similarities between the two of them. Was my longing for Chris so intense that any Western foreigner could potentially resemble him? Despite this nagging paranoia, I couldn't resist speculating on how they may have met. Perhaps it had been in a pub, where he flashed his pearly whites and whispered sweet nothings into her ear. Or maybe they had locked eyes on the street and just known…

Perhaps they had met at the train station while waiting for the same train? Although the woman didn't strike me as particularly stunning, he seemed to have eyes for only her. Slightly irritated and lost in my own presumptions, I was jolted back to reality by Masami's voice.

"Wow, there are so many people here!" She quickly suggested buying snacks before the show started, as we had ten minutes to spare. Most of the people wore short-sleeved shirts and summer

attire since the weather was perfect—warm, but not too hot with a mild breeze that occasionally brought a hint of chlorine from the pool.

After the crowd clapped in unison, they fell silent when a woman in a diving suit, adorned with a whistle on a string around her neck, stepped forward with a wide, banana-shaped grin and introduced herself as Michiko.

The Westerner seemed to not understand Japanese, as his companion whispered translations in his ear after each of Michiko's sentences, I presumed as I involuntarily peeked at them again.

The show was about to begin, and as I looked around for Masami, I saw her rushing back to take her seat. She offered me dark red pieces of fish from a carryout tray. Before I could decline Masami's offer, the loud crowd's sudden gasps of astonishment drew our attention to the pool.

The stars of the show had made their entrance—fast as arrows, leaving four shadows at the bottom of the water as they spun and jumped while Michiko introduced them one by one to the delight of the crowd.

The trainer wrapped up the introduction by exclaiming, "And now, Lila, our bottlenose dolphin!" The blaring Japanese pop music from the speakers, ineffectively muffled by the thick ferns nearby, gradually swelled into an ovation from the crowd.

This was the sign for the dolphins to follow the other presenter, Emiyo, who smoothly jumped into the azure-colored water of the pool. Swimming on their backs to the rhythm of the energetic melodies, the dolphins formed a flawless circle around her. The touching act prompted loud expressions of awe and admiration from the audience.

The excitement grew louder as Michiko, now equipped with purple-and-pink-striped hula hoops attached to a long pole brought the dolphins' attention to her. They jumped through the hoops with such accuracy that not one origami artist could envy their precision.

But it wasn't just their accuracy that intrigued me; it was their liveliness and playfulness! The dolphins were fast and intelligent, comprehending and obeying their proud trainers as they effortlessly executed each command. In their excitement after completing each task in the program, which included catching a frisbee, sliding their bellies in circles on the slippery platform, spinning hoops around

their noses, and others, they eagerly awaited their prizes—shimmering fish from poolside buckets.

The atmosphere in the crowd grew livelier as dolphins leaped high, moving together in stunning synchronization. They splashed the front rows of clapping, mostly amazed spectators, although some were annoyed at getting soaked and taken by surprise.

A few children moved to the front, some even standing up before sitting down again due to their parents' intervention. Despite their attempts to contain their excitement, the anticipation was palpable.

But a bigger surprise awaited us.

"Now, ladies and gentlemen, I need one volunteer."

Mixed feelings of anxiety and excitement washed over me. It felt as if Michiko's words had been directed at me.

In the span of a few seconds, I found myself following a few other people and raising my hand. Deep inside, I had an intuitive feeling that she would choose me. And she did. Masami cheered loudly, joined by others. With shaky legs, I made my way down the stairs toward the beaming trainer.

"Hello. What's your name?" she asked.

"Aiko." I heard my voice tremble into the microphone that had been passed to me.

"Beautiful name! Aiko, have you ever seen a live dolphin before?" Michiko inquired.

"No, this is my first time."

"So, you haven't received a kiss from a dolphin before, correct?" she clarified with a smile.

"No, I haven't."

Now, Michiko turned to the audience.

"Ladies and gentlemen. Dolphins are very affectionate animals and they love kissing." She giggled. "Now, Aiko, nothing in this life is for free, not even love." The laughter from the audience grew louder, but I didn't find it funny. Still, I was too excited to really react. "So, I need you to throw this ball, and if Lila retrieves it and brings it back to you, you will get a kiss from her on the cheek."

She anticipated the audience's encouragement, but I required none. As I gazed at the dolphin, I sensed she knew what was going on.

Her vibrant eyes fixated on the ball as I received it from Michiko and hurled it into the water. There was no need for patience as Lila swiftly swam toward me, propelling the ball through the splashing waves. The crowd erupted in jubilant cheers, but my attention remained captivated by Lila's companionship, rendering the applause unheard.

"Yay! Bravo to Lila!" Michiko exclaimed. "Now, Aiko, are you ready for the kiss?"

I smiled and, encouraged by Michiko, leaned down to feel Lila's moist beak on my cheek.

"Big applause for Lila and Aiko!"

As I took my seat among the clapping audience, Masami couldn't hide her excitement. "Oh my God, you were chosen out of all the people, wow! How was it?" she asked.

"Wet," I replied, and we laughed and followed the rest of the show.

Dancing with the trainers to the music, the dolphins jumped on the platform and wagged their tails in perfect synchronization. Some performed unexpected moves like backward flips or spins. These breathtaking jumps were just an introduction to the grand finale, where four trainers were propelled by dolphins on a high-speed, choreographed ride along the surface of the pool. It looked like an incredibly fun and thrilling experience as they darted through the water, only to suddenly emerge on top, creating a majestic sight akin to the parting of the Red Sea by Moses. The audience erupted into applause and cheers, marveling at the spectacular performance of the trainers and their dolphin partners.

Like followers of a savior to the Promised Land in the Bible, the mesmerized viewers in the audience could contain their awe no longer. They stood from their seats, mouths agape and eyes wide open. I, too, found myself standing in astonishment, envying the trainers for their incredible work and briefly wishing I could be in their shoes, or rather, their marine park swimsuits.

The dolphins waved goodbye with their slippery flukes, as if in perfect precision, urging the public to join them in bidding farewell.

As with most shows, when it came to an end, people began to rush toward the exit in a mass, following one another like sheep behind their shepherd. The little girl who had dropped her ice cream on the hungry pavement, and the foreigner who didn't quite

resemble Chris flashed by in my peripheral vision. However, I remained seated, feeling a profound sense of emptiness and slight confusion about my feelings toward the show.

I found myself unable to leave. A boundless urge kept me cemented to my seat for a reason I couldn't comprehend.

Masami stood and waited for me to do the same, asking if I was fine, but as soon as she perceived I was not going to leave, she sat back down, imparting me a bewildered look.

After everyone had left, Masami's patience wore thin. "Aiko, shall we go?" With a hesitant nod, I reluctantly got up to follow her toward the exit but still felt a strong craving to see one of the dolphins up close again, face to face. Just before we reached the park exit, I stole a final glance at the smaller pool in the corner and noticed a lone dolphin swimming in circles. It was as if my wish had come true, and I could hardly believe my own eyes.

"Masami, can we just take a quick look?" I asked, noting the tempered politeness that she flashed my way.

As we approached, the dolphin immediately swam toward us, making clicking noises. Upon realizing we had nothing to offer him, he turned around and made his way toward the dirty white, slippery platform that connected to the pool. And then, like a small, excited child, slid back to it, splashing drops of water which, with the help of wind, reached us.

As he repeated his clumsy slides several times in a row, I found myself pondering the reasons behind his antics. Was he trying to show off to gain our attention? Was he simply having fun, or acting out of boredom? Despite my lack of knowledge about dolphin behavior, I was captivated by his innocence and the potential fun that he seemed to possess.

"I think we have to go back," Masami said.

At that very moment, the dolphin swam toward us again, this time coming closer. It was as if he understood her words and was begging us with his gaze to stay longer.

For a moment, he looked me straight in the eye, sending goosebumps all over my body. We continued to gaze at each other as if struck by an electric shock. His eyes seemed so human, filled with deep, hidden stories. "Masami, do you know where these dolphins come from?"

"From here, from our waters, Aiko," she replied.

"Please tell me more about dolphins. You are from Taiji. You must know about them," I pressed.

"I don't know much, Aiko. I am sorry."

It was hard to believe, yet there was nothing I could do but think of another source of information. There was no way I could let go of these long-forgotten feelings. Feelings of excitement and a leap of hope that I thought I would never feel again.

"But if you like them so much, they are all around us. I mean, Taiji is full of them. Katashi and—" She stopped abruptly and changed her sentence. "There are even programs where you can swim with them."

"Really?" I exclaimed, my excitement mounting at the thought. "Have you done it?"

"I never did it, but I know where you can do it."

"Take me there, please… now," I insisted.

"Now?" she asked, taken aback.

You're more fun after a few beers, I mused as we walked toward a nearby bus stop.

"It's the next stop, Aiko, at Moriura Bay. Inside the hotel, there is a Dolphin Base," she said while I gripped the handrail tightly and realized my palms were becoming excessively clammy with eagerness.

"I am sorry that I can't join you. I have to go home and cook for Katashi. Please, forgive me. But your home is not far from here, so I don't think you should have any trouble finding your way back." She felt guilty about not accompanying me, I could tell.

Little did she know, in fact, I felt relieved she was leaving me to my own devices. It was often tiring for me to constantly adjust to someone else's needs. In Taiji, despite feeling lonely at times, I had slowly grown accustomed to my own company, rarely needing anyone for anything. It gave me a sense of freedom.

"It's here, Aiko," she pointed with a long, slender finger at the building that suddenly arose in front of us. Just before the bus door opened, she added, "In the reception, you can also ask them to call a taxi for your ride home." She smiled goodbye, her usual slightly exaggerated makeup adorned with a rare apologetic grimace.

The hotel was an ordinary establishment that gave off the nineties vibes. Despite its simple exterior, the interior displayed various shades of blue adorned with fishing nets, wooden anchors,

and an array of sea-themed paintings of different sizes. The walls exuded a refreshing vibe, proudly showcasing the hotel's location in Japan.

As I approached the reception desk, my attention was immediately drawn to the small dolphin heads that decorated the pens. Unable to contain my curiosity, I inquired with the lady behind the metal steel desk, who greeted me with a beaming smile.

"Excuse me, I heard that I can swim with the dolphins here?"

"Indeed, you can, ma'am," she replied with a warm and inviting demeanor. She then proceeded to inform me of the price of the program and swimming suit, and I reached into my purse to retrieve the money that Hisoka had given me for a substantial grocery shopping. Without dwelling on the need for an excuse to spend the money, I placed it on the counter, eager to proceed.

"You're in luck," she said with a wink, causing my heart to skip a beat. "You'll have all the dolphins to yourself."

It was a mystery even to myself why I had developed such a strong desire to be around dolphins. In retrospect, I remembered seeing them as plush toys, on stickers, key chains, TV commercials, and even on a cheesy toilet seat in Madoka's apartment some years back. My knowledge and interest had ended there. So how was it that one day, a single look in a dolphin's eye could trigger such indescribable desires within me? Desires to be in their presence, to interact with them.

Despite not understanding the source of this newfound fascination, one thing was certain: being around them brought a genuine smile to my face, one that had been absent for a long time.

Not only was I the sole participant in the swimming program, but I was also fortunate that they didn't make me wait for an extended period of time.

"Hi, I am Erika. I will be your guide for today." The lady who appeared out of nowhere showed me into a changing room. Clad in a snug dark blue and black wetsuit layered over my swimsuit and fitted with a mask, fins, and snorkel, I appeared more akin to a professional diver than the clueless amateur I truly was.

I followed in her footsteps, my excitement growing with each step, but my impatience also increased as I knew I was getting closer to seeing the dolphins up close.

What I beheld was beyond my expectations. Behind the unassuming facade of the hotel, stretched hills of various shapes, sizes, and shades, created a serene and peaceful ambiance that seemed straight out of a dazzling postcard depicting heaven on Earth.

At the front, there they were, mystical creatures. Their fins emerged from the pool's surface from time to time, offering a tantalizing glimpse into their enigmatic underwater world. Some of them swam in circles while others performed small hops with an occasional jump toward the open sea.

"Okay," Erika interrupted my thoughts as she walked toward the nearest one. "Now, we'll get closer, inside the water. But first, before you swim with them, you have to observe me." Following her instructions, I stayed behind and watched Erika interact with the six large dolphins that swam in circles in the pool. Despite her reassurance, I still felt skeptical about getting into the water with them.

At first glance, the humpback fins breaking the surface of the water could have made them resemble sharks. But that image quickly disappeared when I glimpsed their approachable smiles.

"In this pool, we have three bottlenose dolphins and three Risso's dolphins." This information was new to me, but I could logically deduce which was which based on their appearances. The ones with longer snouts must have been the bottlenose dolphins, and the others, with oddly proportioned heads and bodies significantly covered with scratches and scars, were the Risso's dolphins.

As I hesitated to step into the pool, I nearly slipped at the edge. "Be careful, please," I heard a voice behind me say, but I managed to keep my balance. "Also, don't touch their blowholes. They don't like it."

The rush of cold water into my wetsuit surprised me. Taking a few deep breaths to calm myself, I ventured deeper into the pool. The pressure increased, and I walked slowly toward Erika, who was already in the middle of the dolphins who seemed to appear out of nowhere. Suddenly, I started feeling anxious.

Looking at so many of them from afar was one thing, but being in their immediate presence was entirely different. Their sheer number, size, and strength commanded my respect.

The dolphins seemed thrilled as they swam briskly toward us, getting closer with each passing moment. One of them, in an apparent state of felicity, jumped out of the water, splashing the tiled walls of the pool. I noticed that some of them appeared light blue against the color of the bottom, their enormous fish-like shadows gliding gracefully beneath the surface.

My fears faded. With a mask on, I could see that the pool was quite small for six gigantic mammals. But I pushed aside that thought, my focus shifting to how I could get the chance to touch them. The texture of their skin puzzled me.

They didn't make me wait too long. The dolphins made their way toward me, emitting funny clicks and whistles that were slightly suppressed by the density of the water. Summoning my courage, I stretched out my hand to feel the smooth and rubbery skin on my palm.

At times, while swimming, it nearly seemed as if we would have a head-on collision. However, I underestimated them, and they were cleverer than I presumed. Just when I would envision a potential accident with blood from my head, stitches at the hospital, and irritation on Hisoka's face, the dolphins would instantly change their trajectory and swim the other way. It made me wonder if it was some sort of play or teasing on their part.

To see them again from a different perspective, I lifted my head above the water. The rather calm surface of the pool belied the energy it bore below.

"If you are lucky, you can grab them by their fin, and they will take you around the pool," said Erika, whom I heard just before I dove under the water again. That idea had struck me before her encouragement, but I was too shy to ask. Now, with an open invitation, I was determined to hunt for any of their fins.

As they turned out to be cheeky and swift like a rocket, it wasn't as easy as it seemed.

They would often speed up when I approached as if they were teasing and playing a cat-and-mouse game with me. Despite their mischievous behavior, I felt a sense of camaraderie with them as I swam underwater. It was as if I were gradually becoming one of them. It somehow seemed that they had accepted me into their pod, I wanted to believe.

They would come close, swim below or underneath me, and let me touch them. Sometimes, they would playfully nudge me with their beaks or tails when I least expected it, seemingly provoking me to play along or seeking attention or contact. It was an exhilarating experience, and I couldn't help but be captivated by their playful antics.

Finally, I managed to clench onto one of the closest fins that appeared in my way. I held on tightly, determined not to let go. In this union, he became the leader, the driver, and I, a passenger in the back seat, surrendered myself completely.

We swam faster than I had imagined, making sharp turns due to the small confines of the tank. As we swam, the water foamed with little bubbles, reminiscent of a hot tub. But more importantly, there was an overwhelming sense of laughter and joy. Initially, I felt a little scared, but soon, I found myself briefly merging into their space, fully embracing the moment and the experience.

Enchanted by their authentic vigor, endless curiosity, positive energy, and child-like happiness, I forgot about my responsibilities, pain, and emotional baggage from the adult world. In their presence, I lost track of time and of the rest of the world and felt like I was a part of their kingdom. A realm of understanding, synchronicity, respect, and connection exceeded my wildest imaginations.

The pinnacle of this extraordinary encounter arrived when, during my dive, a Risso's dolphin gracefully approached me and came to a halt just inches from my face. I was taken aback, a mixture of confusion and astonishment washing over me. Yet he remained motionless, fixing its gaze upon me. Its intense scrutiny never wavered, and in that enchanting moment, a profound and infinite union formed between us. It felt as if the dolphin possessed knowledge about me. This extraordinary connection persisted until Erika's voice shattered the spell, announcing the conclusion of our time together.

After this timeless moment, it was difficult to go back to reality, yet I had no choice, as after swimming with them, the ticket also included a show.

She called each of the dolphins by name, but I couldn't tell them apart, as to me they all looked alike. However, it seemed as if they had their own unique characteristics. There was a shy one who didn't move around much but rather swam in circles in a corner of

the pool. Then there was a vocal one, frequently emitting a series of whistles to communicate with others. Another was a cheeky showoff that I could identify by the scar below his left eye, always vying for attention. Interestingly, they all had one thing in common—jealousy. They were hungry for nestling and affection, competing and pushing each other for the touch of a human. It was evident they craved interaction and attention, displaying their eagerness to connect with us.

But for the show, despite their different personalities, suddenly they merged into one obedient, neuter entity. Erika, along with other trainers, taught them to jump, wave their tails, give kisses on people's cheeks, and exhibit their comically separated teeth. She even made them "sing" to her hands as she moved them like a maestro conducting a symphony. Others imitated the sounds of pulling fishing rods in her demonstration. Their vocalizations and tricks were impressive, but sitting at the edge of the pool as the sole audience member brought a sense of oddness and déjà vu to me. Just a few hours earlier, I had been watching similar tricks and experiencing similar strange feelings. The only difference now was that it was all just for me.

Instead of feeling honored, I felt the connection between me and the dolphins fade away. I couldn't help but wonder if Erika would let me jump in with them again, to once more experience that unique bond that I had just tasted and now craved. I didn't think there was any reason for my simple request to be refused, even though it required some courage on my part. However, I was disappointed by Erika's steady smile and lame explanation that my ticket only included the swimming program and the show.

It was all orchestrated. Part of the plan, I thought to myself, finding it reminiscent of the Japanese way of doing things. *No exceptions to be made, no rules to be broken*, I mused, realizing there was no room for variation.

But what was even worse was the realization that after the show ended, as I closed the sky-blue main door of the hotel and left the dolphins behind, I had no idea when I would see them again.

Before placing my weary feet on the mat, I glanced into the mirror with newfound courage. In the dim light, I saw a stranger staring back at me. Her young face bore the marks of exhaustion with two new parallel wrinkles between her eyes, giving her a stern expression. She seemed like she was about to look away, but then she gathered strength from within and kept staring. Her eyes looked burnt out and empty. Despite struggling to recognize myself in her, I knew that underneath this facade, she was me. With a bashful smile, I finally lay down in bed ready to confront whatever was ahead.

Blurred memories of wild nights at karaoke, often culminating in dancing on tables, a kaleidoscope of laughter on my friends' faces, and happy tears while fooling around Tokyo's nooks flooded my mind. The delight of seeing a sparrow taking a dry bath in the sand, the satisfaction of savoring my favorite ramen, Sayaka's brilliant sense of humor thrown at me when most needed, and the warmth of Chris' hand on my cheek—all reminders of a life I once cherished. Details which, it seemed, meant everything to me.

I wondered what had happened to me. I had lost my zest for life; I found myself adrift in a sea of low vibrations and frequencies, caught in the clutches of the devil with no energy to resist. This was not who I was.

As Hisoka's loud snores filled the background, I glanced out the window and caught sight of a shooting star streaking across the dark sky. I felt a wave of confusion wash over me as I wondered what to wish for. In a moment of whimsy, my thoughts shifted to dolphins, creatures I knew little about but felt strangely familiar to me. I recalled the piercing gaze of the Risso's dolphin that had locked eyes with me, and I tried to piece it all together. What had that dolphin seen? Was he trying to communicate something to me? Did he perceive my pain? The questions swirled in my mind as I gazed at the sky, lost in contemplation.

Undoubtedly, I needed to get to know them better, learn about their lives, and find out who they truly were. I longed to share my excitement with Sayaka and Chris, but I had no idea where they were or what they were doing.

I wish I could spend more time with the dolphins, I finally declared to myself. Still looking up at the sky, I added, *Would I be greedy if I asked? Why did Chris leave me?*

For the first night since arriving in Taiji, Hisoka's snores dissolved into an offset of my thoughts…

Chapter 11

千里の道も一歩から。
Senri no michi mo ippo kara.
A journey of a thousand miles begins with a single step.

HISOKA'S OUTDATED AND BIGOTED VIEWS on relationships forced me to learn to surrender through clenched teeth. Hisoka was adamant that he was the provider and I was the recipient. He ensured that by paying for groceries and meticulously keeping track of the bills and other expenses, most of which I was not privy to.

However, I knew that he could afford more than that. In profitable months, I learned from Masami that he could make "very good money." Still, he chose to live a frugal life.

Despite being lost and uncertain about my desired profession, I was determined to work. I felt ready to break free from the confines of the house and earn my own income, regardless of the job. Most of all, however, I wanted a way to visit the dolphins that didn't require me to rely on Hisoka's money.

But reality tinged with déjà vu struck me once again. I was met with resistance from Hisoka, who insisted that my place was at home.

Occasionally, when he was in a better mood, he would give me some leftover yen for what he called "woman's stuff," though I wasn't exactly sure what he meant. I would place the money in one of the dusty and smudged Chinese cups that, like many other neglected objects in his house, never fulfilled their true purpose. It perched on top of the old-fashioned dresser that towered above Hisoka's eye level and became my makeshift piggybank—and a source of hope for an uncertain future. Though I had no specific objective in mind, I subconsciously believed that it would come in handy when the time was right.

Early one morning, before Hisoka embarked on his fishing expedition, I awoke with a newfound determination to break free from my usual routine and visit the bookstore located at the end of our street. My eagerness to learn more about dolphins fueled this spontaneous decision. As soon as he departed for the docks, the sound of his aging *keitora* fading into the distance, I slipped into my trusty red sandals reserved for my infrequent solitary strolls. Filled with anticipation, I embarked on my journey to the bookstore, eager to immerse myself further into the captivating world of these enigmatic creatures.

Upon pushing open the door to the store, the chime of the tiny bell resonated more loudly than I had anticipated. It was a place that had piqued my curiosity numerous times, yet I had never mustered the courage to step inside. Behind the counter, a woman sporting metal-framed glasses cast a brief glance in my direction, evoking memories of my stern microbiology professor back at Hamamatsu University. However, her warm smile and quiet "*Irasshaimase*"* quickly dissipated that image. The hypnotizing smell of fresh books stirred up old, melancholic yet somehow unrecognizable memories.

The shop was filled with books of different genres—some cheerful and others less jovial, some knowledgeable and others less wise, some factual and others fictional—all adorned with polychromatic images and various stories, creating a fresh and mysterious kaleidoscope of print. But I knew exactly what I had come for, and I made a beeline for the section dedicated to "Animals." To my surprise, there was only one book on them; it was entitled *Behaviors of Dolphins.* Whispering the title to myself, I instantly knew I could spare some yen from the Chinese cup and that I wouldn't leave the store without it in my hands.

As I flipped through the pages of the book, my thoughts consumed by the captivating photos of dolphins, some in close-up, others in their entirety, I couldn't shake off a memory that had been

* (いらっしゃいませ) *Irasshaimase*: Welcome in.

lingering with me since the other day at the pool. Lost in my thoughts, I suddenly heard a familiar laugh, and even before I looked up, I knew it belonged to Masami.

"Hello. How are you?" I asked as I approached her, noticing that there was something out of place about her. The usual strained smile that I had come to recognize had been replaced by a genuine, beautiful one. Excusing herself from the sympathetic seller and taking a brief glance at the book I had in my hands, she gently pulled on the sleeve of my cotton shirt to ensure we were at a safe distance from prying ears and eyes before whispering, "You won't believe it…"

"What?" I asked just as softly.

"Shingo broke it off with the shopkeeper," she revealed, pausing for a moment before continuing. She knew she could trust me more than anyone else; I didn't judge her. She didn't need to explain to me that she still loved him despite her being married. Although she didn't know the details of my love story with Chris, she sensed there was no one else who could understand her like me. "But that's not all," she added with even more excitement. "He asked about me. His sister told me herself."

"And? And?"

"Well… I am married. How could I leave Katashi? I would break his heart. But am I not allowed to dream?" She smiled, though it seemed less authentic this time.

"You are breaking his heart every day by not loving him. And your heart too…" I responded solemnly.

A deep, synchronized sigh escaped us both, returning us to reality. It was true, nobody could take away her dreams. But where were they leading her? I knew the answer I had given her was for both of us.

Instead of dwelling on my past and Masami's choices, I shifted my focus to the book I held in my hands. I thought of a place where I could immerse myself in it. It seemed like the perfect moment to change the heavy topic.

"Oh, Masami, I'm actually glad we crossed paths today! You seem to know all the hidden gems in Taiji," I said. It seemed to work as she smiled proudly. "Do you know of a quiet beach where I can relax?"

True to form, Masami didn't disappoint me this time either.

With vivid descriptions, she guided me to a place I had only dreamed of. After a twenty-minute bus drive, I found myself nestled among the thick hills of the cove.

Nearly deserted and exuding an aura of tranquility, I found myself by the aquamarine expanse of the mirror of the tender sea.

With the May wind barely stirring, gentle waves caressed my feet along the shoreline. The water possessed a refreshing coolness, but the early afternoon sun compensated for it with its warmth. The farther my gaze extended, the deeper the sea seemed to grow in hue, acting as a subtle reminder that venturing too far from the safety of the shore might not be wise.

As I took a seat on the earth-colored tiny pebbles, I was startled by a voice calling out, "Aiko." Turning my head in surprise, I felt slightly embarrassed when I realized the voice wasn't directed toward me but at a young girl.

Despite her fringe covering half of her bright eyes, I could see the little girl's cute grin and guessed she was around seven years old.

Carrying small stones that shimmered in the sun, she ran to her mother who sat not far from me. "That's for you, Mommy."

Her mother smiled at the present and placed them by her side.

"Mommy, Mommy, look!" Little Aiko called.

Instead of indulging her child though, her mother opened a sunscreen's lid. "Aiko, stay still. Close your eyes."

"Mommy, look!"

"Aiko, please, I need to put sunscreen on your face."

Aiko obediently closed her eyes as her mother precisely spread a fat, white cream on her daughter's skin.

"Mommy… Oh no," I heard her whisper. "He is gone…"

Turning to follow her gaze, I managed to catch a glimpse of it, a splendid butterfly. I was close enough to observe its black body decorated with symmetric, magnificent, neon blue rectangles that grew toward its body's center.

My thoughts transported me to a hidden realm of animals. I was glad that, in place of succumbing to the allure of the olive-green, silky-looking dress that had caught my eye in the boutique next door to the bookstore, I made the conscious decision to invest my money in "women's stuff" of a different kind—an insightful book. As I flipped through the pages, I felt affirmed by my choice.

With awe and astonishment, I immersed myself in the pages of the book, learning about dolphins' remarkable intelligence, compassion, and social bonds. What truly captivated me was their uncanny similarities to humans. Not only were they warm-blooded mammals like us, needing air to live, but their daily lives seemed to mirror ours in many ways. It was fascinating to discover how much we shared with these majestic creatures of the sea.

While they haven't lived on the land for about fifty million years, they didn't have to deal with banks, city halls, or other bureaucratic offices or have to understand governments, borders, schools, or religious worship buildings, their social needs were not much different from our own.

Dolphin offspring established the most profound bond with their mothers, staying by their side until they were about eight years old. During that time, they would learn how to find and hunt prey, familiarize themselves with their surroundings, navigate their way home, and survive the dangers of the underwater realm. But that was not all. The need to be in their mother's presence went beyond that; it was about cuddling and nestling close to her. The kind of peace they needed could only be found in the company of their moms.

As mothers mingled to gossip and catch up, slightly older youngsters would frolic with their peers, but never stray too far from watchful eyes. Teenagers often gathered to surf the waves or indulge in mischievous activities like getting high on pufferfish to experience hallucinogenic rides. Meanwhile, the more mature ones went on dates, charmed each other, and even fell in love.

And to relax, but most importantly, to heal their skin from infections, they visited "spas," as humans did. They would scratch their backs, tails, and bellies on a rainbow of corals while receiving five-star treatment for their skin and getting help with their dermal problems.

Some of them were more courageous, manipulative, funny, bossy, shy, or affectionate than others. Just like humans, the palette of characters among them was limitless with a wide range of personalities and traits.

And just like people, dolphins had their dark sides too. It wasn't uncommon for dolphins to form gangs and intimidate female dolphins, often by surrounding her in a way that she couldn't escape,

jumping and leaping around her. In some observed cases, if the female dolphin managed to escape, the male dolphins might even chase her, bite her, and, once she was returned to the confines of their group, hit hard to discourage her from trying to flee again in the future.

Or, sometimes, right before their dinner time, just for fun, they would toss prey into the air like a ball. This habit, like many others, was not yet completely understood by scientists.

None of their unsavory behaviors made me love them less. In fact, I felt an even greater connection with them. As humans and animals, I hoped that with our imperfections we would be able to understand each other more and learn from one another.

While all the loud squeaks, whistles, trills, moans, and grunts were a language they used to communicate with one another, just like us, they also called each other by names through distinctive individual signature whistles. Each had its own name within a pod.

On top of that, they possessed a superpower that we did not. Just like bats, dolphins used echolocation. With their high-frequency clicks, they were able to locate objects by interpreting the echoes of sound waves that bounced off objects. This allowed them to precisely explore the shape, size, and speed of those objects, even hundreds of yards away.

And what's more, for decades dolphins have undergone military training to carry out diverse tasks such as detecting and marking underwater mines, finding sunken ships, aiding divers in underwater search and rescue missions, and even playing a role as an armed forces spy.

But what touched me the most was their special connection with one another. For them, being together in a pod was everything. There was nothing more valuable than the safety and happiness of each other, often helping one another when in trouble. As social animals, their entire lives revolved around being in a collective kingdom. It made me wonder who the dolphins I swam with were to each other.

I had just a few more pages left to finish the chapter when I suddenly realized that the beach was empty. I had been so engrossed in my book that I hadn't even noticed little Aiko and her mom leave the beach. A sense of panic washed over me as I glanced at my watch; Hisoka could return home any minute.

In a hurry, I brushed off my legs and sprinted toward the bus stop. When I arrived home, I was relieved to find that Hisoka was nowhere in sight. The absence of the plate in the sink confirmed that he hadn't returned yet. However, I had also skipped lunch. The only thing on my mind had been continuing to read my book.

The more I delved into the world of dolphins, the more my curiosity was piqued. I felt like I was barely scratching the surface, standing atop the tip of an iceberg while the vast expanse of knowledge lay hidden beneath the ocean. My hunger for understanding grew with each turn of the page, leaving me with an insatiable appetite for more. So much so that when Hisoka called on the landline to inform me he wouldn't be coming home until late, I didn't pay attention to a reason why.

The bedside lamp was my only source of light as I struggled to read the last sentence of the chapter about fun facts about dolphins. It was late. My watch showed one o'clock. The words on the page were becoming blurry. Rubbing my eyes, I read, "While sleeping, the bottlenose dolphin shuts down only half of its brain, along with the opposite eye. The other half of the brain stays awake at a low level of alertness."

Eminently clever. I wished to have such control over my brain. How weren't they fatigued while half of the brain stayed awake?

With that contemplation, I yawned and finally, with a sense of tranquility, traveled into a dream world, closing my eyes. Both of them…

Chapter 12

躓く石も縁の端。
Tumazuku ishi mo en no hashi.
Even the stone you trip on is part of your destiny.

June 2009

FOR DAYS, I HAD BEEN reading about what I wished to see and explore for myself. Taiji was home to many dolphins, and knowing that fact only fueled my longing to encounter them firsthand.

As I walked around the town, images of dolphins and whales seemed to be everywhere. Their likeness adorned the mosaics on the walls of hotels, posters in restaurant windows, and murals on random buildings. Their miniature beaks held letters with their contours drawn on the sides of mailboxes while rice was shaped into their forms for children visiting eateries. Enormous, life-size bronze statues with detailed tails and smiling faces were erected on many town pavements. I could no longer indifferently pass them by as they increasingly swirled through my mind's evocation.

Remaining in bed, I took a good stretch and then opened my book to the next chapter, which delved into the topic of human-dolphin collaboration.

"A modern human-dolphin partnership currently operates in Laguna, Santa Catarina, Brazil. Here, dolphins drive fish toward fishermen waiting along the shore and signal the men to cast their nets. The dolphins' reward is the fish that escape the nets."

I caught myself repeatedly returning to the same sentence, unable to concentrate or grasp the meaning of what I was reading. A glimpse of a vivid memory from the pool the other day flooded my thoughts, leaving me with goosebumps. There was an indescribable uniqueness about them that lingered in my mind.

Reflecting on it, I realized their mere presence brought me immense joy.

Suddenly, a huge desire to see them overwhelmed me. The thought consumed me as I sat with my open book in my hands. Finding I could no longer sit still, I ran to the Chinese cup to check for yen. Counting them in a rush, I registered with relief that it would be just enough for a visit to swim with the dolphins. Without hesitation, I skipped my morning routine, even forgetting to lock the house before leaving. I felt a twinge of hunger as I remembered my omitted breakfast but quickly pushed it aside as I saw a sculpture of a dolphin through a bus window and took it as a sign to continue to my destination.

As I made my way through the dead town, it felt like the journey would never end, despite the short distance. Nevertheless, I couldn't help but smile at the strange and wonderful feeling that swelled within me, at this strong connection I felt with dolphins.

Filled with excitement and impatience to join them in their world again, I made my way into the same building as two weeks prior. However, a different receptionist greeted me this time and urged me to hurry to make it in time for the swimming program.

Despite my eagerness, my heart sank when I entered the locker room to change into my swimming suit and found myself surrounded by a large crowd of people.

Between them, I saw a mother meticulously tucking her daughter's long, silky coal-black braid under a pink swimming cap, a Chinese couple making loud grunts as they zipped up their wetsuits, and two teenage girls giggling for unknown reasons. I was not the only visitor at the Dolphin Base today. Informed earlier it was the last swim for the day and about to start and left with no choice but to "share" the dolphins with others, I joined six other people as they followed Erika.

As we gathered around, Erika began to explain the rules for approaching the dolphins just as she had done last time. "Remember, don't touch their blowholes. They don't like it," she cautioned at the end. With her speech complete, she gestured for us to follow her.

This time, we went beyond the pools and entered the area in the sea with cages separated by nets and wooden paths for people to walk. I later learned that these were called sea pens. They were bigger and deeper, each housing a larger number of dolphins. At

first, I felt uneasy about getting into the water, considering it was a part of the sea. But dressed in a diving suit and flippers, I thought it wouldn't matter much, as I wouldn't be stepping into the unknown with my bare feet. The water was calm. *It's just like a pool,* I kept convincing myself as I stepped in. In the company of dolphins, I could forget about the whole world for a moment.

Upon a furtive glance, I recognized the small girl with her mom. It was "little Aiko" from the beach.

Watching her and her mother, I couldn't help but smile.

The girl possessed a genuine curiosity, posing questions that even adults often overlooked, displaying a fervent eagerness to acquire new knowledge. Yet simultaneously, she exhibited a remarkable level of patience, content to await answers. She served as a reminder of how much children can teach us—the sheer delight of learning through every sense, rooted in the essence of living fully in the present moment. She reveled in the smallest details, finding joy in the daily gifts life bestowed upon us all.

It triggered a flood of my own memories. Just like some people might find it mildly bothersome, I couldn't help but recall the sound of unwrapping my beloved blueberry lollipop, the one that had always brought me pleasure. The heavenly sensation of hot chocolate gliding over my tongue on chilly winter days. The comforting touch of my cherished plush toy, Froggie, never failed to bring me to ease. I couldn't forget the sight of those incredibly rare snowflakes, perfectly shaped, gracefully descending from the infinite expanse of Tokyo's gray sky as I gazed through winter's window. And the aroma that permeated the air as nature awakened from its slumber, melting away the snow to make way for the magical gifts and transformation that Spring bestowed upon us, marking yet another turn in the eternal cycle of seasons.

But my cycle was now tinged with longing for the innocence and happiness of the past, forever gone. Now, the remembrance of it through Aiko's pure smile brought me a feeling of deep sorrow. Almost… had it not been for the dolphins' company. As I watched them in the pen, I was transported to a moment of bliss and peace that was punctuated with excitement and constant wonder.

I had not once meditated in my life, yet the contentment that seeing the dolphins brought to me ushered me to the edge of Nirvana. If not for the people around me loudly laughing and

occasionally screaming in excitement or fright, I would have transcended.

In my semi-Zen state, feeling the familiar touch of the Risso's fin on my palm, I heard another series of chuckles from a group of teenage girls. As I turned to look at them, I suddenly realized that Aiko, the little girl, was gone.

My head swiveled in every direction, but she was nowhere to be found. As I scanned my surroundings, I found her mother engaged in deep conversation with Erika while two teenage girls tried to clasp a dolphin's fin. Then my eyes were drawn to a couple in the corner of the pen who appeared to be recreating a scene straight from a fashion magazine photoshoot. The woman, with her long, thin legs and model-like appearance, posed for her boyfriend who played the role of a photographer. The backdrop of dolphins and the lush, shamrock and parakeet green hills made for a perfect billboard setting. But my mind was far from admiring the commercial-like scene. Now, close to panic, my heart racing uncontrollably, I continued to search for little Aiko.

Recognizing that there was only one other place she could be, I dove beneath the water's surface and discovered a dolphin dragging a little motionless body by the hem of her wetsuit toward the surface. As I powered toward the dolphin, it accidentally dropped the little girl and then circled back around to try again. Knowing who it was, I swam hard toward the limp body as the dolphin attempted to push her upward.

With an unknown force of will and power driving me, I found myself in the middle of the scene within seconds. As the dolphins opened a path, I grabbed little Aiko from her rescuer and struggled to the surface before dragging her to the wooden dock. My heart raced as I realized with terror that Aiko wasn't breathing.

Mouth-to-mouth resuscitation was as indoctrinated into me as eating breakfast, so I wasted no time in starting CPR. During a brief pause in chest compressions, I shouted for someone to call an ambulance and bring an AED. With exhausted lungs, I continued to give her puffs of air, all while hearing muffled shouts, sighs, and grave encouragement from behind me.

Aiko's mother, who had collapsed on the floor in front of us in shock, nearly dragged her daughter away from me. Although she didn't mean to, her actions were disrupting the entire process.

Luckily, someone finally moved the girl's hysterical mother out of the way, although not without her protesting. Despite a few shouts, tears, and the overwhelming scent of anxiety and sweat, no one offered to help me.

As I continued with the chest compressions and rescue breaths, I began to feel dizzy from the exertion. Despite this, I knew I couldn't stop. Exhausted, I caught a glimpse of Erika's pale face out of the corner of my eye. She had been frozen in shock only moments before, but now she was running toward me with the small, red suitcase—the AED.

However, before she could even set it up, Aiko's mother suddenly screamed her daughter's name in triumph. Aiko had awakened! I rolled her onto her side to allow her to cough up a significant amount of water from her small, tired lungs.

It is said that when someone is dying, they often see a kaleidoscope of their entire life and of all the people they have crossed paths with. Although I was not the one on the brink of death, as I performed chest compressions, I saw the faces of people from my own life flash before me: Minoru and my mother, my friends, Sayaka… Chris.

Just before Aiko coughed the water out, I saw the same beach I had sat on a few days ago. I felt a sense of pity for her mother, who would never know what Aiko had wanted to show her there.

Next time your daughter wants to share a special moment with you, please give her your attention. It means everything to her. These moments are the most precious to cherish. They won't repeat and life goes by so quickly.

As I looked back on the memories from the cove, I regretted not sharing this advice with her mom. *Now, I wish I had told her that,* I thought to myself, but I never did.

As I lay in bed later that night, I felt like I was reliving a dream as I recollected the day's events. It had started like a nightmare with Aiko drowning, but thankfully, it had a happy ending.

I later learned that she was the best swimmer in her school. Her overconfidence had led her to remove her snorkel so she could give a kiss to a dolphin underwater. It was during this moment that she choked and lost consciousness.

Despite being hailed a hero, I couldn't help but feel that the dolphins were the real saviors. Questions raced through my mind as I tried to make sense of everything that had happened in the pen, and I struggled to piece it all together.

The sight of the dolphin trying to bring Aiko to the surface while two others circled her left me absolutely awestruck.

Witnessing their actions with my own eyes, I couldn't help but wonder—how had they known Aiko was in danger? What had driven them to try to save her?

It was as if dolphins possessed a level of empathy beyond what we typically expected from animals. Perhaps they could sense Aiko's distress, or maybe it was their sixth sense at work. Or, I wondered, had they somehow been aware that they might be witnessing a tragic event?

Their presence exuded a magical and otherworldly aura, almost unearthly in nature. It was overwhelming to behold their radiant energy, and it felt like something beyond human comprehension. They seemed almost celestial as if they hailed from an alien planet.

As I perused the books I had purchased, I couldn't help but feel that the texts were but a mere drop in the ocean of knowledge. There was still so much to learn about them.

Another thought eventually set in to nag me. Had destiny brought me to visit the Dolphin Base that day?

A series of what-ifs flooded my mind. What if I had gone back home to lock the door and missed out on the chance to swim with the dolphins alongside Aiko? Would I have even paid attention to her if I hadn't seen her at the beach before? And what if her name wasn't Aiko and she didn't remind me of my younger self? And what if I hadn't studied medicine and didn't know how to perform CPR? Was there anyone else there who could have saved her?

As a result of my actions, I received an unexpected and humbling offer. An invitation to the dolphin's world… A sentence that I, not in my deepest desires, would have imagined hearing: "You are more than welcome to visit our Dolphin Base anytime you want." The manager, Ryota, who sported a clean cut and wore sports sunglasses, bowed in appreciation and added, "Of course, you don't have to pay…"

Amid the vibrant colors of the rainbow, I glided through the water, exploring the hidden treasures of the coral reefs. I moved with grace and poise, like a geisha, but instead of the streets of Kyoto, I was beneath the ocean's surface, breathing in the crystal-clear water like any other sea creature. Beaming with joy and ecstasy, I felt like the Queen of the Ocean. I had tasted the freedom of a world unknown to most humans—a world of harmony, order, wholeness, perfection, and peacefulness.

The world beneath was a kaleidoscope of colors with alluring, pastel-brown and verdant sea turtles, graceful seahorses, and rosy-pink octopuses moving in unison. They danced together, creating a beautiful spectacle that gave way to the stars of the show—dolphins. The majestic mammals took the forefront, and the other creatures followed their lead, all moving in harmony to the melodies of their whistles and clicks.

Gazing downward, a breathtaking sight unfolded beneath me: a sea of dolphins converging like the undulating waves of the ocean. They swam harmoniously, interweaving and stacking upon one another. Some formed couples, their closeness unyielding, while others maintained a strategic distance for agile maneuvering. A few traversed the waters in a slalom-like dance as others darted forward in a straight trajectory, engaged in playful competition. I marveled at the diligent mothers attending to their precious calves. It was as if a three-dimensional fairy tale was transpiring before my very eyes, a magical tableau brought to life.

Fixing my gaze upon them, I noticed a particular dolphin decelerating as if to extend an invitation for me to join the pod.

Without hesitation, I reached out and grasped its fin and was instantly pulled downward. And there I was, swimming among the pod, enveloped by the vastness of the ethereal, crystal-clear waters. At that moment, a profound sense of contentment washed over me. Their allure, elegance, and infectious joy were all testaments to their sheer perfection.

The highlight of the experience was their impeccable synchronization as they skipped through the water effortlessly. It was a free performance for all to see, unexpected and beautiful. Their jumps were like torpedoes launching into the air, spraying water on the mild wind of the never-ending horizon of still blueness.

Between sleep and wakefulness, I opened my eyes to the squawks of seagulls outside my window. The realization hit me with cruel force as feelings of insufficiency and longing for something indescribably close to my heart were taken away. It had been a long time since I had had any dreams, but even harder to recall such intense and heavenly ones.

As I glanced at my watch, I felt a sense of amusement seeing that it was already eleven o'clock. Normally, this would be the time for Hisoka's random lunches at home, but lately, he had been busy with preparation for what he called his "massy fishing" and wouldn't return until two or three in the afternoon, giving me some much-needed freedom. This meant time for introspection and reading, both of which consumed my days. While introspection could be painful, I preferred the alternative.

Since I still had a few hours before Hisoka's return, I decided to skip breakfast and prioritize searching for the new book I had bought some time ago. I looked everywhere, hoping to find it in the drawer next to the tatami mat. Instead, I noticed a corner of some papers sticking out of my atlas from Sayaka. I pulled it out, only to find my old drawings inside.

I couldn't control the tears that streamed down my cheeks as I reminisced about the good times that had passed. The drawings had almost been forgotten as if they had never existed. They depicted our secret places with Chris, including the rusted brown bench where we used to feed the always-hungry pigeons and watch Japanese wagtails. The other drawing portrayed our favorite wisteria tree dressed in magical all-purple shades, which we used to hug together to give it some love and receive good energy in return, and

a collection of multicolored stones and intricate shells from Miho Beach.

As I looked at each drawing, memories flooded me, but the one that hit the hardest was a portrait I had made of Chris. After he disappeared, I had nothing left of him. Ironically, even though he was a photographer, I didn't have a single photo of him. The sketch in my hand was the only portrait I had of Chris. And boy, did he look real.

Unconsciously, I praised my talent as every line captured the imperfections of a human being. Yet for me, with his tiny wrinkles around his eyes, slightly disproportionate nose, and a few pimples on his oily forehead, he was perfect.

The memory of that day was rather blurry, but I still vividly remembered Chris' stubbornness.

"Come on! You took so many photos of me! Now it's your turn! Let me draw you, Chris!" I had pleaded. We were lying on a black-and-red checkered blanket, and I had to beg him to pose for the portrait. "That's why I prefer to draw you when you're sleeping!" I added, feeling frustrated.

"What?" His eyes had squinted as he had playfully thrown me onto my back, tickling me until I laughed with tears of helpless joy.

But he had eventually agreed. Sitting with a proud posture, almost like Van Gogh in his self-portrait, I had managed to capture his composed face.

As I gazed into the portrait's captivating, lifelike eyes, a sharp pang of pain pierced my chest. To prevent myself from succumbing to the familiar darkness, I quickly set the portrait aside where I had found it.

Beneath it lay an untouched drawing pad and a set of pencils that required sharpening. Untouched, it had been there all this time. I decided to pack it into my backpack.

Chapter 13

あなたのそばが、私のお気に入りの場所です。
Anata no soba ga watashi no oki ni iri no basho desu.
Together with you is my favorite place.

August 2009

"AIKO, COULD YOU BRING ME the bucket of fish, please?"

It had been more than seven weeks since I started coming to the Dolphin Base. Despite my limited time and movements, being in their presence "behind the scenes" felt like a whole new world.

You are more than welcome to visit our Dolphin Base anytime you want. Ryota's words rang in my ears like the sweetest symphony as I made my way toward Hayato with a heavy bucket of fish. But as much as I longed to be with the dolphins every day and every single moment, there were aspects beyond my control that I couldn't neglect.

My main concern was Hisoka. I knew he wouldn't understand my desires and would undoubtedly forbid me from visiting the Base. His frigid views on sentimental topics were crystal clear, and to make matters worse, he didn't like me leaving home. I felt deep inside my heart that I had to keep yet another secret.

Furthermore, I didn't want to take advantage of Ryota's goodwill and cross any boundaries. I didn't want to ruin the glory of the opportunity given to me.

However, despite the incredible privilege bestowed upon me, the manager's suspicious and occasionally unwelcoming glances coupled with his reserved and distant demeanor served as a constant reminder that, in the eyes of him and most of the trainers, I was an outsider lacking any prior experience or background in marine life.

Consequently, I tried to give them their own space while making myself useful. However, it was not always easy to determine what I should or shouldn't do, and the boundaries often blurred.

Despite these obstacles, I remained undeterred from visiting the Base. Typically, I made my way there three times a week and left Moriura Bay by mid-afternoon to time my departure based on Hisoka's return home. Every minute spent away from the dolphins felt like a waste.

As time passed, I began to believe the dolphins would recognize me by swimming dramatically toward me with a distinctive whistle and showing excitement through their body language. While it seemed like a minor thing, it was a significant bond that I felt gradually grow between us. It was strong enough to break the protective shell I had built over the years.

Something was changing underneath the surface. Slowly and gently, I recognized that I could endure once again, a feeling I had lost when I had last seen the post office box in Shizuoka. I began to realize how much I had missed being able to feel, sense, and experience. The world brightened with colors, flavors, and sensations.

All these experiences gradually brought me back to my old self, the person I had forgotten a long time ago. It felt like a part of me that had been lost was slowly resurfacing.

And to my surprise, it was thanks to the animals.

The real-life stories of dolphins that I read were truly inspiring. Their behaviors, such as cooperative hunting in different parts of the world and living in peace with humans, brought me tears of joy, awe, and wonder. However, behind the scenes and beyond the applause that accompanied their captivating tricks, it was a novel experience for me to witness these magnificent and untamed creatures up close in face-to-face encounters.

The more time I spent around them, the more incredible surprises were unveiled. What struck me the most was their unspeakable intelligence.

And while some of my questions unfolded by themselves, I was led to even more complex inquiries.

I sensed that these creatures were not as simple as they seemed. Despite their indisputable intelligence, there was more. But I didn't know what. And I hoped they would reveal their mysteries in time.

I adored them, yet it was Riki, a Risso's dolphin, who captured my heart. I could swear it was him that had looked me straight in

the eye on that first, memorable day of my swimming with them. The day when everything changed.

It was always him, eagerly swimming toward me, or sometimes even awkwardly leaping into the air upon my arrival at the Base, his gaze filled with curiosity and wisdom. Occasionally, I caught a glimpse of sorrow within those eyes, despite the constant presence of his never-fading smile, which always left me unsettled.

"Tell me, what's going on in that little brain of yours, huh?" I spoke to him as if he comprehended every word. And somehow, I believed he, like the others, truly did. "I sense a deep connection between us. At times, you seem wounded and lonely… just like me. Am I correct?" I whispered to Riki when we were alone.

Most of the days, when the horizon was aglow with hues of green and blue akin to a painted canvas, a condensed, dark orange sphere emerging in the east, I would arrive as early as six o'clock alongside a few trainers, eager to catch a glimpse of their daily routine. However, for me, it went beyond a mere responsibility; it was an utter delight.

Despite their constant reminders that I didn't need to assist them, I insisted on standing in the back kitchen myself, undertaking what the trainers referred to as one of the least pleasant tasks in their line of work—preparing and sorting fish and vitamins for the dolphins. Regardless of the monotonous nature, the grueling effort, sporadic backaches, and, above all, the overpowering smell of seafood that I still hadn't grown accustomed to, I loved the work. The trainers failed to understand that I wasn't doing it for them, the people. Ultimately, I wasn't there to socialize with them either. I was there to observe and learn more about my beloved animals.

As I watched them, I couldn't help but contemplate their reliance on our grace. Not being a mother myself, I wasn't equipped to fully comprehend the bond between children and parents, nor had my parents provided me with the finest example of it. Nevertheless, I imagined that my love for these dolphins was comparable in some manner. Not only because they were innocent

and cute. There existed an eternal obligation to nurture them, to provide sustenance, and to love them unconditionally. And in some inexplicable way, I sensed that it worked reciprocally.

Despite the trainers driving the daily rigid agenda at the Base, it was evident that the dolphins lived their own lives, and each day held unique experiences.

Every dolphin possessed its own character and exhibited varying moods depending on the day, which was a manifestation of their individuality and evoked in me a sense of alertness, curiosity, and vitality. Some trainers, I noticed, treated these changes like obstacles or annoyances.

Most of them were not fond of dolphins' spontaneity, I observed, especially when it disrupted their meticulously planned timetables, schedules, or tasks, particularly when in front of the tourists. As a result, I occasionally witnessed them resorting to displeased tones or withholding treats as a form of punishment.

Though it may have seemed insignificant, I could sense that it was a genuine punishment for the dolphins. It wasn't just about missing out on the food itself; it was about losing the trust of their caregivers and creating a sense of confusion.

At times, astonishingly, it seemed to me the trainers preferred working with robots over living beings with emotions. Amid the five trainers and other personnel working in the pens whom I merely recognized by sight and exchanged brief greetings with, there was Kairi.

"You're mistaken. Dolphins don't have small brains. In fact, theirs are larger and more complex than ours," she asserted one day.

"Pardon?" With those being her first words directed at me, I initially couldn't comprehend what she was referring to until it dawned on me. She must have overheard my monologue with Riki the other day.

Feeling slightly embarrassed by my ignorance, I watched as she departed with a smile. At that moment, I knew she shared the same deep affection for dolphins.

As the youngest among us at nineteen and a part-time employee, she held a position below Jun, Hayato, Erika, and, of course, Ryota. Hokkaido-born and raised, she had only been at the Base for two months, but her level of knowledge appeared superior to most.

Her slightly crooked teeth somehow emphasized her friendly, anime-like face and made her exceptionally approachable. However, it wasn't just her amiable demeanor that drew me to her. As time went on, a sense of mutual trust and a hint of apprehension began to develop between us.

As she passionately recounted stories about the neighbor next door whom she had fancied for weeks, her narratives brimmed with vivid details and that familiar spark in her eyes. I couldn't bring myself to share my own tales of love and heartache, nor could I express my skepticism on the matter. I chose to preserve her innocent perspective, one that I too had once been ensnared in, and instead directed the conversation toward other topics that naturally revolved around dolphins.

"Did you know that dolphins can sense when a woman is pregnant or when someone has cancer?" Kairi exclaimed one day. "It's almost as if they have x-ray vision. Some even believe they can perceive people's energies. Isn't that incredible?"

During Kairi's break, I joined her and we found solace in sitting at the farthest corner of the dolphin's enclosure where nothing but the expanse of an infinite horizon greeted us. The strong wind brushed against my face, and at those moments, I felt truly alive.

As we observed seagulls and black-winged petrels soaring above the massive rocks, we inhaled the ocean's scents carried by the cool breeze and pondered what lay beyond its expanse. What activities occupied the lives of people on the other side? What conversations echoed through their days? How did they pass the time? Our laughter floated through the air, yet simultaneously, someone on the opposite side of the globe might be shedding tears.

Amid this paradoxical contemplation, we couldn't help but think of individuals who might harbor similar emotions, thoughts, pains, and destinies but who felt isolated in their belief that they stood alone. In truth, we were more interconnected than we ever comprehended.

Whether in tranquil silence or animated conversation, Kairi and I cherished each other's presence and, above all, the company of the dolphins.

When she wasn't at the Base, she assisted her mother at the local grocery store. Every now and then, she would bring me a snack, my favorite onigiri rice ball with tuna, from the store.

However, deep down, I knew her ultimate calling lay at the Dolphin Base. It was evident that she devoted her time and wholeheartedly immersed herself in understanding dolphins and their requirements. Above all, she cherished her moments in their irreplaceable company, and I comprehended that completely.

I couldn't envision it any other way. In a sense, I experienced a slight pang of envy, harboring a secret yearning to one day join their ranks.

The astonishing stunts dolphins performed, like playing ball while wearing amusing hats and oversized summer glasses, proudly displaying their eighty to one hundred teeth at the command of their trainer, leaving affectionate kisses on visitors' cheeks, surfing on their backs, or leaping out of the water, all for an audience of amazed onlookers or those eagerly anticipating a swim with them, didn't exactly align with my dream. Instead, what truly brought me immense joy was being in their presence, experiencing the freedom of swimming alongside them, feeling their skin against mine, and making eye contact. That was what I knew would truly fill me with happiness.

I loved catching glimpses of what Kairi described to me: the mesmerizing underwater flips, the thrilling and exuberant whistles, the playful opening of their mouths to blow bubbles, and even the actions of sticking their tongues out or recognizing themselves in the mirror. That very mirror, which many troubled souls lacked the strength to gaze into with honesty and introspection, was something I yearned to encounter one day.

And beyond that, there was so much more I longed to discover along my future journey.

However, I was well aware that becoming a trainer required more than what I currently possessed. The trainers' extensive knowledge, education, and experience indicated that there was a long road ahead for me to achieve my dream. Yet I couldn't shake the feeling that I had an advantage. My connection with the dolphins seemed stronger than that of most trainers, and that persistent thought lingered within me.

When in the oblivion of my passion I heard countless times about the difficulties of earning a living through art, it wasn't a strong enough reason for me to abandon drawing. In a world filled with endless replication, I yearned to be a creator. I craved to produce something new, something authentic, and above all, something that belonged uniquely to me. I understood that this was what brought me true contentment.

There are certain matters in life where the heart possesses a wisdom that surpasses the intellect. Unfortunately, we often find ourselves disconnected from our hearts, struggling to listen to their guidance. However, as a gentle breeze caressed my skin, my heartbeat served as a reminder of my true passion.

Since Chris departed from Japan, I hadn't touched a pencil and paper until last Monday, when I finally retrieved the A3 sketch pad and pencils from my bag. At first glance, they appeared to simply require a bit of sharpening, but for me, it meant much more than merely holding them between my fingers. It demanded mental strength to confront and take a step toward the painful past and memories. It had been such a long time, and I almost felt awkward as I gripped the pencil. But as I pressed it against the paper, the familiar and soothing sound it produced brought forth my first stroke, and I realized just how much I had longed for it.

Although there was an overwhelming urge to document the dolphins, I knew I needed a few good days to reestablish my natural rhythm for sketching.

Despite the undeniable challenge of capturing the constantly moving dolphins in my drawings, I adored having them as my muses. The perfectly symmetrical flukes, along with the dorsal and pectoral fins, seamlessly came together to create a harmonious whole. Their sleek skin, darker at the top and lighter at the bottom, gleamed under the radiant rays of the sun. Often, this silky appearance was marred by intricate lines of scars, each with its own story, adding an air of mystery to their beings.

Their ever-present smiles served as warm and inviting invitations to their underwater realm, a world that was even more extraordinary and enchanting.

What fascinated me the most, however, were their eyes. A single gaze into those depths was enough to imprint an indelible

mark on one's memory, a depth that many Homo sapiens seemed to lack. It was as if they possessed knowledge beyond our comprehension. Even with my eyes closed, I could vividly recall their every intricate detail.

Thus, often I found myself partially sketching them from the evocative memories etched in my mind.

But there were certain events that I would rather erase from my memory. The most devastating of all was the day Ryota unexpectedly announced his incomprehensible decision to sell Chika, another Risso's, to the Sea Aquarium in Shanghai. It felt as if a bolt of lightning had struck us out of nowhere, leaving us completely unprepared for such a turn of events.

Shortly thereafter, we found ourselves gathered, staring in disbelief at the imposing stretcher that carried poor Chika's thrashing body like a bag of rice. Slowly, it was hoisted high into the infinity of the sky by a roaring, bright yellow crane truck before being carefully placed into a crate.

A profound sorrow consumed us, although it wasn't readily apparent on the trainers' stoic faces. It hung heavily in the salty air, manifesting as a collective, subdued energy of despair and helplessness.

Chika must have been consumed by immense fear as she soared high above the sole place she had ever called home, leaving behind the dolphins and people who had been her companions throughout her entire existence.

Even though I caught a glimpse of her dorsal fin nervously twitching from within the crate that resembled a somber coffin, serving as a stark reminder that she was still alive, I couldn't shake the overwhelming sense that deep within her being, her soul must have felt as though it were gradually fading away.

The name Riki meant "strong," but I could see that he grew weaker with each passing day. His appetite diminished, and he began isolating himself from trainers and the other dolphins.

He spent most of the time in the same left corner of the pool. We knew Riki and Chika had been inseparable. Although we weren't certain of the genesis of their familiarity, we had no doubt there was a strong connection between them.

In the hopes of recapturing our shared connection, I attempted my usual playful antics, running around the pool and even approaching the edge to kiss Riki. I ached for his usual responses, expecting him to chase after me and intermittently emerge from the surface, his gracefully curved fin disappearing beneath the water for a few suspenseful seconds before surprising me with a magnificent leap. I also longed for him to swim toward me to return the kiss that I cherished.

However, this time, he simply floated in place, seemingly apathetic to my presence. It was as if I didn't exist to him anymore, and his lack of a response left me feeling disheartened and perplexed.

I could sense his emptiness, agony, and pain seeping into my very being, etching itself onto my skin and piercing my heart. Throughout my life, I had experienced the loss of loved ones, and each time I had been confronted with the unbearable weight of the unknowns and unanswered questions—how, where, and why. Yet even with this understanding, the most challenging part was that I felt utterly powerless within the confines of the Dolphin Base.

I made an effort to be understanding, acknowledging that there may be aspects beyond my grasp in certain situations. But there were moments when it became difficult to overlook the illogical and peculiar behaviors and decisions displayed by some of the trainers. It almost seemed as if they were driven by hidden motives. What surprised me most was that when I shared my knowledge about dolphins that had been acquired through books and my own observations since joining the Base, it was largely unknown among the trainers and met with little interest or curiosity. This not only led me to question their qualifications but also their capacity to experience genuine feelings.

Unlike dolphins, who were emotional beings, the trainers seemed like robots, using any means necessary to mold the dolphins into machines as well.

The despair of witnessing one of the most joyful dolphins in the pin succumb to depression was utterly unbearable. No matter

how much effort I exerted to uplift Riki's spirits, I couldn't shake the realization that I would never be able to replace Chika.

Drawing from my own experiences, I hoped the gift of time would aid in his healing process.

Chapter 14

どれだけ遠くまで行っても、自分自身からは逃げられない。

Doredake tookumade ittemo, jibun jishin kara wa nigerarenai.

No matter how far you travel, you can never get away from yourself.

Haruki Murakami
UFO in Kushiro

KOYASAN, September 2009

MY FIRST JOURNEY OUTSIDE OF Taiji took me to Koyasan, the place where Hisoka's parents had been cremated. It had been exactly thirteen years since they tragically passed away in a car accident, and for every anniversary during those thirteen years, Hisoka had faithfully made the six-hour pilgrimage to Koyasan to offer his prayers.

The details of their death were one of Hisoka's many taboos, so I refrained from prying for further information. But I assumed that it must have been the reason why he chose to travel by train instead of by car as it was a quite long journey. Personally, I didn't mind it. In fact, I had an affinity for trains with their steady and soothing rumble and preferred their routes that ventured into the wild rather than the monotonous and often dull highways.

As I voluntarily glued my gaze to the train window, I became captivated by Japan's diverse flora, abundant lush green mountains, and wild landscapes that covered over seventy percent of the country. I had learned that from Chris, an outsider to my own country, but one who had made me appreciate the natural beauty of my land even more.

It has been exactly three years since I last laid eyes on him, yet I found myself frequently caught in thoughts of him as if there still

existed a lingering connection between us. This sensation, however, was draining as I struggled to comprehend its meaning. It was as if my mind were playing tricks on me. He left without remorse, and logically, I should have allowed him to fade from my memories. However, an uncontrollable bond persisted, one that I couldn't seem to sever.

This bond contrasted starkly with the connection I shared with dolphins. I could feel their unwavering love, and the mere thought of leaving Riki in anguish filled me with sadness and guilt. Even if my departure from Taiji was temporary and necessary, it weighed heavily on my heart for those coming few days.

Like a blossomed eight-petal lotus, Koyasan was encircled by a majestic range of mountains consisting of eight peaks. As we ascended via a cable car a steep hill adorned with a mesmerizing display of varying shades of green, towering trees of diverse dimensions, and delicate blooms, I remained captivated. The cable car journey served as the renowned and fulfilling means of reaching the town.

But that was just the beginning of what Koyasan had to offer. Along the way, we encountered many rigorously maintained temples that exuded serenity as if they had been created to calm the wildest souls in the dense forests. One of those souls belonged to Haru, Hisoka's old school friend who had become a monk many years ago. As I glanced at him now, I remembered Hisoka's reserved yet honest story of Haru being a "school heartbreaker" who underwent a drastic change after falling in love with Emi. Ironically, the same girl turned out to be the very person who had led him on with false hopes, callously leaving him to endure deep suffering in the end. After years of denial and despair, Haru eventually found peace within the teachings of Buddhism.

He graciously extended an invitation for us to stay at the *shukubo** at Koyasan Temple where he served. As we entered, we were greeted by the sight of its expansive open-air corridors, constructed with deep timber and cedar and adorned with delicate rice paper sliding doors. The architectural design of the entire sacred structure exuded simplicity and embraced traditional elements to the fullest. Mindful of the customary practice, we removed our shoes and placed them on the designated shoe rack at the entrance before stepping into the hall.

Haru calmly gestured, "On the right side, you'll find the rooms, and on the left is the entrance to the terrace."

A few timid rays of afternoon sunlight filtered in from outside, mingling with the warm glow of the spherical lamps suspended from the wooden ceiling that cast a gentle radiance along the seemingly endless corridor. The walls, pristine and white, were adorned with dark timber barrels arranged in perfectly symmetrical patterns, dividing the space into sizable squares of equal dimensions.

With its mathematically precise arrangement, everything appeared harmoniously organized, instilling a sense of tranquility in the soul. Despite the temple's millennium of existence, the well-preserved wooden floor panels looked as though they had just been newly installed and exuded a pristine allure. The tendrils of incense, like the arms of an octopus, wafted through every corner of the lobby, leaving a lingering aroma of sandalwood in their wake.

"This is your room," Haru said while sliding a door open. Seeming to sense the question forming in my mind, he preemptively answered, informing us that Hisoka and I would be staying in separate rooms. A wave of relief washed over me, accompanied by a quiet sigh.

At first glance, Haru appeared strict and stern, but within seconds, his true nature unfolded before me—warm and welcoming, much like the meaning of his name, "sun."

As I stepped into my room, a sense of goodness, lightness, and liberation enveloped me. Walking barefoot on the meticulously woven straw tatami mat, every inch of the floor covered with precision, provided a soothing sensation for my tired feet.

* (宿坊) *Shukubo*: Visitor's or pilgrims' lodgings in a temple.

Haru slid open the *shouji*, allowing rays of sunlight to stream into the room, revealing its true colors. On the east side of the room was a neatly coiled mat; atop it rested perfectly ironed and tightly folded pajamas.

On the left side of the room, I noticed the presence of a *tokonoma*,† a recessed space in the wall adorned with calligraphy art. A solitary vase held fresh flowers, adding a touch of vibrant color, while an incense holder completed the simple arrangement. Apart from these elements, the room remained devoid of any other furnishings, adhering to the minimalist aesthetic that defined the temple.

Haru spoke, breaking the silence, "Have a rest now. You must be hungry. Shortly, a monk will bring you a vegetarian bento box. Afterward, I will take you and Hisoka around the town and to the cemetery. How about in an hour?"

Hisoka nodded on behalf of both of us. Haru excused himself and led Hisoka down the corridor, leaving me alone in my quarters.

As I gazed through the expansive window, a breathtaking sight extended before me—a Japanese garden in its peak of blooming glory, enhanced by the September season. The presence of several small ponds caught my attention, not merely as a source of water, but also as a haven where native birds were taking their royal baths.

Cedars, Canadian hemlocks, and Himalayan white pines competed with one another, each displaying unique beauty, majestic size, and graceful shape. Meanwhile, azaleas, Japanese maples, and Ilex crenata adorned the landscape, their vibrant colors contrasting against the golden sandy paths that intricately wound through the garden. In a paradoxical blend of order and chaos, meticulously trimmed bushes with small pagodas nestled within them formed precise lines, seemingly transforming into miniature fountains by some enchanting magic.

The leaves of the trees appeared to be the epitome of vibrant greenness! It was reminiscent of the image Sayaka had painted in my mind of lush Irish grass. Now, I had the privilege to witness it with my own eyes, to take in its beauty firsthand.

The birds seemed to share in the appreciation of this magnificent landscape, making their homes among the branches and

---

† (床の間) *Toko no ma*: An alcove where art or flowers are displayed.

treating everyone, without exception, to captivating and enchanting concerts.

After a delicious meal, as I closed the *shouji* before embarking on a walk, I couldn't help but think to myself that this picturesque setting had a profound impact on me. It could *almost* convince me to become a Buddhist nun.

At exactly three o'clock in the afternoon, the three of us gathered outside the entrance of the temple.

As we strolled through the town, I couldn't help but notice that Koyasan rested in the heart of a valley, encompassed by majestic hills that were festooned with wild, towering trees that boasted impressive, proud trunks.

"Did you know that UNESCO has included Koyasan in the Sacred Sites and Pilgrimage Routes in the Kii Mountain Range on its World Heritage List?" Haru explained as he gave us a guided tour of the town.

I recalled Hisoka mentioning it during our train ride, so its recognition didn't come as a surprise in its tangible presence.

Living in Taiji, I had found it difficult to fathom a quieter place, but Koyasan seemed to rival it effortlessly. With its impressive count of one hundred and seventeen temples, the highest number in all of Japan, it truly earned its reputation as "the mother" of temples.

After Hisoka's parents were cremated, their ashes were placed in a ceramic urn and interred in the sacred Okunoin Cemetery. Following Hisoka's lead, I walked leisurely on the paved cobblestones, taking in the strength and height of the ancient cedar trees, their barely visible crowns capturing my attention. While Hisoka appeared rushed, nervous, and stressed, I rediscovered a sense of peace that had eluded me for years. Nature's power reminded me of its might, but it also revealed the strength of human faith and determination, evident in the countless *Jizo* statues‡ and *torii* gates that adorned the surroundings, enveloped in a thick, humid, and overgrown deep green moist.

Hisoka stood in front of his parent's tombstone, offering his prayers. Respectfully, we stepped back a few meters, allowing him a moment of solitude. Haru smiled warmly at me, and I saw it as the

---

‡ (地蔵) *Jizo* Statues: Small, childlike statues made in the image of Jizo Bosatsu, the guardian deity of children and travelers.

perfect opportunity to ask him a question that had been on my mind for a while: "Do you ever feel lonely?"

As if he had anticipated my question, Haru wasted no time in responding. "Look around you, Aiko. Can you see?" he replied.

"See… what?"

"Anything," he replied cryptically.

"You mean…" I hesitated, trying to grasp his meaning, "Birds? Trees?" I scanned my surroundings, attempting to identify anything else that caught my attention. "Graves?"

"But can you *truly* see them?" Haru pressed.

I was puzzled. "What do you mean?"

"Are you looking or seeing?"

I had never really considered the distinction between the two, and before I could respond, I found myself hesitating. Sensing my uncertainty, Haru continued.

"We live amidst too much chaos. Constantly preoccupied, we fail to truly see what is right in front of our own eyes. We look, but we do not see the true beauty that surrounds us, let alone acknowledge one another. People do not even spare a moment to gaze into each other's eyes. Even when we find ourselves alone, we quickly seek distraction to occupy our minds—newspapers, games, phones—anything to divert our attention from… ourselves," Haru continued, his voice quiet and filled with a tinge of sadness. "We often blame lack of time, but it's mostly no desire to truly know ourselves. Often deep down, we fear what we might uncover or we are afraid of opening the wounds of our life experiences. So, we keep ourselves busy, pretending that this is how it is meant to be. And yet…" Haru paused, his gaze drifting beyond the confines of our current location. "We cannot fathom what lies beyond the realm we inhabit. We live as if we have never truly been born."

With every word the monk spoke, I felt a shiver run down my spine. The weight of his message settled in, and there was a brief silence before I broke it.

"It sounds so sad," I remarked, reflecting on my own life. "Is this why so many people are unhappy?'

Haru nodded, a solemn expression on his face. "Indeed, it is a sorrowful truth. The main problem lies in the fact that people search for happiness externally. We rely on others and outside circumstances to bring us joy. But true happiness resides within

ourselves. It may sound like a cliché, and people may hear it repeatedly, but it is undeniably true. The issue is that many do not want to help themselves. They are too idle to look inside their souls," Haru remarked with a hint of disappointment. "If only they would understand that it is enough just to be who they are without constantly judging themselves and others. And to see the enlightenment and inner light that we truly are."

He paused, taking a deep breath before continuing. "When we truly see that inner light, we realize we don't often need the assistance of a psychologist, guru or healer. We have the power within ourselves to find our own healing. We just need the courage and willingness to embark on that journey."

The monk gestured to me. "Do you know who your worst enemy is?" His eyes were filled with wisdom. I sensed it was a thought-provoking inquiry, and although I couldn't immediately find the answer, I shook my head in response. "You are your own worst enemy. But here's the good news: you can also be your own best friend. Learn to truly love yourself."

Haru paused in thought before saying, "And to answer your question, Aiko, I have never felt more complete than I do now, and I never feel lonely. How could I be lonely when our Earth has so much to offer? We are truly fortunate to be granted this precious gift called life, don't you think?"

Soft wrinkles appeared around the corners of his eyes, accompanying his gentle smile, as if they were old friends. After a few breaths, Haru spoke again.

"Of course, we are social creatures, and having others around us is important. However, we must understand that our happiness and the remedy for our loneliness do not solely rely on them. Once this realization dawns upon us, true suffering diminishes," he explained.

"What if…" I hesitated, unsure whether to voice my concern. But when I met the monk's gaze, brimming with wisdom and understanding, I found the courage to continue. "What if someone is suffering because of their past or lives in fear of the future?"

Haru's expression remained serene as he pondered my question, and then he responded, his voice filled with compassion.

"There is nothing like the past and the future. There is only now. It serves no purpose to dwell on something you cannot change

or to worry about something you are uncertain of experiencing. It is a waste of precious time. Embrace the present moment," he emphasized, pausing briefly to let his words sink in. "Allow me to share with you the wisdom of Lao Tzu: 'If you are depressed, you are living in the past; if you are anxious, you are living in the future; if you are at peace, you are living now.'"

I absorbed his words, contemplating their significance. Still, one concern lingered in my mind, and I cautiously voiced it. "But what if one can't forget their past?"

"You are right, Aiko, it's not easy. Each of us embarks on a distinct path, facing our own struggles and carrying burdens that may remain unseen by others. It is true that the healing process varies from person to person. Some may find solace in delving into their past, confronting the wounds, and finding closure. Others may choose a different road, letting go in their own way without revisiting it. However, it is crucial, in order to avoid falling into a state of depression, we should not dwell exclusively in the past. While the healing journey may take different forms, it is essential to embrace the present and find ways to move forward, regardless of the approach we choose. And remember, it's not about the problem, but how we deal with it."

I contemplated his words, finding comfort in his comprehension and sagacity. The path to healing might be diverse, but the importance of living in the present resonated deeply with me.

"Daily meditation, appreciation for what we have, and, above all, mindfulness can deepen our self-awareness and our connection to the present moment. Through these practices, we can gain a deeper understanding of ourselves while also appreciating the world around us. By cultivating mindfulness, we can detach ourselves from the relentless stream of thoughts that often contribute to our pain," Haru affirmed. "Instead of feeding our minds with negativity, we can choose to nourish them with positivity. Open your mind to any possibility. Free yourself from all taught beliefs. Observe the world as if you were a curious child."

He passed an appraising eye over me. "You have the power to manifest anything you desire in life. The key lies in knowing what you truly want and trusting that the universe will align to fulfill your wishes. Everything unfolds as it should."

As Haru spoke, a radiant glow emanated from his eyes. It wasn't the sun's reflection as it was hiding behind the clouds, but rather something deeper—a profound hope he held for humanity. It was as if I could read his thoughts, and he confirmed them with his next statement.

"Always remember, Aiko, that you can shape your own reality. People often forget just how much power they possess," he emphasized, his voice filled with conviction.

But monks don't forget, I thought. With their bald heads, spreading all around the town and cemetery, they were like little ants in their kingdom.

Their synchronized prayers echoed through the air, permeating every corner and reverberating among the trees, shrubs, plants, and flowers. It was as if their collective devotion created a powerful force that resonated with the beating of each person's heart, effortlessly touching the depths of one's soul.

Upon our return, I opted for a tranquil evening while Hisoka and Haru decided to continue their conversation over a cup of tea on the terrace in the garden.

Gathering a freshly folded towel, lavender-scented soap, and a zesty lemon shampoo and adorned in my red yukata, I left my room and descended the stairs to the *onsen.* I had always cherished the experience of hot springs. The warm water enveloped every cell of my body, stimulating my senses as blood circulation surged to completely revitalize me. Never had I felt so refreshed and invigorated as I did after indulging in the tranquility and serenity of an *onsen.* It was more than a mere cleansing of the physical self; it felt like a purifying ritual for the soul.

Unlike that one day in Shizuoka…

Similar to Koyasan, it wasn't *konyoku*,§ but rather one of those where men and women had separate pools. In the serene ambiance, I found myself swimming amid blooming lotus flowers, unclothed and in solitude, feeling akin to Eve in Paradise. Surrounded by lush greenery and the soothing melody of a small-scale waterfall cascading over majestic volcanic rocks, I basked in the blessings of the moment, overwhelmed by contentment. Yet my tranquility was abruptly shattered when I caught sight of a shadowy man's figure

---

§ (混浴) *Konyoku*: Mixed bathing.

slowly approaching the women's *onsen.* Panic surged through my veins as my heart raced, conjuring up worst-case scenarios and preparing to cry out for help. But then, with immense relief, I realized it was none other than Chris!

Approaching me with cautious steps, tiptoeing as if to conceal his presence, Chris wore a mischievous smile and placed a finger to his lips, signaling his awareness of the "crime" he was about to commit. In a land governed by strict principles, his actions would be deemed a grave offense if discovered by anyone. However, Chris never quite understood why people blindly adhered to all the rules, often proclaiming that rules were meant to be broken, particularly those that lacked rationale. While I couldn't fully grasp his perspective on this particular rule, he was fortunate that I was the sole occupant of the *onsen* at that moment.

Entering the pool with great care and deliberate slowness, Chris startled me, leaving me in a state of shock. He disappeared beneath the crystal-clear water, only to resurface right in front of my lips, engaging in a passionate and lingering kiss. Then, as if nothing extraordinary had occurred, he gracefully leaped out of the water, walking away with a proud chest and upright posture, as if returning from a victorious battle.

Reflecting on those memories now, I couldn't help but smile to myself, although at the time, the thought of the potential consequences had filled me with dread. Immersing myself, I allowed the water to purify both my soul and body.

With the fragrance of purple flowers lingering on my soft skin, I stepped into my room and was greeted by the sight of freshly fluffed bed sheets meticulously arranged by the monks atop an open futon mat that had been strategically placed in the center of the room. The tranquil symphony of chirping crickets provided a comforting backdrop, evoking a heavenly and familiar ambiance from the garden. The navy-blue sky festooned with shimmering stars held a captivating allure that radiated a sense of pure perfection. Mesmerized by their celestial beauty, I couldn't bring myself to close the *shouji*, as if it would be a disservice to the enchantment and mystery they held. Lost in contemplation of their ancient astronomical wisdom, my mind wandered back in time to that memorable evening under the stars with Chris as we used Minoru's old telescope.

"Can you believe that all these lights we see are from the past?" he asked, gazing at the stars.

"What do you mean?" I inquired, struggling to grasp the question.

"Can you believe that each of these stars emits light that may have traveled for ten, fifty, or even one hundred million light years to reach us? Yet we witness them all simultaneously, in the same moment," he explained.

He attempted to simplify the concept, but it took me a few minutes to fully comprehend it. Time was indeed relative, I concurred.

Ironically, I could now feel it in my skin, the relentless passage of time. In the best moments, it slipped through our fingers despite our fervent wishes to hold onto it. But in moments of boredom or hardship, it dragged on mercilessly. Lately, in Taiji, I had found myself spending an unprecedented amount of time alone. The experience of solitude was no longer new to me. I couldn't help but ponder how the monks had lived in such seclusion for years. Now, even though I was married, I felt as if I were walking a similar path.

And then it hit me. It didn't matter where you were, who you were, what you did, or how you lived; what truly mattered was being content within yourself and feeling loved. Deep down, we all yearned for love, even if at times we were too wounded or too proud to admit it and ended up creating a protective shell. Love manifested in various forms, and perhaps I had rediscovered it once more—in dolphins.

And in that moment of complete silence, a realization struck me like a bolt of lightning. I had completely lost control of my life! Was it the refreshing evening breeze from the garden, the new surroundings that offered a different perspective, or Haru's resonating words that echoed in my ears like a solemn bell calling for prayer that had brought on this revelation?

I had had occasional glimpses of it before, but I failed to fully acknowledge or recognize its significance. The worst part was that I had allowed something I had vowed to myself for years—never to repeat my mother's mistakes—to come to pass. Unconsciously and tragically, I had followed in her footsteps. I had married a man I didn't love and become nothing more than his servant.

And what's more, I had forgotten. I believed I had moved on. I convinced myself I was stronger. I pretended not to care. But the truth was I hadn't forgotten; I hadn't moved on. I wasn't as strong as I had thought. And deep down, I *did* care.

"Why?" I sobbed, my voice choked with tears as if hoping my words would reach a kindred soul somewhere out there. My heart, after a long period of dormancy, pounded with full force, and I couldn't help but ask the same question over and over. The rhythm of my heartbeat felt dissonant now. While in the past, it had been joyful and content, now it was filled with misery and pain.

Why did he leave me? Why did he never explain the reason?

That unfinished chapter of my life had torn me apart from the inside out, and it was only here in Koyasan's temple that I had allowed myself to admit it. If only I could receive an answer, perhaps then I could find the strength to move forward. But no answers would come. The closure I desperately sought was elusive, never to be granted. I felt betrayed by the only two people I had truly loved and trusted in my life—Chris and Sayaka.

Overwhelmed by an unexplained sense of guilt, I had blamed myself for years, tirelessly searching for answers. Now, my entire body trembled with the weight of my emotions, and a lump in my throat made it impossible to swallow the heavy tears that streamed down my face. Collapsing to the floor, I wept for the brevity of life, for its delicate nature, and for every precious minute I had lost without Chris by my side.

At that moment, all I could do was sob, hoping that somehow, by releasing my pain through tears, I could find solace, to cry this pain out. My lament echoed into the night as I continued to gaze at the blurred, flickering stars. Exhausted and overwhelmed by the mental anguish, I succumbed to unconsciousness.

In the tranquil warmth of the morning, where the sun replaced the moon and the stars hid for the day, I received an invitation to attend a dawn ceremony. Still clad in my *yukata*, stirred awake by the gentle rays of sunlight streaming through the open *shouji*, I couldn't quite recall when I had drifted off to sleep.

It was only six when I noticed myself on the outdoor patio of the main hall, seated in one of the chairs, facing a statue of a bronze Buddha. My back ached, likely a result of the uncomfortable wooden panels I had unwittingly slumbered upon. Deciding to

alleviate my discomfort, I settled into a seat a few rows behind Hisoka, hoping he wouldn't notice me.

The *jyuushoku*[**] and the monks began to chant Buddhist sutras, their voices blending harmoniously as the scent of incense wafted through the gentle breeze, penetrating my nostrils with its potent aroma. Each resonating sound from the colossal golden gong reverberated through the fibers of my being, imbuing a sense of divine presence, even for those who doubted its existence.

Yet amid this solemn atmosphere, I couldn't shake the feelings of anger and disappointment that swelled within me directed toward Chris.

Despite the cloudless azure sky and the gentle breeze caressing our bodies, creating the perfect atmosphere for a late afternoon walk that Haru had invited us to, I excused myself. I wasn't feeling quite right. I was sleepy, somewhat dizzy, and above all, lacking the motivation to join them. Instead, I closed the door and settled down on the mat, surrendering to the desires of my heavy eyelids as I allowed them to gently close.

Random thoughts disrupted the tranquility I yearned to embrace. Sleep initially evaded me, but gradually, a sense of calmness washed over me. Instead of engaging in a mental battle with my thoughts, I chose to accept them and let them pass by peacefully. And eventually, they did just that. The moment I stopped giving them my attention, they began to fade away, like leaves on a stream. As a result, my heart grew calmer, and my heartbeat discovered its ideal rhythm. Despite feeling as though an invisible force restricted my movement, I found myself in a state of relaxation.

The darkness transformed abruptly into a vivid display of dancing, colorful wires. Some appeared thick, while others were thinner. Some moved swiftly while others had a slower pace. Among

---

** (住職) *Jyuushoku*: Buddhist monastery chief priest.

the apparent chaos, a sense of synchronicity and harmony permeated every cell of my body. The wires grew increasingly vibrant, rapid, and distinct, captivating my attention with their clarity.

Their power mesmerized me, engulfing me in an overwhelming sensation, yet the thought of opening my eyes and relinquishing that unfamiliar feeling was far from my mind. With each passing second, a growing sense of harmony enveloped me.

Soon, the sutras recited during the morning prayer played in my mind like a repeating melody, further soothing my spirit and bringing contentment. In this very moment, only the present mattered, holding all my attention and focus.

Just as I was immersed in this semi-conscious state of bliss, a sudden knock on my door startled me, causing me to quickly rise and sit up.

"Aiko? Are you okay?"

"I'm fine, Hisoka," I responded, recognizing the concern in his voice as I replied through the closed door, eager to dismiss his worries. "I just need some rest. I didn't sleep well last night, and I still feel tired after waking up early for the morning prayer. I'll lie down for a bit longer."

As I heard the echo of his footsteps fade away, I settled back in a hurry onto the mat and closed my eyes, hoping to return to the mystical realm I had experienced moments ago.

But as much as I tried that realm was slipping away from my reach, so eventually, I gave up and instead shifted my focus toward the window.

As time slipped away from my awareness, I was surprised to realize that evening was drawing near, indicating that I must have been lying on the mat for a considerable number of hours.

Throughout the rest of the evening, I tried to comprehend and unravel the events that had unfolded; unfortunately, answers never came. The understanding I sought seemed just out of reach.

The following morning, using a headache as an excuse, I once again declined to venture out of the room. Overhearing Hisoka

whispering to Haru that I might be unwell or even pregnant, I allowed them to hold onto that assumption and opted to remain secluded.

This time, to prevent unwanted thoughts from flowing, I closed my eyes and focused my full attention on the deep and resounding breaths I took. And then, just as I was on the verge of giving up, my patience wearing thin and my breaths becoming rapid and uncounted, I suddenly became aware of merging white lights. They shimmered and glowed, moving in a rhythmic dance together. It felt as though the moment lasted an eternity, yet I lost track of time once again. And then, the deepest understanding, something I had only read about in spiritual books, manifested itself.

Words could not capture its essence; they had to be experienced firsthand. The sensation of disconnecting from my physical body, perceiving it as a temporary vessel while recognizing the soul as the true essence of who I was, overcame me. Every cell in my being resonated with this realization. And in that fleeting instant, the insignificance of trivialities became apparent. I felt a profound sense of belonging to the vastness of the Universe, just like every other being.

Despite the artificial borders that people create, separating one another based on race, religion, or any other factor they can think of, we are all connected. Instead of recognizing this unity, we choose to perceive divisions. And although I knew it all, now I could sense it through my whole being. Love binds us.

At that moment, I realized the power of taking control of my own happiness. I felt a strength within me that I had never experienced before. I felt satisfied and content. There was no room for fear, only acceptance, love, and most of all self-love. It was an unparalleled feeling, one I didn't want to end. The light surrounded me, casting gentle rays of security and abundance. I felt an incredible closeness to God, Energy, the Universe, or any name one might call it, like never before. As if I became one with God. Though I couldn't quite define the feeling, I knew I didn't want to let it go. But everything that begins must also come to an end.

Contrary to Hisoka and Haru's concerns about me falling ill or being pregnant, I felt rejuvenated. Just like any other human, I understood that it was natural to have both good and bad moments. However, the secret to achieving enlightenment was to hold onto

the good ones for as long as possible, almost reaching the point of eternity.

Time seemed to slip away from my grasp as I became completely engrossed in the present moment. There was an indescribable invisible force that bound me to that space.

On the final day of my trip to Koyasan, I participated in the morning prayer once more. It felt like a sense of déjà vu as if time had stood still since my last visit a few days prior. Just like before, the *jyuushoku* and the monks recited Buddhist sutras. The fragrance of incense filled the air, evoking a familiar scent, if not the same one, and the resonance of the gongs reaffirmed the presence of divine existence.

Except for today, as I listened to the sounds of their power, I noticed a gradual dissipation of the anger and disappointment I had been harboring toward Chris. Surprisingly, it felt as though I was embarking on a journey of forgiveness and appreciation. Appreciation for the fact that I had been fortunate enough to experience love, even if it had been for a fleeting period.

Now, with clarity, I could discern that my affection for Chris had transformed into an unhealthy obsession. It had become an addiction. I had developed an insatiable need to constantly know his whereabouts and actions, placing excessive reliance on him for my own happiness. What's more, I realized I hadn't loved myself and had tried to find validation through his feelings. At that moment, I recognized the lack of balance in our dynamic and understood that it was detrimental to my well-being.

"Do you know the meaning of your name, Aiko?" my mother once asked.

"It means 'love child,'" I had replied.

"That's right. A child of love."

As if in response to the old memory, Haru's words from the other day suddenly overcame me. "Don't forget who you are, Aiko. Open your heart and remember. Only through pure love will you find the right path."

To liberate my heart from pain and gain clarity, I realized it was crucial to release and forgive Chris, as well as myself.

As the resonating sound of the final gong dissipated, a high-frequency vibration lingering in the air, I experienced an overwhelming sense of inner peace, unlike anything I had ever felt before. More so than in moments shared with Chris in his comforting embrace or savoring each delightful lick of matcha ice cream with Sayaka. More so than while nestled in my mother's lap with Froggie warmly hugged in my embrace as she read aloud the adventures of *Guri and Gura.* Yet this was the first time I experienced such profound tranquility in solitude. And I felt wonderful. I felt complete. I felt content.

Although Koyasan felt like a surreal dream, a cathartic experience on every level, I couldn't shake the longing I felt for the dolphins, who had become like family to me. I pondered whether they shared the same sentiment.

They alone compelled me to return to Taiji.

Filled with hope, especially for Riki's life in Taiji and Chika's new beginning in Shanghai, I tightly clutched the *omikuji*†† I had picked on my final day at the Koyasan temple. The note bore the words "future blessing," and from the depths of my heart, I fervently wished for my destiny to take a turn for the better in this unknown future.

†† (おみくじ) *Omikuji*: Fortune slip usually bought at a shrine.

Chapter 15

知らぬが仏。
Shiranu ga hotoke.
Not knowing is Buddha.

TAIJI, September 2009

SIDDHARTHA GAUTAMA'S WEALTHY FATHER LIVED in constant fear for his son's well-being and sheltered him within the confines of their opulent palace. Of course, it failed to satiate Siddhartha's inquisitive spirit. After he saw for the first time an old man, a sick man, and a corpse being carried to the burning grounds, he was determined to discover the true nature of the world and ventured beyond the palace walls for good. In his quest, equipped with nothing but an open mind and heart he delved into the depths of the real world, seeking the essence at its core. Abandoning material luxuries, he acquired the invaluable treasures of understanding, wisdom, and truth that no amount of money could procure. Above all, he attained inner peace—and became the first Buddha.

The story of Buddha, which I had chosen as a topic for my high school final exam, came flooding back to me.

The journey to Koyasan may not have mirrored Buddha's transformative experience, but after years of familiarity with his life, its significance began to resonate with me. Surprisingly, there was something our respective journeys had in common. Over time, I had learned to relish and even value my own company. Silence became a teacher, compelling me to push the boundaries of self-discovery and seek inner peace.

I came to understand that life holds so much more if we open our minds and hearts. Venturing beyond the safety of our comfort zones can be both daunting and terrifying, yet it also brings numerous rewards and enlightenment. It marks a new beginning,

and though I was only at the onset of that path, I was grateful for taking the step to introspection, to perceive beyond the surface.

True freedom can only be found within oneself; no one else can grant it. I witnessed this firsthand in the lives of the monks. They possessed nothing materialistic, yet they exuded a sense of profound deliverance and genuine happiness. It became evident to me that contentment does not stem from possessions but from the state of one's inner being. Happiness, after all, is a state of mind. The more objects one accumulates, the more one craves, as people are boundless and easily grow bored. The never-ending desire for more is a reminder of the importance of seeking fulfillment within rather than through external acquisitions.

Reflecting on Haru's words and my flowing tears, I realized it was time to release the accumulated pain that had burdened me for years. It was time to surrender and let go. I had spent far too long trying to evade the truth within myself; the time for avoidance had passed. Now, I couldn't wait to share my newfound understanding with the dolphins. Despite our language barrier, I knew deep down they would comprehend me better than anyone else.

Among the participants in the dolphin swimming programs, different motivations were at play. Some were consumed by an obsession, making it their life's mission to come as close as humanly possible to these majestic creatures. Some sought the perfect shots for their social media accounts, yearning for a picturesque moment or a framed dolphin-kissed cheek photo to adorn the walls of their salons. Others joined with a casual mindset, treating it as another item to check off their touristy to-do list, akin to riding Asian elephants in Koh Samui or encountering orangutans in Bali, as Sayaka had mentioned. Then, there were those who, out of sheer boredom and an excess of disposable income, participated for the sake of amusement. And lastly, there were the individuals who found themselves in these programs without understanding what had drawn them there in the first place.

However, only a select few truly understood the genuine needs of the dolphins. Among this group, there were individuals who possessed a profound love for these creatures, dedicating themselves to extensive research to comprehend their true requirements.

Still, for some, it was sufficient to delve into the depths of their hearts to grasp the genuine nature of dolphins.

It was a cloudy morning, but that didn't stop me from visiting Moriura Bay. I chose to wear a breezy liputa dress, one that had been tucked away in my closet since I had last seen Chris. As I looked at myself in the mirror, I noticed a newfound freshness. Cat eyeliner accentuated the small glimmer in my eyes, reminding me that putting in a little effort to look good was solely for my satisfaction. This realization was liberating.

With no time to waste, I followed my usual routine of seeing Hisoka off to work. Afterward, I hailed a taxi to finally embark on the long-awaited visit.

As I crossed the threshold of the Dolphin Base—the sharp steps under my feet, the familiar scent of salty breeze filling my nostrils, the echoing sounds of loud splashes, and the humidity of the air—an unexpected sense of belonging washed over me. It was amusing how quickly it felt like home.

It was difficult to believe that I had been away for only four days. It seemed like an eternity had passed.

Rushing toward the dolphin pool, my feet slipped clumsily on the wet floor, causing my sketching block to tumble out of my bag. After I regained my footing, I quickly retrieved it, remembering my determination to complete the drawing of Riki that I had started a week ago. However, upon reaching the pool, I realized that he wasn't among the dolphins performing for the audience. Panic gripped my heart, fearing that something bad had happened to him.

Frantically, I spun around, scanning my surroundings, until my eyes settled on Kairi, who was waving at me from the far dolphin pens. Closing the distance between us, she understood my concern

and pointed toward Riki. *There* he was. My relief was palpable as I found him nestled in the corner of one of the pens.

Observing his sluggish movements, I couldn't help but think that he would make a perfect model. But as I looked into his dull eyes and realized he showed no reaction to my unexpected arrival, my artistic inspiration vanished. Feeling a sense of sorrow, I reluctantly set aside my drawing tools.

Initially, I entertained the thought that perhaps he didn't recognize me, but deep down, I knew it was impossible. The vibrant spark that had once resided in his eyes just a few weeks ago had disappeared. He continued to avoid making eye contact with me, showing no reaction as I approached him, and remained motionless. Time had yet to serve as a healer. A disquieting notion crept into my mind—there might be something more pressing at hand.

"Is he sick?" I inquired, raising my voice slightly as Kairi approached.

"We're not entirely sure. He has been floating motionless like this for days."

As I gazed upon him, I sensed his anguish as my own. I had finally grasped the concept of empathy as a disease, just as Sayaka had tried to explain to me.

Amid our shared solitude and mutual suffering, I felt the weight of someone's eyes fixed upon me, just over my shoulder. It was an unsettling sensation, so I turned my gaze toward the source to confront this audacious intruder. However, my act of defiance proved insufficient. Unrelenting, the guest continued to stare at me without remorse. Positioned a few meters away, sporting a silver baseball cap that obscured much of his face, I could discern that he was a foreigner.

"Who's he?" I inquired.

"Oh, just a tourist who wanted to see our program. Or perhaps catch a glimpse of… you?" Kairi replied mischievously, while feeding fish to the dolphins from the rusted bucket before giving me a sly smile. She seemed determined to lift my spirits and continued teasing me. "Why do you ask? Could it be you're interested in him?"

"No, no, not at all. It's just… I think I've seen him before," I lied, trying to dismiss her comment and ignore his persistent gaze.

As Jun approached the pen to begin the swimming program with a big group of people, she called Kairi over to fetch a bucket of fish. This left me alone, and I felt a sense of relief as I wasn't in the mood for Kairi's playful banter.

From a distance, I watched the dolphins gracefully swim in their familiar circles. Their captivating glances fixated on the bucket of food, eagerly awaiting their reward for performing their tricks. Miyako, along with the newly arrived dolphins, anxiously splashed water, aiming at newcomers while Jun, slightly embarrassed, attempted to brush it off with a laugh. As I silently mouthed the words, she recited the monologue I had memorized by heart, concluding with the reminder, "Don't touch their blowholes. They don't like it."

On the surface, everything appeared unchanged, but deep within me, a sense of unease stirred. Something felt off, though I couldn't quite comprehend what it was.

As my thoughts drifted into the background, I observed Jun's customary professionalism as she orchestrated the show for the group. Their laughter echoed through the dolphin pens, filling the air as the majestic creatures swam in their circles, occasionally leaping toward the fragmented clouds in the navy sky.

A sudden roar of thunder punctuated my thoughts, and I couldn't help but think, *It will rain.* The ominous sound signaled the impending arrival of a typhoon.

The long-awaited meeting after four days turned out to be far from what I had imagined. With a heavy heart and another warning of thunder, I made the decision to leave to gather my thoughts. To my surprise, the foreigner, who had been observing me, was nowhere to be seen. Just as he had appeared, he had dissolved into the dense, humid air. *Perhaps the approaching rain had scared him away*, I speculated, noticing others rushing toward the safety of the hotel as Ryota shouted over the megaphone to get back inside the building.

I held onto hope that tomorrow would bring a better day. Casting one last glance at Riki, I let out a deep sigh, overwhelmed by my helplessness.

"Tomorrow, I'll be back," I whispered, my voice filled with a mix of love and desperation. "Don't forget that I love you, Riki. Okay?" It had been a long while since I used those words 'I love

you,' but what mattered was that I knew they held a meaning. I hoped Riki knew it too.

As thick clouds cast shadows, the colors around me began to fade. Gentle raindrops started to fall, adding to the somber atmosphere. On my way to the bus stop, a few meters away from the hotel's corner, I noticed a shadow trailing behind me, but this one belonged to a human. As I quickly glanced back, I recognized the silver baseball cap from the pool.

A sense of unease crept over me, and I instinctively scanned my surroundings, searching for anyone who could assist me if needed. Realizing that I couldn't turn back now and regretting not calling a taxi, I hastened my pace. To my alarm, my follower, with his inseparable, terrifying shadow, did the same thing, matching my every step. The tension became unbearable, weighing heavily on my nerves, until he suddenly shouted in English, "Wait!"

Startled, I stumbled over my own feet and instinctively broke into a run. Unfortunately, there was no one else in sight except for a few rowdy seagulls. Dark scenarios flooded my mind within seconds, but I tried to stay calm and reassured myself that no one would harm me in the middle of the day in a small, safe town.

"Wait! I need to talk to you! It's important. I know you love dolphins! That's why I chose to talk to you!" he called out urgently. His words struck a chord within me, causing me to slow down and gradually release my fear. I came to a stop as he added, "We need to save them!"

"What is it?" I asked, still panting while maintaining a safe distance. Now, I could see his face clearly. However, it wasn't his sharp cheekbones or his large hazelnut-colored eyes that caught my attention, but the genuine distress on his face.

"We need to save them," he repeated, his voice heavy with breath.

"Who?"

"The dolphins," he replied, capturing my full attention.

The rain continued to drip onto his jeans and cotton shirt while I stood protected under my polka dot-patterned umbrella.

"Can we talk somewhere?" he requested.

We took a seat in a small restaurant by the road, facing each other. I ordered green tea, and Steve, the name he had earlier introduced himself with, followed my choice.

"Listen. You're not one of them, right?" Steve asked, his tone serious.

"What do you mean by 'one of them?'" I responded, feeling distressed. It had been a long time since I last spoke English. Chris, like most Dutch people, had exceptionally good English skills, albeit with a noticeable accent.

The stranger's English, on the other hand, flowed smoothly and effortlessly as if straight out of a Hollywood movie, leading me to assume he must be American. It turned out that my belief was correct. Guessing the age of foreigners had always been a challenge for me, just as it was in this instance. However, in close proximity, his visible wrinkles and a few white hairs peeking out from under his cap suggested that he might be a middle-aged man. Whenever he spoke, his anxious, somber expression and pallor became evident. He appeared to be in good shape, dressed in sportswear reminiscent of New Yorkers I had seen jogging around Central Park in American movies.

"I don't know if my instinct is right, but I sense a deep love for dolphins within you. I could see it in the way you look at them," he remarked.

"I do..." I replied, uncertain about where he was leading the conversation. Impatience began to creep in, and I could conceal it no longer. "Excuse me, but what do you need from me?" My irritation may have caught him off guard, but over time, with my experience, I had grown more reserved and skeptical of strangers.

"Aiko, do you know what is happening in Taiji? Do you know what they do to the dolphins here?" he asked. I was taken aback by his question, realizing that I had no idea what he was referring to. His last words were whispered, and he glanced around to ensure no one would overhear. There was no need to worry, as the place, aside from the partially deaf elderly owner and a few bothersome flies, was completely deserted.

"What I am about to tell you may shock you, and I apologize for being the one to reveal this truth. A terrible truth," Steve began, taking a deep breath. My impatience and nervousness grew, and in the background, I could hear the pounding of my own heartbeat. "From September until March, every year, around one thousand five hundred dolphins are slaughtered here in Taiji." He paused to gauge my reaction or give me a moment to process his words. However, no amount of time could help me digest such a deceitful revelation.

"You're lying!" I couldn't contain my frustration. Why would he fabricate such lies? What was his motive? Who had sent him here?

"I am not lying. It is the truth," Steve insisted. "Fishermen corral them by the hundreds, using barriers to disorient and drive the panicked pods away from their natural migration paths into hidden lagoons."

Partially in denial and partially in shock, I was ready to leave. However, some indescribable force kept me rooted to my seat, and I remained there, listening despite the growing pain in my chest.

"Later, they are pre-selected and sold off for upwards of a hundred and fifty thousand dollars per dolphin," he said, raising his voice slightly. "They are sent to marine parks around the world, where they are kept in captivity and forced to perform circus acts, like the one you have here in Taiji. They have to pose for photos, their tails held high, walk backward on the water using their flukes, wave their tails as a goodbye, and 'sing' to their trainers… all just to receive fish to satisfy their hunger. If you watch them closely, how they follow the buckets with food, you'll understand that everything they do is driven by their desperate need for food." He looked into my eyes with sorrow, let out a sigh, and went on. "In the bay, some dolphins are chosen for marine parks; the remaining ones are mercilessly slaughtered in what can only be described as a massacre and later sold for five hundred dollars for their meat. The water bay turns completely red… from their blood."

Attempting to grasp his words, despite my vivid imagination, I struggled to believe what I was hearing. Masami had mentioned that there were thousands of dolphins in our seas, so it shouldn't have surprised me that the ones in our facility might have been taken from our waters or sold overseas to other countries like Chika had been. However, the idea that it was a systematic business involving such a staggering number hadn't crossed my mind. And the worst

was to think that the rest were being mercilessly slaughtered in such a cruel manner—I simply couldn't fathom it.

"It is still legal in Japan. Your government defends dolphin hunting as part of your cultural heritage," explained Steve, interrupting the turmoil of thoughts in my head. "You must wonder, who I am… Who we are…"

I was in shock; I could not respond.

He continued. "We are activists who come here with a mission to put an end to this cruelty. We are dolphin lovers. We just know how unique and special they are. We understand their needs."

It was difficult not to believe him. The anguish in his eyes as he described the bloodbath and the love that emanated from him while talking about their uniqueness could only be understood by another dolphin lover. And by choosing to speak to me, he must have recognized that love in me as I stood at Riki's side.

"I'm with the Dolphin Project—maybe you've heard of it in the news? We come here every year with Ric O'Barry, its founder and director, with the intention of stopping it all. We collaborate with various local Japanese activists who are working to end the hunts. In fact, Dolphin Project is funding several lawsuits which are currently in litigation in Japanese courts." Suddenly his eyes appeared glassy, and I prayed that tears wouldn't start streaming down his face like the raindrops falling outside the window next to us. If they did, I feared I would join him in weeping, unable to find solace. "Arghhh, Aiko, the way they kill them…"

As his narrative unfolded, every word cut through me like a succession of haunting nightmares. Each new revelation felt like a piercing spear, surpassing the previous one in agony, and leaving a sickening sensation in the depths of my stomach. *One thousand five hundred!* The magnitude of that number eluded my comprehension. However, even the loss of a single dolphin would remain an incomprehensible tragedy.

"What can I do for you?" I asked, a mixture of anger and shock brewing within me. I remained composed despite the sudden and unexpected deluge of new information.

"We need people to find out the truth about this massacre. As many as possible!" Steve replied fervently. "Most people aren't even aware of what is happening here in Taiji! We have to inform everyone about the atrocities taking place! Not only the Japanese but

people from all around the world! We can gather individuals to sign petitions, spread the word through national and international news and social media, and organize demonstrations. Even those who can't physically come here can make a difference by raising awareness."

Time was of the essence, and as Steve spoke, my mind raced, envisioning the various roles I could play in aiding the dolphins.

"Aiko, they are so innocent and defenseless. They drive them to a sloping beach where the water is shallow and force them onto the sand, then drive a spike into their heads! It's an incredibly cruel and agonizing process for them, and that's just the beginning," Steve continued. "Unfortunately, they've expanded the traps to prevent anyone from witnessing or documenting the killings. No matter which angle you approach from, it's almost impossible to see, photograph, or film the brutality. The only evidence we have is a recent film called *The Cove*, directed by Louie Psihoyos. It shocked the world and received numerous awards. I urge you to watch it; it will help you understand what I'm talking about," he continued, taking a deep sigh before proceeding.

"The most painful part is being here, so close, yet unable to directly help them." Steve looked away as he became lost in his thoughts. Slowly, he added, "Yes, we're here, and they're dying in agony right before our eyes, but we can't stop it… not yet."

"It's September. That means the hunting season has begun," I remarked. The question formed in my mind, and despite my hesitation, I mustered the courage to ask, "Are all the fishermen involved in hunting the dolphins?" Was I sleeping in bed with the "enemy?"

"Not necessarily," Steve replied, seemingly unaware of who my husband was. I grappled with the decision of whether to disclose that information, but fortunately, he continued without prompting. "The biggest issue is that they don't see anything wrong with it. They argue that it's been their tradition for centuries. They claim to use dolphin meat as food, conveniently ignoring the fact that the animals carry high levels of mercury, posing a risk of poisoning. Furthermore, much of the expensive whale meat they purchase is *actually* mislabeled toxic dolphin meat. This so-called 'tradition' has *severe* health implications for the people!

"And one of the most dreadful and paradoxical things is that people eat dolphin meat as a snack at the aquarium while watching the dolphin show!" Steve exclaimed. "They delight in their performances, applauding and admiring their adorable nature, all while chewing on their flesh! Can you imagine it?" His laughter held a mix of irony and sadness, questioning both the logic and morality of such actions.

I stared into the distance as a memory resurfaced—Masami offering me an unusual snack at the dolphin show. It suddenly dawned on me that it must have been dolphin meat. The mere thought of consuming it churned my stomach, and I desperately hoped I wouldn't vomit. I wondered if Masami was aware of the dark reality behind it all.

Does she know about dolphin hunting? Is she aware that our husbands may be involved in killing dolphins alongside other fishermen? She was born here and was married to a fisherman; she must have at least heard about it! Although mere assumptions, I already felt betrayed by my first human friend here. And what about Kairi? I couldn't bear to entertain that thought, but thankfully, Steve interrupted.

"Swimming programs like the one you were in today also contribute to dolphin hunting. The more people participate in those swims, the higher the demand for dolphins." Steve must have seen the mixture of fear, pain, and guilt that adorned my face, prompting him to let out a deep sigh before continuing, "It's truly incredible… It's difficult to put into words.

"I understand firsthand how fantastic it feels to be around dolphins, Aiko. I used to work as a dolphin trainer myself." He shocked me with this revelation, and it was evident that he carried his own share of guilt. "It's never too late to educate oneself and join the right path. We all make mistakes. The important part is to become aware of them, learn from them, move on, and not repeat them." He gave me an encouraging smile. "It's not where they belong. As dolphin lovers, we can always find alternatives. We can study them or support educational dolphin reserves that house injured or abandoned dolphins. We can seek encounters with them in the wild. There are ways to watch and interact with them that ensure both humans and dolphins coexist happily." Steve smiled. "Did you know dolphins can travel up to one hundred twenty-eight

kilometers per day? It's the freedom they truly cherish and, above all, need." He slumped in his chair.

"I wanted to believe they enjoy swimming with people," I confessed, trying to convince myself with my own words. However, deep down, I knew it was a lie.

"No, Aiko. What they truly desire is freedom, not to be coerced into performing tricks and rewarded with lifeless fish," Steve replied with conviction. "Are you aware that they are forcefully separated from their families, which often leads to their depression? They are highly social and family-oriented creatures. Did you know that calves need to stay with their mothers for several years? A female dolphin may even carry her deceased baby for days, sometimes until only the head or a part of the body remains as she mourns the loss. Can you imagine the never-ending suffering they endure being confined in those cramped tanks? In captivity, dolphins are deprived of the space to swim freely. They are frequently deprived of food by trainers to enforce obedience, teaching them ridiculous tricks and so forth."

"Steve… I could sense it. Deep down, I knew it wasn't right to close them in those small pools and pens. I could sense so many things, but I ignored my instincts," I confessed, placing blame upon myself.

He listened attentively, not through mere nods but by locking eyes with me. He truly understood.

"Sometimes, we simply aren't prepared to face the truth," he remarked. His words seemed almost like an excuse, yet I knew he genuinely meant it. A profound silence enveloped us for a long moment before he said, "Aiko, when a dolphin is injured, another one comes to its aid and refuses to leave its side. Dolphins even stay with injured or ill individuals, assisting them by bringing them to the surface to breathe if necessary."

"Now I am certain!" I exclaimed suddenly. "They were trying to save the drowning girl!" A vivid memory of little Aiko's rescue resurfaced in my mind. "I always knew there was something human-like about them!"

"Human? Humans can be cruel." Steve paused as if gazing into the depths of the universe before returning his focus to me. Locking eyes, he continued, "Yes, humans help others, but often for their own gains. Dolphins, on the other hand, do it purely out of

empathy. There are numerous stories, dating back to Ancient Greek mythology, where dolphins were known for saving people! To this day, there are countless documented stories of dolphins protecting swimmers from sharks by encircling them or bravely confronting the sharks to drive them away."

Despite their altruistic acts toward humans, we were still causing intentional harm to them. I yearned to uncover those responsible for it. "So… it's the fishermen. And the government… Who else?"

"Fishermen, the government, sometimes dolphin trainers when they want to check for suitable or beautiful dolphins for their facilities."

Dolphin trainers? I thought incredulously, trying to maintain a stoic facade as Steve continued to unveil the truth about 'the torturers'.

"*Yakuza** sometimes roam the place too. It seems they're part of the business. And even some of the policemen. The coastguards ensure that no one interferes."

"What?" I whispered in shock.

"Fishermen drive the dolphins for hours, wearing them down until they are utterly exhausted. Then, mercilessly, they run them over by the skiffs. It's a barbaric act! Or they kill them with long, sharp hooks or spears. The pain the dolphins suffer is heart-wrenching and often lasts twenty to thirty minutes. Some are aware of it, yet they feign ignorance, pretending that nothing is happening in Taiji."

"Please, Steve, I can't bear to hear anymore," I pleaded, my voice trembling. The weight of his detailed descriptions had become too much to endure. Tears streamed down my face, and the weight of my heart felt almost unbearable. But it wasn't just sorrow that consumed me; anger compelled me to action. Fury not only toward those involved in this cruel slaughter but also toward myself stirred in me. I resented his words, but deep down, I knew I carried a sense of disgrace in my heart. I felt ashamed to have been a part of it, to have unknowingly supported the horrendous business. Even though I wasn't aware of what was happening behind the curtains, I had had doubts about the dolphins' happiness for months.

---

* (ヤクザ) *Yakuza*: A transnational organized crime syndicate.

Being in their presence was a truly magical experience, but now I questioned myself. Was my love genuine? Had I scrutinized my doubts enough? Or was I deceiving myself, deliberately turning a blind eye to the signs along the way, desperately hoping the dolphins were truly content?

Each time I visited the Base, the size of their tanks and pens became more apparent, cruelly contrasting with their majestic bodies. I couldn't ignore how cramped they were, confined within those small spaces. Their happiness, or rather, their mere survival, seemed to hinge on the meager offering of lifeless fish they received during shows. The tricks they performed held no joy for them, contrary to the misguided belief of the ignorant masses. No, they performed the learned skills to stave off hunger.

The sight of trainers leaving them stranded on the bare concrete, devoid of water, while cleaning the tanks, surrounded by chemicals, was utterly appalling. Often, they would endure scorching sunburns and suffer without water for agonizing minutes.

Steve explained to me that the scars on the dolphins could have resulted from their biting each other. When dolphins from different pods are brought together, conflicts arise, and in such an artificial and stressful environment, their aggression toward one another may intensify. The once mysterious scars I had wondered about now appeared less enigmatic, sadly. Given that it wasn't their natural environment, and they were, after all, wild animals, which meant nobody could fathom their behavior, attacks, even on people, happened occasionally. The dolphins had been taken away from their home, separated from their families, confined to small tanks, and forced by starvation to perform ridiculous tricks. How could they not grow angry?

Their profound social needs and family bonds were something humanity struggled to fully comprehend. Like Riki and Chika's relationship. Riki's worn-down teeth, which I now understood were likely a result of him chewing on the tank lining, were a manifestation of the stress he had experienced after being separated from Chika.

I recalled feeling uneasy, and dare I say, even envious of how the trainers at the Base behaved as if they owned the dolphins. Yet the realization that there was a timeframe and financial constraints determining whether I could spend time with them made me

recognize that I was part of a system where even nature was not exempt from human control. Unfortunately, I had been mistaken in thinking otherwise. People had dominion over it all.

Indeed, I had been cocooned within my own sphere of pain, isolating myself from the world, and avoiding TV news. Yet in a small town like this, why had I not pieced these clues together? How had I been so oblivious?

The flashbacks of Masami attempting to convey with her unfinished sentence something about the dolphins and our husbands, their long-awaited "massy fishing" endeavor, the peculiar pieces of meat she offered me, and the unexplained business surrounding Chika all swirled through my mind.

However, what truly caught me off guard was my visit to the Whale Museum one rainy day. Its eerie atmosphere, the model of a whale being pursued by a boat crowded with spear-carrying men suspended from the ceiling, the puppet show that depicted historical cetacean hunting methods, and the gallery that displayed specimens of preserved dolphin and whale parts left a disturbing impact on me.

As much as I had initially witnessed happiness in the dolphins, the more I delved into reading about them and spent time with them, the more I had sensed that things weren't as ideal as they seemed. Their perpetually smiling mouths, designed to deceive, became paradoxical, a curse, an illusion that many unwittingly fell for—including myself.

Somewhere deep within my heart, I had known it all along, yet I had consciously chosen to ignore the warning signs. I held myself accountable.

Aching pricks in my chest slowed my heartbeats, and all I could hear were my own heavy, uncontrollable sighs, echoing the pain that the dolphins endured.

Now, with Steve's words, it appeared that things were falling into place. I sensed we belonged to the same group who "delved into the depths of their hearts to grasp the genuine nature of dolphins."

Lost in my thoughts, I watched raindrops fall. Eventually, Steve drew my attention back to him. "You know a typhoon is on its way, right?"

"Yes, I'm aware," I replied, my voice tinged with fear, unsure if I was ready to hear his next statement.

"Do you know what that means for the dolphins in the tanks and pens?"

"No," I uttered.

"They will be confined to their cages, left alone to the mercy of God..."

We continued to talk, but the weight of the situation lingered. After paying, we left behind untouched tea and broken hearts.

It was a long night, one of those nights where I tossed and turned only to realize that a seemingly promising position was actually more uncomfortable. Where my bed felt so unfamiliar that it no longer felt like mine. Where the pillow became more of an obstacle than a solace for my weary head burdened by the day's troubles. One of those nights wherein every murmur became like a squeaky door, maliciously attempting to disrupt much-needed rest. Where alternating between sweaty discomfort and cold chills, I became confused, clouded by my body's needs.

The unsettling sounds of the approaching typhoon with its howling winds and relentless downpour instilled fear deep within my soul. And it didn't help to fall asleep.

Despite my restlessness, my consciousness finally drifted away.

As the sun descended, painting the horizon with hues of pink, purple, and orange, I found myself swimming in the pristine waters of a crystal-clear cove, surrounded by lush green foliage. Submerging my head beneath the surface, I was greeted by a wondrous sight—a pond filled with a diverse array of dolphin species.

They playfully interacted with one another, creating bubble rings that they would swim through as the air expanded. It was a never-ending game, bringing joy and amusement to all, regardless of their age differences.

A calf swam near its mother, clumsily imitating the movements of the older dolphins. I felt as if I had stumbled upon an extraordinary party with the dolphins serving as gracious hosts.

Suddenly, they approached me, their curious eyes fixated on my human form, yet I could sense that they saw beyond the surface into my soul. After a brief inspection, they drew closer, encouraging me to join their games, an invitation I gladly accepted.

In that moment of pure bliss, I realized I needed nothing to find happiness.

However, the serenity was short-lived as gray clouds gathered, shrouding the once-clear sky. Raindrops pounded the water's surface, plunging it into darkness and enveloping the atmosphere in a chilly embrace. An air of unease hung palpably in the surroundings.

And then I witnessed in sheer horror spears and knives emerge from the shoreline above to ruthlessly pierce anything moving beneath the water's surface. But their target was unmistakable… the dolphins. I tried desperately to scream and warn my hosts, but every attempt was stifled by water that flooded into my lungs, leaving me gasping for air as if I were drowning. Trapped in place, my body paralyzed, I could only watch the tragedy unfold.

Amid the terror, the dolphins' cries and pleas for mercy swelled, their sorrowful voices penetrating the chaos.

Trapped within the tumultuous vortex of water, I felt helpless. Desperate to shield my eyes from the horrific scene, I could only watch as their lives were mercilessly taken away.

My gaze fell upon a calf, who moments ago had been joyfully playing within the circles of bubbles in the clear water. Now, separated from its mother's comforting presence, it stared directly into my eyes, silently begging for its life. I mustered all my strength, frantically moving my limbs, but I remained immobilized, unable to swim to him. With harrowing intensity, I watched in silence as a spear punctured the small dolphin's vulnerable belly. The once crystalline water transformed into a macabre shade of crimson, obliterating my vision.

With a start, my clammy head propelled my body into a seated position in my bed, leaving the pillow damp with sweat. It had all been a nightmare.

Yet it wasn't merely the nightmare itself that shook me to the core. It was the painful realization that the cruelty inflicted upon these magnificent creatures by humans was a horrifying reality.

Chapter 16

全て理解していると思ったらそれは勘違いである。
Subete rikai shiteiru to omottara sore wa kanchigai de aru.
If you understand everything, you must be misinformed.

IN MY CURRENT LIFE IN Taiji, there existed an extraordinary amalgamation of thrill, impatience, and eventual relief coursing through me—it was when Hisoka departed from the house. This granted me the freedom to lead a life on my own terms, a life so markedly distinct from his that he could never truly understand. Being with someone who felt more like a stranger than a partner every passing minute was suffocating; my life with Hisoka was a punishment.

However, this time, this sensation surged even stronger within me. The pressing need to understand the revelations I had heard the day prior overwhelmed me while a pang of consciousness toyed relentlessly within my thoughts.

I couldn't remain calm with the multitude of questions swirling in my mind. I knew I had to promptly seek answers. Without time to spare, I knew a person who might offer me a better understanding of the situation. As I heard the click of the closing door and caught a glimpse of Hisoka's car fading into the distance through the window, I knew it was time to confront Masami.

Half-awake and wrapped in a long dressing gown, she slid open the *shouji* and widened her eyes in astonishment as she discovered me standing on her doorstep at six in the morning.

"Hello, Masami. Can I come in? I know it's early, but I need to talk to you about something," I said in one breath, my words reflecting a sense of urgency.

Her initial hesitation was evident in her body language, as she perhaps expected me to apologize for disturbing her with an

"*Ojamashimasu*;"* but such an apology never left my lips. Cracking the door open, her inviting gesture signaled for me to enter.

"You look worried. Is everything okay? Would you like some tea perhaps?" she offered.

I declined with a shake of my head, indicating that there was no time for tea, and instead, still standing at the *genkan*,† I asked with a hint of accusation in my voice, "Did you know, Masami?"

"Did I know what?"

"Did you know about the dolphins?"

"What about the dolphins?" Her astonishment grew, but I couldn't tell if it was genuine or if it was her acting skills playing the role.

"Did you know about the massacre happening in Taiji? Did you know they kill dolphins here? Up to even two thousand per year? Did you know that?"

A long silence followed, and a sudden sense of consternation washed over her delicate face as if she were searching for the right words to respond.

"Please, just tell me the truth," I said, my patience wearing thin. Another long silence ensued, but this time our gazes locked, and she understood she could no longer evade the truth.

"Yes, I knew," she confessed.

"What?" Somewhere deep inside, a glimmer of incredulity remained, hoping that she would be just as shocked and unaware as I was. That we could both grieve together and find a way to rescue the dolphins.

"Masami! You knew all this time, and you never said anything? How could you? How could you?" She had seen me with the book about dolphins in the bookstore. She had known how I talked about them, looked at them, cherished them, and adored them.

"How could I what, Aiko?" Her voice held a mix of defiance and confusion.

"How dare you know and not tell me the truth about what's going on in Taiji! You are a traitor!"

---

* (お邪魔します) *Ojamashimasu*: "Please excuse the intrusion…"

† (玄関): *Genkan*: Entrance, front door, entryway.

"A traitor? And what is the truth, Aiko?" She paused for a few seconds, then said even louder this time. "That this is our tradition? That this is something we have done for centuries that keeps us and our town going? If that is the case, then *you* are the traitor!"

"But how can you call it a tradition?"

"What do you know about Taiji? What do you know about our culture, Aiko?"

"I don't care about a tradition that is cruel and kills innocent, beautiful, highly intelligent animals! Just because it's a tradition doesn't mean it's right. In some traditions, humans eat humans," I said passionately. Masami's face displayed a look of disgust, but I disregarded it and continued without hesitation. "Does that mean it is right? Besides, look at what tradition does to Japanese people! No one speaks up. We don't talk about our feelings. We work constantly and have no time for meaningful life experiences. Why is the suicide rate so high in Japan? We have one life, and it slips through our fingers. And do you know where it leads us? To miserable, robotic lives!"

"Who told you all that, huh? Was it one of those foreigners who comes here to save the dolphins, who invades our land and dares to dictate what we should do? And what do they do in the West? Have you ever thought about it? Are they any happier? And don't they kill their cows and chickens? Aren't those living beings too?" Masami held my gaze. "And you know what's more? Their livestock live wretched lives in small cages before they are sentenced to death!"

"It is the same for the dolphins," I agreed. "They live in those small tanks—that's cruel. It's a slow, painful death for them."

"And how would you know? Can't you see how happy they are? It doesn't appear that anyone harms them there. They seem to be well taken care of. Weren't you the one who told me they are so content around you?"

I sighed, feeling the weight of my own realization. "Because I thought I saw it in their eyes. But I was too blinded by my own pleasure to see their suffering."

Masami's voice softened. "I'm sorry, Aiko, but the well-being of my family is more important than dolphins or strangers from overseas who know nothing about us."

"Masami, they were given an option. If they stopped hunting the dolphins, they'd receive the same amount of money they usually made by selling them." I lowered my voice. "They said it's not about the money; it's a form of pest control, claiming that dolphins consume too much fish in the ocean. But that's not true. The truth is it's people, and we don't want to acknowledge that. They're just searching for excuses."

"And it's our tradition."

"You keep talking about tradition," I argued, "but slaughtering thousands of dolphins isn't tradition. Taiji is a *whaling* town. In earlier times, a lone whale would be directed into a net by crews of men rowing boats. The meat was distributed among the local townspeople, and only a small number of whales were hunted annually.

"It wasn't until the 1960s when they started using motor boats to corral hundreds of dolphins," I said, repeating Steve's words with the assumption that she already knew what I was telling her. "The fact that these captured dolphins are sold for thousands of dollars for live exhibitions in captivity suggests that this is a business rather than a traditional method of subsistence hunting for the survival of the community."

Masami fidgeted uncomfortably.

"Do you know why you're stuck in your ways?" I pressed.

She appeared disinterested in my opinions, but I continued nonetheless.

"Because you want to belong somewhere. Which is understandable. We all do. But when we cling to it at all costs, it obscures universal truths. It hinders thinking outside the box and caring for one another on a larger scale. We are all one family. We are all connected."

"Tell that to your dolphin lovers! Aren't they the ones who come to our country with their shoes on when they should be walking barefoot?" She paused, giving me a cold glare. "Why don't they fix their own issues first?"

I paused to reflect on what she had just said. She had a point, and I knew that even people from the Western world were not without fault and did not always set the best examples. However, this wasn't about "them" or "us." It was about the dolphins, and I needed to stay focused on conveying that message.

"They don't want trouble. They can see how special dolphins are and want to end their suffering peacefully," I insisted.

"By taking away our livelihood and traditions!" It seemed Masami wasn't interested in my earlier explanation. "Aiko, whaling has been a part of our heritage for centuries. It's something my grandfather, then my father, used to do, and now it's Katashi's turn."

"And... Hisoka? Is he one of them?" I didn't need her to answer. Her compassionate gaze and nod were a confirmation of what I already knew deep inside. Now I was certain what "massy fishing" was about... She smoothly changed the subject, leaving me with a heavier heart.

"Those people choose their target. They wouldn't go to Iceland, Norway, or Denmark," she remarked. "You're right, we Japanese don't know how to speak up." She thought for a moment and then looked me in the eye. "And you know it better than anyone, Aiko."

I knew she was referring to my life with Hisoka and perhaps even to herself subconsciously. But at least we were aware of it. Awareness was the first step toward progress.

"That's not true. The Dolphin Project participates in physical protests around the world as much as possible." I repeated Steve's words. "Masami, I love our country and its traditions. I love our people, and I care deeply. That's why I speak the truth. I appreciate the richness and uniqueness of Japan, but we must re-evaluate some of its practices. We can find alternative solutions that don't harm the innocent." I pursed my lips before saying, "Masami, your husband has brainwashed you."

"So, the foreigners *have* gotten to you," Masami retorted.

"No. These issues exist worldwide. This problem exists in many countries. That's why they don't blame a specific group of people, including the Japanese. It's about taking action to address the problem. It's a global issue, but we can make a difference at the local level," I explained.

Masami's smile appeared forced, prompting me to continue.

"Masami, the only similarity between you and dolphins is that deceptive smile. The difference is that they cannot change their circumstances; it's how they were created—that's their curse. But you have the power to change. Stop pretending everything is fine like many of us do. Be honest with yourself—I know deep down this isn't the life you truly desire. And you know it yourself. You're

just afraid to take that step, as I once was. Leaving your comfort zone for the unknown is hard. But how will you know what awaits you if you never try?" I gave her an appraising if not empathic look. "I wish you all the best."

She understood that I was referring to her taking a leap of faith, both in pursuing her acting career and in expressing her love for Shingo. Deep down, she knew he loved her too, and there was a real chance for them to succeed. However, seeing the need to defend herself, she shifted the focus onto me, mirroring a defense mechanism I used to employ myself.

Masami sighed. "I'm sick of this hypocrisy. They shed tears for dolphins while consuming chicken for lunch. Aiko, before you pass judgment on others, take a look at yourself first." I couldn't deny the truth in her words.

"You're right," I acknowledged as she lifted her eyebrows in surprise at my response. "I had enough time to reflect on things, all alone, far away from everything and everyone I knew. I had to start over and truly understand who I am at my core. And in the past few days, I've come to realize that I've carried a deep-seated wrath for a long time. I was so angry that I tried to hide my true emotions.

"Suppression, pain, pride—call it what you will. All of it fueled my anger toward the world, the people who had hurt me, and most of all, myself. I had been trapped in a cycle of self-sabotage, burdened by guilt and self-pity. It was as if I had erected a wall between myself and the world, closing myself in a protective shell. But in doing so, I was also punishing myself for sins I had never committed."

As tears welled in Masami's eyes, their presence was both difficult to witness and cathartic. I knew I had to press on, to finally put an end to it all.

"People claim to love animals, but often their affection is centered around their own pleasures. They argue that children will miss out if they don't get to see dolphins up close, but if children knew the suffering behind their captivity, would they still desire visits to aquariums? To truly love animals is to observe them, learn about them, and grant them the freedom to be themselves. It requires being in their presence, experiencing their essence.

"I carried anger within me. But never around the dolphins. I felt lost. Yet never around the dolphins. I was in pain. Yet never

around the dolphins. I had so much fury and resistance that it blocked my capacity to love until *they* healed my broken heart. They were the only ones to whom I could reveal my third face, for a long time. Despite their inability to speak our human language, they not only accepted me into their pod, without judgment or harm, but above all, understood my pain. You may ask how I know. Some things are hard to explain; they can only be felt. And that's how it was with them. Thanks to the dolphins, I no longer felt lonely, for the first time since I arrived in Taiji. How can I stand by and allow them to be mercilessly slaughtered? They are my only source of joy. How?"

"You can't change the world, Aiko." Masami's eyes held a touch of pity, but I refused to feel sorry for myself.

Just yesterday, upon discovering the truth about Taiji, I had been consumed with anger toward Japan, my fellow countrymen, and the system. But then, I had recalled Chris' response to my question about why he loved Japan so deeply.

"Why do I love the Land of the Rising Sun? The land of geishas, samurai, shogunates, ninjas, and sumo? The land of karate, jujitsu, aikido, and more? The philosophies behind them? The land of unique art, painting, calligraphy, profound literature, woodblock prints, origami, and manga? The land of cherry blossoms?" Chris had asked and with a smile, he had shrugged. "How can I not? It's precision and perfection. The land of phenomenal, often exceptionally healthy cuisine. Japan has so many paradoxes and controversies. The strangest subcultures. Harmony yet chaos? The fusion of modern and ancient, entwined in euphony and enchanting beauty. How can I not love it? It captivates me."

And that was all true. But I also understood that a healthy balance existed, not in hating or loving Japan in absolutes, but in admiring its beauty and striving to rectify its flaws. Japan wasn't the sole country hunting dolphins, as Steve had also informed me. Furthermore, most Japanese people were unaware of the dolphin slaughtering practices of their land. No country was perfect.

Masami was right; some Westerners mistreated animals too. Yet there were also individuals dedicated to advocating for the welfare of those livestock. My mission was dolphins, that much I knew. It didn't matter the cause, location, or collective effort involved in fighting for what was right. What truly mattered was for each of us,

as individuals, to walk toward the light instead of succumbing to darkness. While I hadn't shared these thoughts with her, I responded by summarizing them once again:

"You are right, Masami. But I can contribute to changing a piece of it by doing my part. If everyone does their part, we can slowly change the world. *Kaizen*, remember?"

Though Masami remained silent and her final thoughts eluded me, I understood that each of us held our own beliefs and walked our own paths. While I believed wholeheartedly in my case, I couldn't compel someone to share the same perspective. All I could do was express my opinions and raise awareness.

And that's where my role came to an end. But I held hope that she would open herself to other possibilities and consider different approaches…

"Remember, Aiko," Masami warned, "you're embarking down a dangerous road by defending dolphins."

"If what I'm about to do can help even just one dolphin, that's better than doing nothing at all. There are numerous ways to live one's life and choose a path, Masami. Once you make that choice, commit to it wholeheartedly, without any doubts in your heart."

As I reflected on my memories, the image of Riki's eye flashed in my mind, reaffirming the decision I had to make…

Life frequently confronts us with decisions. Some are straightforward, such as picking the book to read or deciding what to have for dinner. But more challenging choices, the repercussions of which will be enduring, hinder our progress.

The mere contemplation of the massacre unfolding in Taiji was excruciating. What if I were to witness it? Despite all the signs pointing in that direction, Steve's revelations, and Masami's confirmation, I struggled to fathom how people were capable of such cruelty. The question that swirled within my mind was whether I could confront such a harsh reality. Simultaneously, I couldn't shake the feeling that it was my duty, and I owed it to the dolphins.

I knew the only way I could get inside the cove was through Ryota.

As though nothing had occurred, I went back to the Dolphin Base. To everyone else, it appeared to be an ordinary day. Despite my efforts to maintain my composure, I was aware that I could never view the Base in the same light again. Now that I knew the dark secret it harbored, nothing seemed as it once had. Particularly, the trainers…

Kairi, who remained the solitary newcomer to Taiji and had spent only a short time at the Base, offered a glimmer of hope that she wasn't involved. However, since she was nowhere to be found, I couldn't address the matter with her.

Nonetheless, the person I required most at that moment was Ryota. But before I headed to his office, there was someone else I needed to speak with.

"I grasp it now," I told Riki, casting a quick glance at him as he floated in the same spot in the pen as he had been the day before. "I'm deeply sorry for what you and your family have been through, as well as you and Chika."

After several days, he finally turned to me, as if he understood.

"Human beings can be cruel. Sometimes, I find myself ashamed to belong to this species," I lamented in mournful soliloquy, even though the sorrowful look in his eyes made it clear that it wasn't truly a monologue. "But believe me, we're not all like that. Riki, if all of this is true… I'll do whatever it takes to help you and other dolphins."

I discovered Ryota wasn't in his office. An unsettling atmosphere hung in the air, and within moments, I understood why. There he was, with Jun, both preparing to depart from the Base. "Are you heading to the cove?" I asked, hurrying toward them.

He took a step back, his astonishment clear in his expression. "Erghm, yes. How did you know?"

"Because my husband is working there today, at the cove. Remember? He's a fisherman. He mentioned something about the trainers going to choose the dolphins today. Actually, would you mind if I joined you? I've always been curious about how you select the dolphins."

Though Ryota appeared taken aback, I was confident he wouldn't deny my request, given the lingering gratitude he felt for my rescue of little Aiko.

"All right… but you'll stay on the boat," he agreed.

"Deal." I managed a forced smile.

On the journey to the cove, I felt a sense of familiarity wash over me. As we drove past Kujirahama Beach, which was now flanked by a barrier of police officers and trees bearing signs with warnings like NO EXIT, NO TRESPASSING, and FALLING ROCKS, I was certain that this was the very place where I had first encountered little Aiko.

"All right, we're nearly there," Ryota declared.

"Where do you go to select the dolphins?" I inquired.

Jun interjected this time, brimming with enthusiasm. "Can you see that public beach?" I nodded. "There's another small cove just behind it. That's where we choose them." And just when I believed I couldn't be more surprised, Jun shared another revelation, adding, "By the way, Aiko, during certain summer months, you might come across a dolphin here at the beach. Swimming within a pen, he is there to entertain beachgoers, and it's great fun. You should give it a try next season."

Hearing that filled me with a sense of revulsion. I had touched the same waters where a slaughter had taken place—and was going to continue taking place.

With a heavy heart, I pondered on how this town was rife with contradictions. Strolling its streets, dolphin effigies were frozen in statues and mosaics, directing you along the avenues, gazing at you from shop windows, and adorning buildings. Road signs boldly read, "We love dolphins," yet the government was simultaneously profiting from their capture. I recalled the dolphin shows, where people cheered and admired the dolphins' performances while consuming their meat, and the trainers, who professed love for these animals, were complicit in the butchery. It appeared the town's residents lacked a moral compass or an appreciation for the gravity of the situation, leaving me utterly perplexed.

It had been almost a year since I arrived in this town and married Hisoka. Three hundred and thirty days had passed, yet not once had I ventured to his place of work, the very spot in which he callously and mercilessly took the lives of highly intelligent animals.

A brief drive from the beach brought us to the port, and I found myself worrying about what I would say or how I would act if I were to encounter him.

The port appeared almost as I had pictured it. With tired, sleepless eyes, I observed the scratched, weathered, white boats gently bumping against the rocky wall and buoys. Some were equipped with stretchers along their sides. Beyond them, the view that extended to the horizon was nothing but perfect. The scene was utterly bewildering in its simplicity and minimalism. The farther my gaze stretched, the more the mountains in the distance faded their blue haze in the morning fog. In the foreground, the port's entrance beckoned toward the boundless expanse of the sapphire sea.

I mulled over numerous possibilities for this town. Why had they opted for the worst one? Why not create job opportunities within the tourism industry? Instead of doling out harm to dolphins, they could have embraced alternatives like dolphin and whale watching. With its breathtaking natural beauty and an abundance of towering palm trees reminiscent of a tropical paradise, they could have developed resorts to entice people to experience the unique village life of Japan, a stark contrast to the bustling metropolises. Wakayama held more potential than just pain as I believed.

"Hello, Yuto. How's your wife?" Ryota inquired, clearly familiar with the fisherman who proudly displayed his ample belly beneath a Lee t-shirt and rain pants supported by suspenders.

"She has a cold, you know? The weather change got to her, but she's feeling better now," the man responded, his voice hoarse.

"Yes, indeed! And I noticed in the forecast that a typhoon is expected next week, so we're lucky to have caught some dolphins before it arrives," Ryota commented as we approached the changing room. Then he asked nonchalantly, "How many?"

"We've herded a substantial pod into the cove. There should be around forty-five of them. Some are waiting for us from yesterday." Yuto made a hand gesture that resembled counting money. His laughter revealed a few missing teeth toward the back.

Ryota and Jun left to don their wetsuits while I remained behind. I hesitated, having second thoughts about staying in this place and witnessing the massacre. But Yuto interrupted my contemplation, saying, "You're not changing, are you?"

"No, I'm a new trainer, so I'm here to observe from the boat," I responded.

"Well, you look familiar."

I wondered where he might have seen me—perhaps at my wedding, in Hisoka's photographs, or somewhere around town? Fortunately, Ryota and Jun arrived before too many questions could be raised.

"So, let's get going. Minato will be joining us," Yuto announced while putting on his fisherman's jacket. The closer we drew to the boat, the more my head spun and my feet hesitated, reluctant to move forward. Nevertheless, I had to keep moving.

Minato, a compact, weathered man with a cigarette dangling from his lips was dressed in a familiar fisherman's outfit. He nonchalantly tossed pieces of snorkeling equipment and a few pairs of white gloves onto the yellow nets at the turquoise-hued bottom of the skiff boat. "Let's go," he beckoned.

As we departed the pier, the larger and smaller boats, the sprawling trees, the towering electric poles, and the white houses with their colorful roofs seemed to shrink into the distance while my anxiety continued to swell. *There's no turning back*, I reminded myself as Minato skillfully navigated toward the gap in the mountains.

My goal was to maintain as much composure as I could, although it was an incredibly daunting task.

"So, how exactly do you capture the dolphins?" I inquired, grimly eager to hear it from their own mouth. Minato volunteered to explain.

"Eh, we use sound to confuse them and run them aground."

"Then, divers from the 'Fishermen's Union' subdue the dolphins. If they are too far from the shore, they are wrestled into slings and carried by skiffs to us. Sometimes *we* help in this process," Ryota proudly cut in.

"Oh, I see. And what kinds of dolphins do we have in Taiji?"

"Bottlenose, Risso's, striped, pantropical spotted dolphins," Minato mumbled, his hand unconsciously scratching his forehead as if it would aid his memory. "Rough-toothed dolphins, Pacific white-sided dolphins, short-finned whales, false killer whales," he continued, listing the various species. "Did I forget something?"

"Melon-headed whale," Jun quickly recited and glanced at Ryota, hoping to gain his approval. However, Ryota's attention was fixed on the horizon; he seemed distant.

During our brief boat ride, the unassuming, petite cove, nestled amid hills adorned with a fresh green forest coat, came into view. This serene display of Mother Nature stood in stark contrast to the turmoil unfolding just a few meters away in its cove.

From a distance, I caught a fleeting glimpse of dolphins' fins and tails emerging from frothy water.

Now, as we drew closer, I observed them tightly huddled together, like sardines crammed into a jar. The sound of their caudal fins hitting the water's surface reverberated loudly.

Upon reaching the cove, the uncertainty of what lay ahead weighed heavily on my nerves. A short distance from the beach, where a few other trainers had already been waiting, Minato dropped the anchor.

From afar the echo of the loud *kan-kan* sound made with heavy hammers filled the air and the water. Fishermen threw rods tied to metal pipes under the water to chase the dolphins. They split the pod. Some of the captors were already within the cove while others arrived in their banger and skiff boats with more unfortunate victims in tow—a pod of six dolphins, including a baby, which stayed close to its mother. Once near the shore, the hunters deployed nets across the cove's entrance, sealing off all avenues of escape and trapping the new dolphins inside. They separated them into smaller, more manageable groups. The animals' panic echoed between the cove's hills.

One of the fishermen gestured from a distance for the trainers and divers to begin selecting the dolphins. Ryota and Jun prepared to join a few others, wading in the water.

Before they entered, Ryota hastily addressed me. "Aiko, keep a close eye on us. We're about to choose the finest dolphins. Bottlenoses are highly sought after worldwide, but we won't say no to the others." Ryota chuckled as if it were a humorous matter. "We need to measure them and assess their gender, the condition of their fins, beaks, teeth, and overall presentation. The perfect captive dolphin is a young female with minimal marks or scars on her skin."

With each passing moment, I found it increasingly difficult to maintain a stoic face.

The captor's eyes conveyed a hunger for yen, dollars, and dirhams—the currencies of kidnappers. Yet in the dolphins' eyes, there was a distinct aura of fear and panic, perhaps marking their initial direct encounter with a human, and for some, their ultimate one.

Divers pounced on the dolphins, grasping their dorsal fins, beaks, and tails, before dragging them around as Ryota attempted to subdue them. Following thorough examinations by him and Jun, the chosen ones were wrestled into a sling attached to the boat's side by Yuto, Minato, and a few unfamiliar men, as if they were mere pieces of meat. Thrashing wildly, fighting for their freedom, the dolphins were within arm's reach, yet the thought of touching or gazing at them never crossed my mind. Unsuitable catches were marked with a white substance. I couldn't help but feel that we, as humans, were unworthy to share the same planet as dolphins.

But the worst was yet to come. As Ryota and Jun made their way back onto the boat, fishermen took control of the harrowing scene.

My heart leaped in my chest as I spotted, among the group, Hisoka from a distance. My eyes widened in terror as he swung a massive spear and aimed it directly at a dolphin. Suddenly, the dolphin's skin, which a second ago, had shimmered silver in the sunlight, turned crimson with blood. Hisoka repeated his action as if to ensure the dolphin's demise.

Then, with the red spear in hand, he proudly raised it toward the sky like a triumphant warrior. Our eyes locked from afar, and I believed that he recognized me.

Now, I observed other fishermen mirroring Hisoka's actions. They callously targeted the dolphins, striking them not just in the spinal cords but anywhere on their bodies with long, sharp hooks and spears. Others cut their throats.

Hitting the right spot seemed challenging, leading many dolphins to not be killed instantly. As a result, they writhed and slapped the water as their lives slowly drained away.

The desperate cries for help the dolphins emitted were unlike anything I had ever heard before. Their high-pitched pleas overwhelmed all other sounds.

Some dolphins drowned in their own blood, some committed suicide by not taking another breath, and some were hauled out of the water by their tails and put onto boats or in stretchers; the wounded ones were dragged onto the beach and piled on top of each other. Amid this brutality, the fishermen laughed, stepped on the dolphins, and took breaks for a smoke in between.

Right when I believed I had witnessed the worst, nothing could have readied me to witness firsthand the ensuing cruelty.

Suddenly, I saw another skiff boat driving through the crowd of dolphins, leaving them bleeding from their faces, backs, and tail fins, which were cut by the boat's motor. In a panic, some had collisions with the concrete seawall while others rushed onto the rock lining. One of the dolphins, I noticed, bore a horrifying facial fracture, with torn flesh in its mouth, revealing raw tissue as it writhed in agony.

I felt an overwhelming wave of nausea. On the verge of retching, my body trembled. I was struck silent. Much like the terrifying nightmare I had experienced a few nights prior, the massacre unfolded before me. My senses and grasp on reality slipped away, leaving me in a disorienting daze. Suddenly, dizziness overcame me, and my vision blurred into a chaotic dance of spots that coalesced into a vast, inky stain. The rest I didn't remember.

Gradually, as I regained my bearings, I found myself reclining in the boat at the dock in the harbor, my feet elevated. Hisoka's face loomed before me, but it bore no concern—only a hint of embarrassment.

Within moments, I realized that I had fainted. That was a first for me. It hadn't occurred during my anatomy class in medical school, where we worked with preserved human brains, nor during forensic medicine class, where we dissected human corpses to study their various organs, still covered in blood. What I had witnessed here in Taiji, however, had exceeded my emotional threshold.

Ryota, Jun, Minato, and Yuto appeared ashen, standing out against the backdrop of the overcast, foreboding sky that felt as though it was falling in on me.

"Let's go, we're heading home," Hisoka commanded, his tone stern as if addressing a reprimanded child. Once again, his fisherman's suit was drenched in blood, but this time, I understood its source. He firmly gripped my shoulder, and if he hadn't, I might

have collapsed once more. Leaning on his support, I dragged my feet from the boat toward his car while onlookers observed our departure.

The instant we closed the car doors, tears welled in my eyes, and I released my first conscious breath. The horrifying images of what I had just witnessed flooded back into my mind.

"What are you doing here?" Hisoka inquired as he backed out. Shocked, worried, and shaken, I could utter not a single word; instead, I began sobbing uncontrollably.

"Why are you crying?" His question alone highlighted that he would never truly understand the depth of my emotions and, above all, would never comprehend the barbaric act he had just participated in.

At that very moment, I looked at Hisoka and knew I had to end our marriage, no matter the cost.

Chapter 17

時間が経てばいろんなことが分かるよ。残るべきものは残るし、残らないものは残らない。時間が多くの部分を解決してくれる。時間が解決できないことを君が解決するんだ。

Jikan ga tateba ironna koto ga wakaru yo. Nokorubekimono wa nokorushi, nokoranai mono wa nokoranai. Jikan ga ooku no bubun wo kaiketsu shite kureru. Jikan ga kaiketsu dekinai koto wo kimi ga kaiketsu surun da.

As time goes on, you'll understand. What lasts, lasts; what doesn't, doesn't. Time solves most things. And what time can't solve, you have to solve yourself.

Haruki Murakami
Dance Dance Dance

THAT NIGHT, I LAY ON the couch, but sleep eluded me. The disturbing scenes, reminiscent of a live-action horror movie, played relentlessly in my mind. I saw the dolphins' bodies, soaked in blood, their eyes wide with fear and panic, and the water of the cove turning crimson. The sounds of agony echoed in my ears like a broken record, refusing to fade away. Suddenly, my nightmare was interrupted by the shrill, unfamiliar ring of our rarely-used home phone. Listening to the prolonged chimes, uncertainty gripped me, particularly at such an early hour. I pondered on who could be on the other end of the dormant wire and eventually mustered the courage to answer.

"Aiko?" The mournful voice barely registered at first, but it had been nearly a year since I last heard it. Though I couldn't see her face, I could sense the weight of time and the lines etched upon it through the mere utterance of those four letters in my name.

"Mom?"

"Aiko! How are you?"

A wave of vulnerability washed over me, even though it seemed like discussing my well-being wasn't her primary intention. I

attempted to hold back tears and responded that I was fine without delving into her own condition.

"Your dad..." Her voice trailed off as if grappling with how to express what needed to be said. "He's gravely ill. He..." There was a pause, followed by a deep sigh and a tremor in her voice. "He's dying. His final wish is to see you."

Minoru was gravely ill, and his life was fading away. His last desire was to lay eyes upon me. The moment I hung up the phone, trying to piece together my mother's words, I was engulfed by an unsettling sense of dilemma—the perplexing sensation of not knowing how to embrace it all.

As a daughter, it would have been appropriate to succumb to misery, fear, and anger in the face of cancer's cruel clutches. However, an unexpected apathy tinged my emotions. Moreover, I wasn't certain if I harbored a desire to see him, which only added to my mounting guilt. Finally, the weight of this guilt propelled me to a resolute decision—to venture to Tokyo, where they had moved a couple of months ago.

Clutching the paper that bore my parents' address in my sweaty palms, I couldn't ignore the undeniable tension coursing through my being. In stark contrast, Hisoka sat behind the wheel, exuding his usual stoicism and enigmatic aura—a face devoid of expression that was challenging to decipher. It was merely a few hours after the unexpected phone call, and he was driving me to the train station.

Gazing out of the window, I beheld what seemed to be tears shed by the divine. It was as if God was weeping for souls who, instead of forging their own path, blindly surrendered to the whims of the system. People who, out of fear, dared not embrace their true selves and manifest their own reality.

The rain relentlessly intensified, as if divine wrath poured from the heavens. The approaching typhoon drew nearer with each passing moment.

Simultaneously, my anger surged, fueled by the realization that the man seated beside me was one of the culprits responsible for

the demise of my beloved dolphins. Although I was en route to Tokyo to bid farewell to my dying father, my mind fixated solely on the plight of the murdered dolphins who had bestowed upon me an unwavering love I had never experienced, even from my own parents.

As we waited for my train, I understood that this was the time to confront Hisoka.

"How can you do that? How can you kill innocent, highly intelligent animals in such a cruel manner?" I lamented, telling myself not to cry.

"I'm a fisherman. It's my job," he replied with a cold demeanor. "What other choice do I have?"

I knew he wouldn't easily comprehend my perspective, but I had to make an effort. "I wish you and others would open your eyes and consider a broader view. You don't have to be bound to something just because it's all you've known in life. There's more to life," I implored.

"But I am content where I am, Aiko. You're not."

I couldn't dispute that. "How can you be content in such a cruel job?" I asked. Indifference emanated from his face. "Besides… you know nothing about me."

"Did you ever share anything about yourself with *me*?" he countered.

"Did you ever ask?"

His eyes were dull and unconcerned.

"Anyway, it doesn't really matter. I don't want to play a blame game. I've made up my mind. I can't continue… I can't continue in this marriage." A heavy silence enveloped the train station. It appeared he wasn't prepared for such a sudden turn of events.

"But you can't…" Suddenly, his passivity transformed into anger and resentment.

"Yes, I can," I interjected, anticipating his argument. "All my life, I have been told what to do. Now, it's time for me to make my own decisions. I can't keep deceiving myself. I'm not truly living; I'm just surviving." I paused to reflect on my own words, the very words I'd dreaded for so long that had been echoing in my mind for months but had remained unspoken. "I don't love you… and I know that you feel the same. We have nothing in common. We are two different people with different goals. Our marriage was flawed

from the beginning. I was blind to it for many reasons, letting fate make choices for me. I hoped for a change but I know now that it will never come. It's time for me to reclaim control of my life." Relief washed over me, but a look of horror descended upon Hisoka's face.

"But, but… It'll be a scandal!"

"That's what concerns you the most? A scandal? That in itself says a lot about our relationship."

"I can't let you go. I…"

"You have no choice unless you intend to kill me, just like you've killed the dolphins." I held no fear of death; living with him had been a slow death, after all.

"What… what are you planning to do?" he stammered.

"I've managed to save some money, so I don't want your financial help." I thought of the yen from the Chinese cup that I had taken with me. "I'm not returning to Taiji. At least not to you."

This was the Aiko he had never known. And perhaps, I never had either.

The sound of an approaching train brought another wave of relief. Hisoka grabbed my arm, but I jerked free from his grasp. Without looking back, I boarded the train.

Trapped within the confines of my thoughts, I found myself revisiting my conversation with Masami. Amid this sea of misery, I begrudgingly acknowledged her partial truth. It muddled my mind further, a burden I least needed at this juncture in my life. Nevertheless, I understood that anyone, if they so desired, could unsettle another's thoughts and moral compass with their own perspectives.

Above all else, I understood that change must commence from within. How could we strive to better the world when we neglected to address our own issues at home? How could we pass judgment on others when we ourselves were far from perfect?

I had reached this revelation long ago while talking with Sayaka but had yet to fully embody it. However, despite the trepidation that enveloped me, I recognized that waiting any longer was not an option. It was imperative that I initiate reforms in my own life. And so, I resolved to begin by posing a series of introspective questions to myself.

The most challenging of which was whether I could advocate for the rights of certain animals while consuming others. I reminisced about the injured dove I had once aided as a child, only to devour *torikatsu** later that evening. Wasn't that the epitome of hypocrisy?

What did I truly believe in? What did I genuinely desire? Who was I? And where was I headed? As the answers eluded me, I came to realize that each of us must navigate and discern what resonates within ourselves and follow our unique path. Every individual possesses a distinct destiny.

As I embarked upon this new journey of awakening, I found myself increasingly adrift, yet paradoxically, more attuned in a peculiar, indescribable manner.

Given the solace of time, I needed to process all that I had seen at the cove. But how? I knew the macabre images would stay with me forever. Confusion washed over me, obscuring my perspective and shaking the foundation of my beliefs. It clung to me persistently throughout the arduous six-hour train journey toward the capital of Japan.

However, even after traversing the length of the country, six hours proved insufficient to untangle the labyrinthine corridors of my mind and discover the elusive answers, let alone find inner peace.

A profound sense resonated within me that humanity remains largely ignorant. We merely skim the surface of the vast depths that life holds. Following the revelation concerning dolphins, the world appeared stripped of the ability to astonish me any further. It felt as though humans dwelled within their own limited realms, oblivious to the hidden wonders that lie beyond their sight. We exist amid a web of deceit, fed falsehoods by the very systems we rely upon, the media we trust, and the politicians we follow. What else remained concealed from our understanding?

But human cruelty shook me more than anything. Once we crossed a line, the next one seemed thinner. A dangerous road ahead. A trap we engage in, under the blurring boundaries. Where else could we venture to acquire pleasure, money, status, and power? Yet I yearned to believe that as much cruelty existed, so, too, must there

---

* (鳥カツ) *Torikatsu*: Chicken katsu; chicken cutlet.

be goodness, propagating a kind of duality. Was there a possibility to exclude evil at all?

The bustling crowd at Shibuya Station proved to be overwhelming, exacerbating my existential ponderings and leaving me feeling even more adrift and desolate. It was as if I had been transported to an alien realm, a world where I no longer belonged. *Where*, I wondered, *do I truly belong? Was there anyone within this vast expanse who could comprehend and empathize with me?*

To my astonishment, my heart hammered as I caught sight of my mother waving fervently amid the sea of unfamiliar faces. Her stride quickened, propelled by the recognition of my presence from a distance.

Almost a year had elapsed since we last had any form of contact; it felt both long and fleeting. It was difficult to ascertain which sentiment carried more weight. Throughout that year, I had experienced a tumultuous journey—emerging from a broken heart, marrying a stranger and living beside him, grappling with loneliness, and cloaking myself in a protective shell. Gradually, however, I had begun to dismantle those barriers and uncover a broader perspective of life, one that surpassed my previous perceptions. It was a year of embracing acceptance on various levels, a time of both comprehension and perplexity.

And over the course of that year, she had not visited me—once. I had never truly expected it, but she hadn't even bothered to call. Yet there she was, maneuvering through the bustling crowds with urgency.

As if she had been present in my life all this time, she sprinted across the station through the throngs of travelers to me. And still, understanding her remained as challenging as ever.

We embraced, and the strength of her frail, bony hands was alarmingly palpable. She appeared thinner than when I had left.

During our journey to their apartment, after she disclosed that Minoru was battling lung cancer and, despite reaching a critical stage, had chosen to remain at home, our conversation remained sparse.

Before we stepped into the cramped studio, my mother offered me a reassuring nod, as if she could discern the mounting anxiety within me. At first glance, the apartment they resided in appeared minuscule, and the scent of stale rice mingled with the pungent odor of cheap cigarettes that permeated the air. Was Minoru still

smoking despite his illness? Considering my mother's disdain for cigarettes, it seemed highly unlikely that the smell originated from her.

And there he lay, reclining on a mat positioned in the corner of the studio. His head was nestled into the softness of a pillow, but the sunken cheeks and pallor of his wrinkled face revealed a profound sense of lethargy and decline. This new, brutal, and jarring image of Minoru proved difficult to grasp. It was astounding to witness the extent of change that could occur in just a year. Sickness and time were merciless adversaries, showing clemency to no one, including him, the self-proclaimed "king." At that moment, an unexpected surge of compassion and sorrow washed over my heart.

Weak and with a voice that often cracked, he began, "Aiko, I know I wasn't the best father. But all I ever wanted was for you to be articulate, educated, and successful in life. I dreamed of you becoming a respected doctor. I wanted you to live to be a proud Japanese." He paused, struggling to gather his strength, and I had thoughts of regret coming there.

Attempting to delay the conversation, I interjected, "It's late; we can talk tomorrow."

However, he disregarded my remark and continued speaking. "Sometimes in life, clarity only arrives at the time of death. It strikes you like a torpedo. And though you may not have enough time to fix everything, you can strive to mend the most crucial aspects. Some people don't get this chance. I do. And I am grateful for it. Thank you for coming." As he uttered those words, tears glistened in his eyes—an unprecedented sight in my entire existence. Yet that wasn't the only surprise. This time, I could hear my mother's sobs openly, unreservedly, with no pretense of hiding in any corner of the apartment.

"Aiko, these belong to you," Minoru said as Mother helped him to rise from his bed to open the old, squeaky drawer of a bedside table. He retrieved a bundle of neatly tied envelopes and with trembling palms, handed them to me. They appeared pristine and were adorned with colorful stamps. I began sifting through them, my eyes immediately gravitating toward one that had already been opened. As I glanced at the sender's name, an intense surge pulsed through my heart, causing my hands to shake uncontrollably. The name that had once been whispered and cherished, the name I had

repeated countless times each day and night but had recently faded from my memory, suddenly resurfaced. It crashed into my consciousness like a hurricane of shock, mingling with fear and excitement to form a single indelible mark of blue ink.

Chris…

With quivering palms, I mustered the strength to shuffle through the envelopes, discovering there were at least ten of them. To my astonishment, the last few were from Sayaka.

A sudden silence enveloped the room as if the air itself held its breath. Amid the stillness, I could hear the thunderous pounding of my own heart while waves of torment and disillusionment coursed through my entire being.

All this time, Minoru had been concealing letters addressed to me. He had orchestrated my marriage to an older man, someone I not only lacked affection for but worse still, a man I didn't even know! He had forced me to wed a stranger despite being fully aware of my genuine love for someone else.

All this time, I had convinced myself that Chris and Sayaka had forgotten about me, perhaps even believing that I had forgotten them. Little had I known that they were trying to reach out, pouring their thoughts onto paper, assuming I was deliberately ignoring them.

I couldn't bear to face Minoru. No words could capture the depth of my disappointment and anguish, except for the lingering thought of him being a "monster" that echoed relentlessly in my mind. However, I kept those words tightly locked within me. I understood that uttering them wouldn't change anything, and once spoken, they could never be taken back. I needed solitude to process the recent turn of events, to digest the enormity of what had just transpired. Above all, I yearned to read the contents of those letters, but not in Minoru's presence.

There was nothing left for me to do but escape from that cramped, odorous apartment that felt like a suffocating prison. It wasn't just the stench of Minoru's freshly lit cigarette that overwhelmed me, but the suffocating weight of his hypocrisy and deceit, which had profoundly impacted my own life.

Clutching the letters tightly in my hand, I rose from my seat without uttering a word. Out of the corner of my eye, I noticed Minoru accepting my decision. It was a stark contrast to the past

when I longed to hear my name called from behind, like that fateful night when I had first met Sayaka. But now, my mother's calls held no significance as their echoes faded swiftly into the closing doors of the elevator. It felt like a sense of déjà vu, yet I was an entirely transformed individual in the present moment.

The fresh air delicately embraced my lungs, providing solace to my restless heart. Overwhelmed, I couldn't contain the trembling of my body and chose to settle on the nearest weathered bench. Hands shaking uncontrollably, I carefully opened the first letter. Nestled within its pages, I discovered a familiar sight—the first photo Chris had taken without my consent, featuring the magnificent Mount Fuji in the backdrop. Tears streamed down my face, and in an attempt to conceal them, I pressed my shoulder against my cheek. I began to read:

Dear Aiko, My Princess,

It wasn't a mere coincidence that your name resembled that of an Emperor's daughter. I often referred to you as my "Princess," knowing full well that my own last name, "Prins," translated to "Prince" in English—a detail I never revealed to you.

I only held you in my arms a few weeks ago as I am writing this, on the plane, bound for Amsterdam. But it seems like it's been ages as so much has happened in such a short span of time.

And as I sit here, watching everything grow smaller and disappear into the clouds, it all feels surreal. But deep down, I know this is not a dream. On the contrary, it is my harsh reality. I can no longer contain the emotions within me... I thought I could endure this pain, but I am too fragile. These past few months have been among the most challenging of my entire life.

When I met you, someone unexpected, someone I wasn't anticipating or waiting for, life once again revealed its unpredictable plans for me. And despite being content and happy in my own solitude, you brought depth to my life on a distinct, indescribable level. You filled a void in my soul that had been silently yearning. I fell so deeply in love with you that the thought of living without you became unimaginable. How can mere words capture the essence of this feeling? Love...

Yet amid this new and unknown whirlwind of emotions, I began to fear that I was losing control of my life. The intensity of my feelings for you started

to overshadow everything else. I found it difficult to focus on my photography, on my passions that once consumed me. For the first time in my life, my work took a backseat. These overwhelming emotions made me afraid. It seemed like I was afraid of love itself.

And the fear of the future gripped me. I was afraid that the beauty of our relationship was too good to be true and that it would eventually fade away. Doubts lingered, especially when it came to your traditional father accepting our love. I worried our connection would cost you your family, and that burden weighed heavily on my heart. I worried I wouldn't be able to provide you with the life you deserved, that my limited means as a backpacker with a camera and no stable job would disappoint you.

But the pinnacle of my fears arrived when I received the news of my mother falling seriously ill. It was a turning point that left me with no choice but to return to the Netherlands and be by her side.

And deep down, I knew you would insist on coming with me, ready to stand by my side, even willing to leave behind your studies, your life, and your family. But I couldn't bear the thought of it. I wanted you to become a doctor, to find stability and a good job. Putting aside my feelings, I wanted you to do things the right way. For a long time, I wrestled with my thoughts, seeking answers to my questions and doubts. My heart urged me to be honest with you, but I listened to my head instead, a choice I now regret.

As much as I yearned for you to be by my side, guilt and responsibility weighed heavily on me. If only you could comprehend the turmoil I was going through and understand my intentions.

I was a coward, allowing my fears to dictate my actions, causing me to disappear without an explanation. I sabotaged not only myself but also you by abruptly ending our relationship. I couldn't provide a rational reason because I knew you would unmask me. I couldn't even look into your eyes because I knew you would see the deceit within them. You know me far too well.

In my misguided thinking, I believed that ending things in such a cruel manner would be for the best. I left you in a state of despair and uncertainty, causing you pain and anguish. I convinced myself that enduring this pain was necessary and that it would lead to a better outcome. I thought it would be best to disappear from your life, perhaps to return under more favorable circumstances.

And now I realize, it was a grave mistake, the biggest one I have ever made in my life. I should have been honest with you from the beginning so that

we could have faced the challenges together and found a solution. Deep down, I knew that we were meant for each other. I felt it in my core, but fear held me back from acknowledging it.

As I gaze out of the airplane window, watching Japan fade from view, I am leaving behind everything I hold dear. Everything I have believed in. Everything I have loved.

All that remains is a glimmer of hope, a faint longing that you will find it in your heart to forgive me.

You taught me so much, Aiko. You taught me how to peel a boiled egg from its shell using a spoon, how to master the intricacies of the washlet, how to be more patient, how to see the world with a broader perspective, how to find joy in the little things, and most importantly, how to love unconditionally and without limits. Through your guidance, I even learned how to love myself and to be a better version of myself.

I vividly recall the moment I asked you why you enjoyed drawing, and your response was that you wanted to capture and preserve fleeting moments. It resonated deeply with me because I felt the same way about photography.

In this letter, you will find our photo from the first day we met. And the first drawing that you sketched of me while I was sleeping. The one you threw into the trash because you felt it was not good enough.

I just want you to know that I always believed in you.

You have always been my muse and inspiration and always will be. I saved that drawing from the trash and kept it as a reminder that we all have to start somewhere and can always improve if we give ourselves a chance.

Today, I implore you to grant me a chance. I cannot alter the past, but I can rectify my mistakes, only if you permit me to do so...

I am asking for your forgiveness. I want to take care of my mom and come back to Japan for you. I want to walk through the torii gate with you, regardless of your father's acceptance. No matter if you decide you want to become a doctor or not.

I am patient now and can wait for you when you are ready. I want you, Aiko. I want you and I need you.

I know that the only answer is love.

And I know that true love shouldn't hurt... I am sorry I have hurt you. But I know that I am ready to show you true love now.

Yours forever, Chris

All that remained was a resounding sob, uncontrollable, as I gazed through my teary eyes at the blue ink upon the pale paper. It was a mere sheet torn from a notebook, its monetary value minuscule; yet to me, it held immeasurable worth. This humble piece of paper embodied everything.

Years of pent-up anger, disillusionment, pain, and resentment toward Chris dissipated in an instant upon reading the first sentence of his letter. In its place, forgiveness and compassion emerged, dispelling the darkness that had consumed me.

All these years, I believed he had forgotten about me, leaving me bewildered and without an explanation. Little did I know, he had done it for my sake. His overwhelming fears had overshadowed everything else, causing turmoil within him as he grappled with which path to choose. The truth emerged: Chris had loved me. But did he still love me today?

I swiftly retrieved the final letter, dated a year ago. After scanning it, I learned that he still loved me back then, signing "yours forever."

But did forever truly exist? Could one truly promise someone the most significant thing they could offer—their own life—forever?

The cacophony of rush hour traffic, the echoing click-clack of women's heels on concrete pavement, and the plaintive cries of a toddler being pushed in a stroller did little to assist in finding the answers I sought. At that moment, all I craved was a serene space where I could process the words I had just read. Escaping from this chaotic environment became imperative, and fortunately, I knew of the perfect place.

Chapter 18

そしてその砂嵐が終わったとき、どうやって自分がそいつをくぐり抜けて生きのびることができたのか、君にはよく理解できないはずだ。いやほんとうにそいつが去ってしまったのかどうかもたしかじゃないはずだ。でもひとつだけはっきりしていることがある。その嵐から出てきた君は、そこに足を踏みいれたときの君じゃないっていうことだ、そう、それが砂嵐というものの意味なんだ。

Soshite sono sunaarashi ga owatta toki, douyatte jibun ga soitsu wo kugurinukete ikinobiru koto ga dekitanoka, kimi niwa yoku rikai dekinai hazuda. Iya hontouni soitsu ga satteshimatta noka doukamo tashika jyanai hazuda. Demo hitotsu dake hakkiri shiteiru koto ga aru. Sono arashi kara detekita kimi wa, soko ni ashi wo fumi ireta toki no kimi jyanaitte koto, sou, sore ga sunaarashi to iu mono no imi nan da.

And once the storm is over, you won't remember how you made it through, how you managed to survive. You won't even be sure, whether the storm is over. But one thing is certain. When you come out of the storm, you won't be the same person who walked in.

Haruki Murakami
Kafka on the Shore

TOKYO, September 2009

JUST LIKE A FEW YEARS ago, I boarded the same bus to Miho Beach. Just as then, following the same footsteps as before, I traversed the pathway through the pine trees, leading me to the once-familiar beach adorned with volcanic gravel.

Yet something was different.

Me.

I was not the same person.

With a fresh perspective, I gazed ahead, taking in the vastness before me.

It was upon this very beach that I had experienced my first joyful and abundant days by Chris' side, days that would be followed by many more. In the heat of the sun, we had played handball, sprinting back and forth along the coastline. We had leisurely strolled along the shore, savoring the mesmerizing sunsets. We had endured sunburns while practicing yoga, soaking in the gentle rays that pierced through the clouds. I had found solace in Chris' protective embrace as if nestled in a cocoon, all while gazing out at the endless waves. And it was here, on this beach, that we had shared our very first kiss.

However, today, I found myself standing alone, clutching the letters in my hands as a chilly breeze brushed against me. These were the very letters I had anxiously awaited, diligently checking my mailbox at every opportunity throughout those interminable years of disappointment and gradual fading hope. Now, almost untouched, it felt surreal as if I were trapped in a dream, and yet here they were, finally in my possession.

Caressed by the gentle kisses of the soft breeze against my warm body, I was reminded that this was no dream. With trembling hands, I settled into our cherished spot and began to open the letters, fully aware of the weight they carried.

I devoured each term, name, expression, idiom, and phrase within them, swallowing every word until I had absorbed the letters' contents. And once I reached the end, I started again, reading them all once more. With every sentence and every word, tears streamed down my face, knowing that they were penned from the depths of Chris' heart.

For years, I had been suffocating beneath the weight of my own buried pain, but now I felt the weight of every grain of his pain as if it were my own. Among the anguish he expressed, his self-blame remained most evident. The reality he had chosen for himself and the consequential pain and torment that had been inflicted upon me were like a boomerang. Sooner or later, they were bound to come back with even greater force, compounding that pain.

And I knew deep down that this was what he felt. I could sense the burden of guilt he carried within him. It pained me more than anything else, perhaps even more than my own grief. In the midst of this cruel irony, where we believed we had caused each other

suffering, we still loved one another and realized that nothing else mattered except being together.

As I held the letters from Sayaka, memories of her bubbly personality and profound sagacity came flooding back. She materialized before me, shrouded in the mist of recollection, and a smile adorned my face while my heart embraced the warmth.

And I found myself laughing through tears as I read her vivid descriptions. She recounted tales of disgusting wads of saliva being spat at her by mischievous llamas; daring adventures with the tamed Amazon parrot Lola in the depths of the jungle who stole fruits from her hand; and accidentally sampling a guinea pig, a Peruvian delicacy, and subsequently feeling sympathy for their unfortunate destiny. And then, I let out a loud sigh of awe as she meticulously detailed a four-day 'Inca Trail' trek through the wilderness, battling high altitudes, until finally reaching the magnificent destination of Machu Picchu.

Her detailed elucidation of the effects of ayahuasca, a holy plant from the jungle, shook me to the core. The brewing process and a ceremony conducted by a shaman guided her to profound self-discovery and revealed hidden truths, indirectly addressing many of her existential queries. As I read her words, I couldn't help but juxtapose them against my own divergent experience in Koyasan, despite the physical and temporal distance between us. Yet a deep sense of connection transcended these disparities, weaving an invisible bond between us.

After my ayahuasca experience, it became clear to me that when you recognize your own light, you begin to truly love yourself. And when you love yourself, you naturally extend that love to others, as you can only offer what you possess within.

I also want to apologize to you. When I saw that light within myself, I realized that I am that light. It's there where all the answers lie. What's more, I came to understand that we are all one with the energy of the Universe. So, when I once told you that you were not the center of this world, I was mistaken. In truth, you are nothing less than the center of this Universe, just as we all are.

The most astonishing part of her letters was her revelation.

> I have momentous news to share with you, Aiko. I made the decision to search for Liam. And guess what? I found him on social media! But here's the unbelievable part… From Ireland, he moved to the northern region of Peru, just a two-hour flight from Lima! Can you imagine? He followed his dreams to work with wild animals and he is researching pink dolphins in the Amazon River!

My heart raced with a mix of joy for Sayaka's reunion and excitement that Liam was now involved in studying dolphins. The interconnectedness of our lives seemed almost too remarkable to comprehend. Taking a moment to process the sheer magnitude of it all, I let out a sigh of amazement and disbelief before eagerly continuing.

> He was absolutely over the moon when he received my message! And he's supposed to visit me in Lima soon! So, despite its flaws, social media isn't all bad. While we can't escape the presence of technology in our lives, it's important to find a healthy balance between the virtual world and real-life connections. If we can achieve that, we can reap the benefits in so many ways. What are your thoughts? Perhaps we can connect through a platform ourselves and talk as if there's no space between us?

Despite the physical distance separating us, I was certain that our spiritual connection had persisted throughout all these years.

It was evident from her heartfelt letters that she missed me deeply and longed for our spirited arguments. While her letters brought me joy, they also stirred anxiety, concern, and sorrow within me. I couldn't bear the thought that she might have believed I had forgotten about her all this time. If only she knew…

Puffy cumulus clouds floated in slow motion in the distance, revealing a glimpse of Mount Fuji and evoking memories of my childhood. I remembered how I used to believe that we could jump

onto their fluffy surfaces. However, adulthood had shattered my innocence, revealing that they were merely masses of condensed watery vapor.

Yet at that moment, a new thought emerged. Despite this reality, it struck me that it's all about how we perceive and interpret the world around us. So, what if we couldn't leap onto those clouds? They still possessed an enchanting and magical quality. And they were so close to heaven.

Wasn't that the essence of processing information? It was about our personal perspective and the lens through which we view things.

With that lingering thought, a peculiar urge overwhelmed me—to have a personal encounter with the sea. Carefully tucking the letters into my backpack which was destined to be left behind on the colorful spectrum of rocks adorned with shades of gray, red, and brown, I entrusted my feet to carry me swiftly toward the chilly waters.

The initial cool sensation on my toes wasn't exactly inviting, but I pressed on, venturing deeper into the sea without any spare clothes to change into or even a towel. As I distanced myself from the shore, the roughness of the stones transformed into the pleasing softness of sand, embracing my bare feet and forging an immediate connection with Mother Earth. Beneath the surface, there seemed to be nothing to fear.

The waves crashed relentlessly, yet to my surprise, fear did not grip me. Moreover, I ventured so far that I found myself tiptoeing and leaping to prevent the waves from engulfing my face. I submerged beyond my waist! My t-shirt and cotton trousers clung to my body, thoroughly soaked by the relentless assault of the sea.

And then with cautious deliberation, almost as if time had slowed down, I lifted my feet from the water's grasp and began moving my limbs toward the infinite expanse. At first, my movements were tentative, but gradually, I grew more confident. The inky blue water deepened with each successive wave, creating an even darker hue.

As the waves diminished in intensity, I executed a fluid turn, effortlessly positioning myself on my back. Embracing a sense of surrender, I freed my hands and legs, placing complete trust in the gentle embrace of the water's grace. The sun, positioned low on the

horizon, bestowed its warm rays upon my exposed face, and even through closed eyelids, I could sense its contours. In a matter of seconds, a profound union occurred; I became indivisible from the sea.

As the realization dawned upon me that there was no solid ground beneath my feet, I experienced an unexpected sensation—nothing but pure freedom. It was a moment I had never anticipated, and the overwhelming emotion that swept over me wasn't one of pride but the triumphant conquering of fear, leaving me content and blissful.

So, this was what dolphins felt in the vast expanse of the open sea—complete freedom.

As the moon gradually emerged from behind a row of verdant trees, its soft glow became the sole source of illumination within my field of vision. Yet amid this serene scene, chaos descended upon my reality.

A wave of uncertainty washed over me. Had Chris been writing all this time? My parents had moved to Tokyo. Was it possible more letters had been left behind at the Shizuoka house? Doubts from the past mingled with a series of inquiries about the future, inundating my thoughts.

What should I do? Should I search for him? Should I compose a response? And if so, what words should I choose? Can I trust him again? What if he has undergone a complete transformation, rendering us strangers? Would our souls manage to reconnect across the vast expanse of time and space? What if he was already married? *Happily* married? What if the love he once felt for me had faded?

Life had taught me that I could survive without Chris by my side, but now that the truth was at my doorstep, I questioned whether I truly wanted to.

How could I find it in my heart to forgive Minoru?

Everything seemed overwhelmingly complex, filled with pain, and above all, frightening. The path ahead was shrouded in

countless unknowns. I still couldn't fathom how Minoru could have committed such an act. Deep within, all I desired was for him to appreciate and accept me for who I was, not just for my accomplishments in life.

I gazed at the half moon, a celestial body that harmoniously traversed its path, gracefully transitioning through its varied phases. Each night, it followed its designated course, an embodiment of serene continuity within the circle of life. As I contemplated its craters, a sense of tranquility enveloped my heart, gradually soothing its unrest.

At that moment, a memory resurfaced. Words uttered by Minoru just before I had hastily departed from the house reverberated in my head and heart.

"And though you may not have enough time to fix everything, you can strive to mend the most crucial aspects. Some people don't get this chance. I do."

Those words offered a glimmer of hope and perspective.

People often say that once a glass is broken, it can never be repaired to its original state. However, in Japan, we have a belief in *kintsugi*,* the art of mending broken pieces with gold. It's a practice that embraces imperfections and creates something more beautiful.

The truth is nothing in life remains constant. Everything is subject to change, flow, and transformation. Often, these changes are beyond our control. But there is nothing inherently wrong with this. It's simply the nature of life; it's a fundamental part of our existence.

In a single moment, everything became clear to me. Life exists on a spectrum rather than a dichotomous scale of black and white. It's a continuum with various shades of gray. Without experiencing the lows, we would never truly appreciate the highs. The contrast between the two allows us to understand and value the beauty that exists in our lives.

Certain matters may have been beyond my control, but there were others that I could influence.

As I reflected on Steve's words about the unfair fate of the dolphins—"No action is also an action. No decision is also a

---

* (金継ぎ) *Kintsugi*: repairing pottery with a lacquer mixed with gold or some other previous metal.

decision."—I realized they held a broader significance. They resonated with me on a deeper level.

I was like one of my dolphins in Taiji—caged!

As a Japanese, I recognized the importance of comprehending my people's actions. However, on a deeper level, I felt a stronger connection to being a child of Earth.

Chris, Sayaka, Little Aiko, Steve, Masami, and even Mahika, whom I had never met, were just a few individuals with whom I felt intimately bonded. They were all a part of my journey toward greater understanding, a path that illuminated the concept of our universal interconnectedness. The concept, which I had first heard from Sayaka so long ago, felt in every cell of my being in Koyasan, finally held complete and profound meaning for me.

And yes, it was true. I felt trapped, just like the dolphins, but unlike them, I had created my own cage through my choices. It seemed that nothing could alleviate my misery, not even a change in circumstances. My own mind held me captive.

I had to reach rock bottom to rise again. I had always had control, even if I hadn't fully realized it. I was going to be a victim no longer! I had only one life, and I needed to do what was right for me and what made me happy. Not others. There was no more time to waste. It was time for me to take charge of my own life.

Perhaps that was the moment when I realized I needed to overcome my rigidity, fears, and stubbornness regarding social media. It had been difficult to remain stagnant while the world continued to progress. I could perhaps use the power of the internet to fight for the dolphins too. I was aware that Kairi was on social media. Unfortunately, I didn't get a chance to converse with her, bid farewell, and most importantly, inquire if she was aware of Taiji's secret. But above all else, I felt the need to search for Chris and Sayaka. It was time for me to embrace the possibilities and connections that technology offered.

This was my path forward! I still had an opportunity! It wasn't too late! I would find Chris and explain everything. I'd express my enduring love for him. Even if, for some reason, we were not destined to be together.

I would share with him the plight of the dolphins, and I would find a way to save them. Now, I knew—it was my *ikigai*,[†] my purpose in life.

With the assistance of a strong gust of wind and the waning rays of the sun, I had almost dried off. Aside from a few hardly noticeable pebbles in my socks, my body embedded with salt, and the remnants of my bold steps into the sea, no other signs of my beach excursion clung to me.

Night had fallen, and I made the decision to return to my parents' apartment.

A complete and eerie silence greeted me as I stood at the threshold of the door. Fear gripped me, but thankfully, it swiftly turned to relief as I met my dad's gaze reflecting in the light of the bedside lamp, assuring me of his existence. He was alive.

With great effort, he extended his hand, whispering my name. I hurriedly took it. Despite the thick wool blanket that enveloped him from head to toe, his touch felt icy cold. My mother held his other palm, and she offered her free hand to me, completing the circle. Energy surged through my body, and I could sense the weight of my parents' regrets.

It is often said that people, on their deathbeds, regret not what they had done, but what they had not. The dreams they hadn't pursued because they had lacked the courage to fight for them and break free from their comfort zones. Fear, the antithesis of love, became a steadfast companion throughout their lives, particularly in the face of the unknown. My parents, too, were no exception. They lived a life consumed by fear, constantly worried about societal opinions and sacrificing their own happiness and that of our family. However, I understood that this pattern was a result of their upbringing, influenced by their own parents and generations before

† (生き甲斐) *Ikigai*: A reason for living, something one lives for; an individual's purpose in life.

them. It was a cycle that needed to be broken—that responsibility fell upon me.

The path to forgiveness required me to transcend the confines of this course and open my heart fully to a state where possibilities were boundless. Perhaps, if it weren't for him concealing the letters, I would have never uncovered the dolphins' misery. Maybe Sayaka had been right after all when she had said, "Everything happens for a reason."

Holding onto resentment was no way to live in peace. It took courage to acknowledge one's mistakes, and it demanded immense strength—often more than one could fathom. At that moment, I couldn't help but feel sorry for him, realizing that he had never truly experienced genuine happiness.

Tears welled up in Minoru's eyes, revealing a profound sense of remorse. No words were necessary. I embraced him tightly, and in his frailty, I could sense the fragility of his bones.

With my hand clasped in his, he shut his eyes, mustering a gentle smile. Amid the weight of despair, he never opened them again.

Just as earthquakes and typhoons strike Japan, causing loss and bringing about change, similar events in our lives constantly shape and reshape our reality. Nothing remains static or eternal. Everything flows, transforms, and rebuilds. It is a reminder that even life itself is transient.

Amid these fluctuations, there is always room for hope. Hope for a new future, for growth, and for the resilience to overcome whatever challenges come our way.

In learning to forgive, I recognized the opportunity to rebuild and embrace hope for a new future.

With a trembling hand, I typed, "Chris Prins" into the Facebook search bar. There were several profiles with that name, but only one belonged to *my* Chris. As his photo appeared on the screen, my heart seemed to lose control. With love, I gazed at his eyes, which had been imprinted onto my memory. They seemed somewhat different, tinged with a hint of sadness.

Summoning the courage, I clicked on "Message," but I was at a loss for words. There was so much I wanted to convey to him, yet I didn't know where to begin.

I typed, "Hello," and submitted the message.

The green active status button lit up, and I noticed the small graphic that indicated the recipient was typing. It felt like an eternity before a response appeared in all caps:

"AIKO! IS THAT REALLY YOU?"

Author's Note

To learn more about dolphins and ways to safeguard other endangered marine species, consider supporting the following organizations' extraordinary endeavors:

The Dolphin Project
DolphinProject.com

Sea Shepherd
Seashepherd.org

Life Investigation Agency (LIA)
Ngo-lia.org/en_about.php

Acknowledgments

From the onset, expressing my thoughts through writing has always felt more natural to me than verbalizing them.

A decade ago, when I embarked on writing this book, I relied on my phone for typing due to an old, dying laptop. Despite its small screen, writing in a language other than my first, juggling motherhood, work, and other passions while finding time for everything proved challenging. Biting my nail cuticles, I endured long hours in front of the screen, often experiencing moments of emptiness. I delved into new information about Japan, dolphins and their fate in Taiji, and philosophy, frequently sacrificing sightseeing during work layovers to articulate a few words and create an authentic experience. Despite the prolonged duration, my determination prevailed, and the book gained momentum when I embraced *kaizen* in my life. Life's myriad options and the allure of trying everything beckoned, but I made a promise to finish what I started, breaking the pattern of initiating but not completing endeavors. The pursuit of perfection gave way to the acceptance that perfection is elusive.

And today, with the finished book in my hands, here I stand. "Never give up on your dreams"—a cliché phrase I can finally utter with sincerity!

I've always dreamed of writing a book. After I watched the documentary *The Cove* by Louie Psihoyos, I knew my novel had to be about the dolphins in Taiji, the majestic creatures I had been fascinated with for so long. Watching the film sparked my personal commitment to 'save the dolphins,' which ultimately manifested in this book. I am grateful for this important movie.

My gratitude to the founder and director of The Dolphin Project, Ric O'Barry, and his team.

I would like to thank Ren Yabuki, a director at Life Investigation Agency (LIA) who consistently and fervently captures

and shares documentation of Taiji's dolphin drive hunts on social media channels.

Further thanks to the Sea Shepherd Organization for its contributions to protecting marine wildlife worldwide. My gratitude also extends to all other organizations, entities, and individuals globally advocating against cruelty to cetaceans.

Special thanks to Brian Kibue, who introduced me to *The Cove* at the most crucial moment and provided invaluable feedback on my book.

Heartfelt appreciation to my parents, Alicja and Dariusz, for bestowing upon me the precious gift of life and looking after me. I express my gratitude to my mother for being a steadfast pillar of assistance. And to my entire family for their unwavering support and love. I love you all very much!

I am blessed to be the mother of Liam and Gaia, the guiding lights in my life who serve as an inspiration to strive for a better future and help me comprehend the depths of unconditional love. I hope their generation will surpass our understanding.

I also owe major thanks to my Japanese friends, most of all, Mochan Wishclub and his wife Erika, for warmly welcoming me into their home, providing an incredible and authentic Japanese experience, taking me on local trips, and assisting me with fact-checking for this book.

To my dear friends in Poland and from around the world—thank you. You know who you are to me! Thank you for adding spice to my life, introducing me to new cultures, hosting me in your homes, and demonstrating that, despite being from different countries, we have more in common than not. My life would not be the same without you!

My heartfelt thanks go to my editor, Kara Wilson from Emerging Ink Solutions, with whom I quickly established a great connection. Her hard work, attention to detail, ambition, smoothness, patience, understanding, time, and effort were invaluable. This book owes much of its essence to her contributions.

Similarly, I extend my appreciation to Mark Kerby and Leina Nyugen, both of whom provided translation work for this book.

Lastly, thank you to *you*, dear reader, for accompanying me on this journey of self-discovery.

About the Author

Born in 1986 in Poland, Dominika Riemer, a Pisces with a penchant for dreaming, has embraced various art forms since childhood. From taking part in amateur movies to writing, drawing, music, and dancing, art has been a constant in her life.

Contemplating life's purpose has been a nightly pursuit for as long as she can remember, juxtaposed with daytime dreams of exploration and cultural immersion beyond her homeland's borders. This desire led her to Ireland immediately after high school, where she landed a corporate job.

Her thirst for travel unquenched, Dominika became a flight attendant in the Middle East, which opened doors to diverse experiences and a global community. Seven years in the Arabian Peninsula offered a blend of challenges, adventures, and unforgettable moments with friends.

Despite initially leaving aviation, the allure of flying drew her back to a private jet company.

While exploring hypnotherapy, she embraces spirituality, guided by beliefs in the interconnectedness of the world, the divine realm, and reverence for Mother Nature. In occasional identity lapses, Dominika's heart becomes a compass to remember who she truly is.

Dominika enjoys the sound of crickets chirping amid tall summer grass. She loves thunderstorms, the tropics, the ocean, the wind on her face, and of course, dolphins.

Printed in Great Britain
by Amazon

61534209R00122